Roxie Holland grew up in a large family and spent half of her childhood with her nose buried in the pages of a book, the other half writing her own stories, escaping off into other worlds. Roxie lives in the UK with her husband and two children. She loves to spend time by the seaside, especially if there is an opportunity to sit down and read whilst enjoying some sunshine.

For my husband, thank you for letting me ignore you whilst I make stuff up on my laptop and for bringing me cups of tea.

For DW, for being my Jas.

Roxie Holland

THE LOVE SHE FORGOT

AUSTIN MACAULEY PUBLISHERS™

LONDON * CAMBRIDGE * NEW YORK * SHARJAH

Copyright © Roxie Holland 2024

The right of Roxie Holland to be identified as the author of this work has been asserted by the author in accordance with sections 77 and 78 of the Copyright, Designs and Patents Act 1988.

All rights reserved. No part of this publication may be reproduced, stored in a retrieval system, or transmitted in any form or by any means, electronic, mechanical, photocopying, recording, or otherwise, without the prior permission of the publishers.

Any person who commits any unauthorised act in relation to this publication may be liable to criminal prosecution and civil claims for damages.

This is a work of fiction. Names, characters, businesses, places, events, locales, and incidents are either the products of the author's imagination or used in a fictitious manner. Any resemblance to actual persons, living or dead, or actual events is purely coincidental.

A CIP catalogue record for this title is available from the British Library.

ISBN 9781035863327 (Paperback)
ISBN 9781035863334 (ePub e-book)

www.austinmacauley.com

First Published 2024
Austin Macauley Publishers Ltd®
1 Canada Square
Canary Wharf
London
E14 5AA

Table of Contents

Prologue	**9**
Beatrice: Then, June	**10**
Matt: Then, June	**19**
Beatrice: Now	**28**
Beatrice: Then, June	**36**
Matt: Then, July	**44**
Beatrice: Now	**53**
Beatrice: Then, August	**59**
Matt: Then, August	**68**
Beatrice: Now	**77**
Beatrice: Then, September	**84**
Matt: Then, September	**93**
Beatrice: Now	**100**
Beatrice: Then, September	**109**
Matt: Then, September	**115**
Beatrice: Now	**123**
Beatrice: Then, October	**131**
Matt: Then, October	**140**
Beatrice: Now	**148**
Beatrice: Then, December	**156**

Matt: Then, December	**164**
Beatrice: Now	**173**
Beatrice: Then, January	**178**
Beatrice: Now	**186**
Matt: January to April	**196**
Beatrice: Now	**206**
Beatrice: The Future	**213**

Prologue

I wake, feeling like I am coming up from being under water, like I haven't quite broken the surface yet. My bones ache. My head is throbbing. There is a sterile smell in the air. *I am in the hospital*, I think to myself, surprised.

I try to think why I am in hospital, but it feels like there are black holes in my memory, and I have no idea why I am here.

I try to focus on what I can hear and what I can feel.

I can feel the heat of another person, sitting by my bedside.

I can feel a hand, holding mine, the back of my hand held against their cheek.

I can feel the weight of their head against my hand like they're bowed over in prayer.

I can feel tears on my hand as they cry.

I hear them whisper, "Please come back to me."

I groan. I'm still feeling half under water, still desperately trying to surface.

There is a sudden movement next to me, the head is lifted, my hand is put down on the bed, and whoever is sitting beside me, they're suddenly gone. I want to call for them, but instead, I succumb to the depths of the water again.

Beatrice: Then, June

When I first told my parents I had quit my job, they were barely able to hide their excitement. I could almost hear them gloating down the telephone line. They didn't bother asking why I'd quit. They just assumed that the pressure and hours of the job had been too much for me to cope with, and they told me it was a good thing I was taking steps to take care of myself.

I followed up the news of my lack of job with the news that I also had a gap in the boyfriend department. This registered with them slightly more than the job news, but they were quick to tell me they had never really liked Ryan, and I was much better off without him. Their declarations had made me want to laugh, as Dad had always been cordial with Ryan and Mum used to keep a stash of fancy biscuits just in case he made an unexpected visit.

Better off, apparently, but homeless, I'd reminded them.

Not homeless! They'd protested, despite it being true. They'd sold the family home earlier in the year and started their long dream of leaving the UK to travel to all the countries on their bucket list, so there is no comforting, familiar roof for me to return to, no bedroom that is still decorated with my childhood wallpaper for me to hide in. Not that I'd said this to them because they sacrificed so much for us, and I know they're enjoying their travels. They send me photographs from every new place they arrive in, even if I have to keep reminding them about how time zones work.

After my announcement, despite being on a different continent, they'd taken everything in hand. A few calls had been made and the next thing I knew, all the arrangements had been made to move in with my brother and his roommates. Moving in with a bunch of twenty-something-year-old men was the last thing I'd planned, but I hadn't planned any of the last few weeks, so here I am, rolling with the punches, trying my best to get my shit together.

I pull my suitcases down the driveway to my brother's house. These two suitcases are the sum total of my twenty-four years on this earth. It appears I travel light, which is a good thing. Ben, my brother, has reminded me I'm going to be stuck in the box room which is apparently only just wide enough to swing a cat in. They'd been using the room for storage, so the fact they've cleared the room and arranged a wardrobe, a bed and a chest of drawers, I'm grateful.

I knock on the door, praying that Ben will be home and the one to answer. I haven't met one of the roommates before, but I know the other one having briefly met them just after New Year when Ben had brought him to the 'we've sold up and are going travelling' party my parents had thrown. Matt had barely spoken to me when I had tried to make conversation, answering me in short sentences and looking annoyed the whole time. I'm hoping the other guy isn't as grumpy as he appears to be.

The door opens and, of course, it is Matt standing in the doorway, looking exceptionally grumpy. I'm not sure why I thought my luck would have changed.

"Is Ben in?" I ask.

"No, he got called into work. I thought you'd be here earlier, I've been waiting for you, so I can go out," Matt tells me.

This is the longest sentence he has said to me though like when we spoke at my parents, he sounds pissed off. He's standing in the doorway with his arms crossed, and I feel like a teenager coming home after sneaking out for a party and being confronted by a disappointed parent.

"I'm so sorry to be an inconvenience." I bite back but then sigh. "Sorry, it's just felt like it's taken me forever to get here."

I've only travelled across the city, but it feels like I've travelled for years, and I'm exhausted. The argument with Ryan when I'd left his house hadn't helped either, I wish he'd just left me to pack up my things, but he clearly didn't trust me not to steal things, supervising my packing, making snide comments the whole time. Heartbreaking, but it has made me feel more confident that it's right for us to be separated.

Matt sighs, and he reaches for my suitcases, taking them out of my hands. He doesn't react to anything I have said, instead he starts heading up the stairs with both suitcases, like they weigh nothing. I step into the house, shut the door behind me and try to catch up. By the time I get to the top of the stairs, he's already down the hallway, opening the door by pushing the handle with his elbow, still holding the suitcases. He pushes the door open and puts the suitcases down.

"See you later," he says. He steps past me.

I look at the room he's put my suitcases in. "Hey, I thought I was staying in the box bedroom?"

"Didn't Ben tell you? Oscar moved in with his girlfriend, so that's your room."

"Oh, okay. Do you know when Ben is going to be home?"

"Nope. Your key is in the dish by the front door. Bye," Matt replies and with that, he rushes down the stairs.

I hear the slam of the front door as he leaves, and then there is just silence.

I spend the afternoon trying to make the room feel like my own. I can tell Ben has put in some effort to make the room feel comfortable. He's painted the walls a soft pink. The double bed is dressed with a thick quilt with a floral design on it. I swear he picked out the most girly bedding possible.

Regardless of the pattern, part of me just wants to climb into the bed and hibernate under the thick covers. I resist the urge. Instead, I unpack my clothes and the rest of my possessions, putting them away in the room. It doesn't take long. I cross the hall to the box bedroom. It still looks like it is being used for storage, so I shove the suitcases in there, hoping Ben doesn't mind that I'm making more mess.

I potter downstairs to the kitchen. I look at the contents of the fridge and cupboards. It's Monday, but it doesn't look like they have been shopping recently, so I grab my set of keys and my purse and walk to the nearest shop to buy something to cook for tea. I've no idea what time Ben is supposed to be home but doing something is better than just sitting and letting my mind wander. Overthinking is the first step to driving yourself crazy, my grandma used to say, and God knows I've been doing a lot of that recently.

"Hey, Beatrice, you're here!" Ben throws his arms around me when he comes into the kitchen later in the evening.

Ben gives me one of his trademark hugs, the one that doesn't squeeze me too tightly, as if he's afraid I'll break. Being so close to family makes me want to cry, but I force myself to smile at him instead as I slip out of the hug.

"I've missed you, dude."

"Are you going to tell me what the hell went on?" Ben asks as he gets himself a glass out of the cupboard. He pours himself some water, staring at me, waiting for me to talk. Quite how I have ended up jobless and boyfriend-less is a topic I haven't wanted to get into with my family. "Mum and Dad weren't very clear on the details, just that you needed a place to stay, and that Ryan clearly doesn't know a good thing. Are you going to fill me in? I thought the two of you were end-game."

"End-game?" I snort. "Have you been updating your slang? Cross-referencing on sites to ensure you have the most up-to-date lingo? If so, please stop."

"Whatever you want to call it. I thought you two were happy."

"Shit happens," I say with a shrug.

"I don't need to go kick his ass, do I?"

"God, you idiot, no, you do not need to speak to him. Nothing to worry about," I try to reassure him. Ben's not the type to throw his weight about, but I want to stop any idea he might have about talking to Ryan. I'm glad they were not close. I'm glad it is unlikely they will ever talk again.

"Well, you're better off without him," Ben replies.

"Yeah, I know," I murmur.

As I say this to him, I'm surprised by how sure I sound. I thought Ryan and I were so well suited, so solid, and I'd loved him, but I know that what has happened can't be undone or smoothed over. I wouldn't want to undo it either. Some cracks can't be smoothed over, some betrayals will always sting.

"As for that job of yours, the hours and the travelling were crazy!" Ben reminds me.

I stare at him with a small smile. "Coming from the guy who chose to become a doctor, you're going to lecture me about long hours? How long is one of your shifts?" I tease him.

"That's different. I'm still working on my rotations," he protests.

"Are you telling me that when you finally get to your ultimate job, it's going to be a cushy part-time number?"

"No, but that's different. You're…" he starts.

I cut him off with a glare. "I'm perfectly able to work long hours. You of all people should know that."

Sometimes it's more frustrating when Ben treats me like I'm going to break under the smallest amount of stress. He has spent years towards becoming a doctor, currently building up his experience as a junior doctor at the local hospital, so he should know better. It is one thing for my parents to ignore my consultant's assessments that I'm now perfectly healthy, but Ben should be able to use his own education to accept this, rather than joining them in treating me like I am made of spun sugar.

"I know, I just…" he sighs.

"I know you love me. I know you care about me, and I know you just want the best for me. So, just for today, I'm going to let it slide. Dinner will be ready shortly. I hope you're hungry."

"Let me pay you back for the shopping."

"Don't you dare! I'm going to pull my weight here. I've got a bit in savings. I'm going to start job hunting tomorrow."

"You don't have to be rushing for another job. If the hours at your old place were too much to cope with, just take it easy for a while."

"It wasn't the hours," I mutter.

"Well, what was it then?"

"How's Lily?" I change the subject.

Lily and Ben have been dating for a year though their relationship is long-distance as Lily is on rotation at another hospital. It's a shame she isn't here as I get on well with her and as my best friend Jas is still working overseas for her own job, I'm down in the girl chat department.

"Lily is fine," Ben replies, and he gets that goofy grin on his face whenever he talks about her.

"God that's quite sickening. Get that look off your face; you'll put me off my dinner," I tease him.

"I doubt that." He laughs.

I start sorting out the rice to go with the madras I've made. "Will Matt be back in time for tea?" I ask.

"No, when he is on shift, he's usually working late. If you've made extra, put it in the fridge, he'll probably eat when he gets home at stupid o'clock. He usually comes home desperate for food." Ben shrugs. "Actually, that reminds me, pass me your phone."

"What do you want it for?" I ask, but I'm already getting my phone out of my pocket and handing it over.

Ben presses a few keys on the phone and then hands it back to me. "Added you onto the Wi-Fi, and I put in Matt's number. In case there is an emergency here and I'm unavailable, Matt can sort it out."

"Please tell me you haven't asked Matt to babysit your little sister?" I groan.

"No!" Ben protests.

"You better not have. I'll remind you, I'm twenty-four. I'm a perfectly capable human being!"

I try to sound outraged but given I've just moved into their spare bedroom, with no boyfriend and no job prospects; I feel it undermines my argument a little.

"I assure you that I asked nothing of the sort." Ben puts his arms up, surrendering.

"Dinner will be half an hour," I say with a sigh.

I'm not sure I believe Ben's protests. If Ben has been nagging Matt to keep an eye on me, it is no wonder he looked so annoyed when I arrived.

"I'm going to have a shower. I'll help you finish dinner when I'm done." Ben promises and then he disappears from the kitchen.

Ben and I catch up as we eat. He tells me about his hospital job, about how Lily hates her new boss, and how he is planning to take her somewhere special for her birthday if they can both get the time off. We talk about our parents, laughing about how Dad had called each of us at four in the morning, both times having forgotten which way the time zones worked. We talk about how Jas is getting on in her job, how much I've missed having her around and how much I've been counting down to the day she is due home. Ben compliments me on the cooking, telling me it is miles better than our mother's interpretation of a curry, and that I'm welcome to cook any time I want.

We do not talk about why I left my job. We do not talk about what happened with Ryan. We do not talk about how I start yawning at seven thirty in the evening like I've been up and awake for days though I do ask him to stop looking at me with his concerned doctor face.

"Let me do the washing." Ben urges after I take the plates back into the kitchen. "You cooked, and I don't want you thinking you have to do all the stuff around the house. We didn't agree for you to move in thinking that you'd be running around after us."

"I like washing up," I remind him. Whenever we'd been given jobs to do at home when we were kids, I'd always bargained with him, so I could wash the pots, especially over something like vacuuming.

"You should go to bed. You look like you should have an early night." Ben stares at me, his head slightly cocked to one side like he is trying to medically assess me.

"Please tell me you're not going to be fussing over me the whole time I am here?"

"You're my little sister; I am going to be fussing over you for the rest of my life," he reminds me.

I stick my tongue out at him, but I let him help me wash and dry the pots, and then I give in and go to bed for an early night.

I wake up and groan to myself. I reach for my phone and squint as I check it to confirm that yes, it is still nighttime. It's one in the morning. I lie still in the bed, curling myself into a little ball under the covers, willing myself to fall back to sleep. Despite my desire to get back to sleep, the room is too dark, and instead of feeling cocooned like I used to in the dark, I feel stifled and anxious. Fifteen minutes pass, and it's clear that sleep is not going to happen.

I get up, taking my cardigan from the hook on the bedroom door, wrapping myself up. I head downstairs. If I am going to be awake, I may as well watch a bit of television. Being awake in the middle of the night and watching television has become a habit over the last few weeks. I don't know why I thought it might change in a different house.

I get comfortable on the sofa and launch Netflix, smiling to myself that Ben has already set up a profile for me. He might drive me crazy sometimes being overprotective, but he's incredibly sweet and thoughtful, as big brothers go.

I search for a film to put on in the background, one that I've seen before, so I don't need to pay much attention to it, crossing my fingers that I am going to fall asleep. Thirty minutes later, I'm still wide awake, watching as the main character is attacked by the masked killer.

"Interesting late-night viewing option you have there," Matt calls from the doorway.

I jump, startled. "Jesus, you scared me! I didn't hear you come in," I exclaim.

Matt smirks. "You're not the most observant person, are you? Ghostface would have it easy with you."

"I like to think I'd give Ghostface a run for his money." I roll my eyes at him. "Are you just getting in?"

"Yeah, just back from work."

"If you're hungry there is some food in the fridge for you," I tell him.

I don't expect a thank you, but I can't help but roll my eyes again as I hear him head off towards the kitchen without another word. I keep watching the film, but then Matt comes back into the living room, a bowl of madras in one hand, a plate with naan bread in the other, and a spoon tucked into the back pocket of his trousers.

He takes a seat on the floor. "I wouldn't have picked you for a horror fan," he comments, putting his plates on the floor and pulling out his spoon.

"I can switch it off if you want to watch something else. I should get back to bed, really."

"Are you all settled in?" he asks. He's got his eyes on the film.

"Yeah, I just am having trouble sleeping at the moment," I admit. "Please, don't tell Ben. He'll just worry and drive me crazy asking questions daily about how much sleep I've had."

"Ben tends to go a bit overboard with looking after people, doesn't he?" Matt's voice has got a tone to it, not as pissed off as he usually sounds, but not cheerful.

"He has a heart of gold, my brother, even if he has questionable taste in paint colours," I muse.

"I told him it was a bit much when he gave me the tin and asked me to paint the room," Matt comments. I can't believe Ben had him paint the room. I think to myself again that it is understandable Matt appears frustrated by my addition to the house.

We fall into silence as he eats his food, and I focus on the film.

"Ben says you're not working?" He asks so casually, but it feels like he's kicked me. I wonder how long it will take for me not to feel shocked about what has happened to me.

"The job hunt starts tomorrow."

"Are you looking for anything in particular?" He stacks his pots together on the floor next to him.

"Just something that pays." I force myself to laugh, to try to sound upbeat like this topic isn't tearing at my heart.

"I can maybe help you there. If you don't mind working evenings, I have a job going at the bar. I manage a bar in town," he explains. "It's just above minimum wage for pay, I'm afraid, but you get to keep your share of tips."

"What is the job for?"

"A bit of everything, really. Depends on what we have on in the night. Waitressing. Bartending. Sorting stuff in the kitchen. Front-of-house stuff.

General dog's body. At the beck and call of everybody else who works there. You could start this week."

He glances in my direction, looking like he's expecting me to say no.

"That sounds great, thanks," I reply.

I feel a wash of relief through me to know that I can take this job without having to use my already limited energy in job hunting, to avoid interviews with strangers, to be asked why I left my last position.

"No problem. I'll leave you to it. We can talk about the job tomorrow and agree on a start date."

He gets up from the floor, carrying his plates to the kitchen. I hear his footsteps on the stairs, and I settle back to watch the rest of my film, crossing my fingers that I'll fall asleep.

Matt: Then, June

When Ben had told me he had wanted to speak to me about something urgent, I assumed he was going to tell me he was moving in with his girlfriend. I thought maybe he was going to ask me the usual questions he does when he's stressed, the ones where he's trying to confirm I am still on the straight and narrow and not about to derail my life and give him a headache. I had a hundred possibilities in my head, but none of them included him asking me if his sister was able to move in with us.

I'd met Beatrice once before; at a party their parents had thrown. Ben had dragged me along to the party, telling me that he didn't want to leave me alone so soon after a breakup. He acted like I was a ticking time bomb of self-destruction. Ben had told me he would introduce me to his sister, and I had expected to find the female version of my best friend, but they were nothing alike.

Ben and I have been roommates for a few years; he moved into the house my great-uncle rented out before I did, and when one of the other tenants left, I took their room. Ben and I have had a steady stream of roommates in the third room, but he and I have been constant in the house. During that time, we gradually moved from roommates to actual friends. He's the person I am the closest to, given I've dropped all my former friends, and he's probably better than all the friends I'd had before, combined. He might be serious, but he's a good guy.

I'd expected Beatrice to be as serious as Ben, but when we'd been introduced, she was friendly, open, one of those people you assume to be full of the joys of spring. Despite the wide smiles she'd given me when we were talking, there was something about Beatrice that made me feel on edge, awkward. Even though our interaction at the party had been brief, she had made me feel like I was at a job interview, one where she knew as well as I did that I was underqualified. Smiles aside, she has a way of looking at you like she knows you're full of shit. I'd spent most of the evening being sullen and anti-social, pissed off that Ben hadn't let me be alone and weirdly bothered by the uncomfortable way I felt around Beatrice.

When Ben had told me a few weeks later that Beatrice was coming over for tea, I'd made myself scarce, making excuses that I had a shift to work. I hadn't been scheduled to work, and going in on a quiet night would have made the rest of the staff convinced I was checking up on them, so instead I'd wandered around, aimlessly, counting down the time until I was sure Beatrice would have left, and I could return home.

Ben had asked if I had minded Beatrice moving in though it didn't seem like there was really any other option. He told me she'd separated from her boyfriend, who I assume to be the guy who had spent the night of her parent's party grabbing her ass, and that she needed a place to stay for a while and get herself sorted out. He told me she was fragile, and he needed to look after her. I'd told him that, obviously, it wasn't a problem for her to be living with us. Oscar, before he had left to move in with his girlfriend, had laughed at the predicament he was leaving me in, as I'd made the mistake of telling him before that Beatrice looks at me in a way that makes me feel like I'm an animal in a research lab.

Yesterday, before she had arrived, I'd been planning on getting the heck out of the house, but then Ben had been called into work and had pleaded with me to stay and welcome Beatrice. Again, he'd told me she was fragile, and that he needed to make sure she was looked after when she arrived. When she arrived, she looked weary and exhausted, nothing like the vibrant, inquisitive girl from the party, perplexing the shit out of me, making me wonder what has happened in the few months since I had seen her that has made her like this.

I'd spent my shift at work convincing myself that I'll have to get over whatever issue I have as, for the foreseeable future, Beatrice and I are stuck in the same space. I can't continue to feel like she's judging me every time she looks at me, so I need to find common ground.

I hadn't expected to come home from work last night and find her watching *Scream*.

I hadn't expected her to offer me food, turning out to be the best thing I'd eaten in ages.

I hadn't expected to offer her a job, signing myself up to spend more time with her.

I certainly haven't expected to be lying in bed for hours, staring at the ceiling, wondering what I've let myself in for.

I wake in the morning, and the house is quiet. I'm used to waking up to a quiet house, as when Ben's not at Lily's, he's either at work by the time I get up, or he's in bed following a night shift. I stretch and get out of bed, planning a shower and then breakfast. I step into the hallway, and then I realise my mistake. I'm not home alone. Beatrice is heading down the hallway from the bathroom towards her bedroom, and I'm standing like an idiot, wearing just my boxers.

"Sorry," I mutter. She pulls the towel closer around her, trying to lift it higher on her body, and it's at that moment I notice the scar on her chest that she is trying to hide. It runs down the centre of her chest, and I remember Ben telling me that she'd had open heart surgery, telling me how she'd nearly died as a teenager. Beatrice looks uncomfortable, still pulling at her towel, using her hand to try to cover her scar. I think that in the few times I've seen her, she's always worn something with a high neckline, and I wonder if she always covers herself up. I gesture at myself. "I'll remember to wear more clothes tomorrow," I promise.

"It's your house. You don't need to change your routine because of me. The bathroom is free." She gives me a small smile. She heads past me towards her room, and I head into the bathroom.

Beatrice is in the kitchen when I get downstairs. She's wearing tight stonewash blue jeans, and a red tee shirt that ends just above her belly button though the neckline is high. Her blonde hair is in a ponytail. She's buttering some toast, so I busy myself making a bowl of cereal.

"Ben had already told you, right?" she asks, breaking the silence between us.

"What, that you are likely to steal the crust from the new loaf of bread?" I ask.

For a moment, she looks unsure of herself, like I have accused her of a major crime and then she rolls her eyes. "Idiot. I meant I'm guessing he told you I've had heart surgery?"

"He mentioned it." I shrug. I pour the milk onto my cereal. "I'm sure he told you things about me, too, right?"

"Yeah," she admits.

I wonder how much he has told her. Does she know all about my past? Does she know how I derailed my whole life four years ago? How hard it had been to put everything back together again? "Coffee?" I ask her.

"Sure," she replies and flicks the kettle on.

"Have you thought about when you want to start at the bar?" I ask.

I take a step towards her, to reach the cupboard where the coffee cups are and as I step towards her, she takes a step backwards, backing into the kitchen counter. She looks at me, an odd expression on her face. At that moment, I realise, she isn't fragile like Ben keeps telling me. She's frightened about something. I back up, giving her space.

She exhales. "I'm sorry. It isn't you," she says. She moves away and takes a few deep breaths. She takes another and then squares her shoulders. "When do you need me to start?" she asks like the previous moment didn't happen.

I follow her lead, taking the coffee cups from the cupboard. "Well, I'm short-staffed as I had a vacancy and then another member of staff has gone off sick, so as soon as you're able would be great."

"When are you next in?" she asks. I put the coffee granules into the mugs. I pour milk into mine, and she nods for her cup.

"I'm in tonight. I work mostly evenings," I explain as I pour the water into the cups to finish the coffee.

"I could come in with you tonight if that's okay. What time do you usually start?"

"Three until midnight tonight. You can do a shorter shift if you prefer, given it's your first one. It'll mostly be collecting glasses and things until your background checks come through."

"No, it's okay. I'll be fine, and I'll be ready on time," she says.

She picks her coffee cup from the side and carries it with her plate towards the living room. I follow her and then sit in the armchair, resting my coffee cup on the windowsill behind me. Beatrice sits on the sofa, her coffee cup on the arm of the sofa, her legs curled under her as she eats her toast.

I glance over at her. "If you have them, a white shirt with either black trousers or a skirt would be best to wear tonight, to fit in, until I can organise you a uniform."

"Okay," she replies. She flicks the television on. "Do you want to watch anything particular?" she asks.

I shake my head. I eat my cereal, watching as she loads Netflix, skipping to her recommendations, finding *Scream 2* and pressing play. I watch out the corner of my eye as she watches the film, shaking my head slightly when I see that she tends to squeeze her eyes shut whenever a murder is about to take place on the screen. I have no idea why she seems intent on watching the film series if she can't watch the scenes unfolding. I can't work out why she seems like she has a dark cloud over her. I think she's perplexing, but instead of trying to figure her out, I turn my attention to my breakfast and coffee, watching the film.

"How's Beatrice getting on?" I shout to Isaac.

The bar has been buzzing. It is busy for a mid-week night, and the queue for the bar looks like it's never-ending though the customers all look happy enough. I get the sense from the crowd that the night is about to turn, that people are getting their last drinks for the evening and the crowd is about to thin out.

"All good, dude. We'd be dying without the extra pair of hands tonight. It's manic," he shouts back to me. Isaac is one of my longest-serving members of staff, and he's been showing Beatrice the ropes for the evening. When we'd arrived, Isaac had treated her like she was his salvation, telling her he couldn't face another night short-staffed. I've barely seen Beatrice all night, just catching glimpses of her through the evening, seeing her clear tables, take people their drinks, and ferry what seems like a million glasses to be washed.

"Tell me about it." I look out to the crowd.

"Do you think she'll come back tomorrow?" he shouts above the din to me.

People think it's glamorous to work in a bar, they don't realise it doesn't take long to feel like your back is killing from being stood up all night, how sick you get of making the same drinks over and over again, how quickly shoes are ruined, how the customers can treat you like crap or a piece of meat depending on their mood or alcohol levels, how many glasses you'll wash throughout a normal shift, or that you constantly feel sticky from drops of alcohol regardless of how fast it is cleaned up. It's not for those who don't enjoy a challenge.

As I finish making the cocktail for the customer I am serving, I spot Beatrice out of the corner of my eye, carrying a tray of empty glasses across the bar. She's smiling at customers as she weaves in and out of the crowd, finding gaps between groups that didn't seem to be there, moving quickly across the room. She looks as happy-go-lucky as she had the day I first met her, and whatever happened in the kitchen this morning seems far removed from how she is now.

I grin to myself. "Yeah, I think she'll be back tomorrow," I reply to Isaac. I try to convince myself that the only reason I'm excited by this thought is because I am desperate for help with the workload.

"You're really hot. I think I could show you a good time."

The pretty redhead reaches across the bar to try to grab my hand. She and her friends are the last of the customers, and despite the times I've reminded them that it's time for them to be leaving, so we can close the bar, they don't seem keen to be making their way outside. They're not very drunk, but the redhead is on the verge of getting a bit too familiar. No matter how many times this happens it always takes me by surprise.

"Come on Kate, we should be going." The brunette tries to coax her friend off the bar stool. She and her two blonde friends keep muttering they're sorry for the way their friend is acting.

"I think he should come home with us," Kate whines to her friends. She leans forward again, still trying to grab my hand.

I take a small step back. "I don't think my wife would like that." I laugh, gently.

"No ring," she says, more observant than I'd given her credit for.

"Time to be going ladies, we need to close," I say, firmly.

Beatrice appears at my side. "Hey, baby." She smiles at me as she runs her hand down my arm, sliding to my hand. She squeezes my hand. Her body language is that of possession, she's angled herself towards me like she is focused on me rather than the women across the bar. "I missed you. I can't wait to get you home," she continues, sounding breathy.

The group of women look at me and then at Beatrice, and then they get up and head towards the door, shouting goodbyes over their shoulders.

I smirk at Beatrice. "You know, if I did that to a woman, I'm sure I'd be called out for it."

"You looked like you wanted out of the conversation. Did I overstep?" She pulls her hand from mine.

I laugh and shake my head. "I will add to your job responsibilities that you can save me from conversations I look like I want to get out of."

"Deal. Right, what do I need to do now?"

"Now, Beatrice, the fun starts. More cleaning!" I grin, and I toss her a clean tea towel.

"Yes, boss."

"You're not sick of cleaning glasses yet?"

"No, I'll do what you need me to. I appreciate you taking me on."

"Well, you're doing me a big favour. You might regret it though next shift, as I'm sure Isaac will appreciate somebody else cleaning the toilets, and it is delivery day tomorrow, lots of crates to carry, bring your muscles," I joke.

"Thank you," she says, but she doesn't sound sarcastic.

"What are you thanking me for?"

"For not treating me like I'm a fragile egg who might get broken at the slightest knock," she says.

"I'm sorry that I don't pander to you," I reply.

In the back of my mind, I'm wondering if I've pushed her too far this evening. Whenever Ben has spoken about Beatrice, he's always told me that she is fragile. I wonder if he's going to be annoyed when he knows I've given Beatrice a job that includes late nights and long hours. I wonder if I've made a mistake offering her a job if I've just set myself up for a lecture from Ben. I look at Beatrice, and she gives me a big smile.

"No, don't be sorry. It gets tiring being mollycoddled by people. It's nice being treated like everybody else because I am just like everybody else, I just can't get my family to see that sometimes. You treat me like I'm normal."

"Well, I wouldn't go so far as calling you normal…" I grin at her, and she laughs. "You have questionable taste in films, for a start."

"What's wrong with horror movies?"

"Nothing at all, but both times, you've watched them with your eyes half shut. Why don't you just watch something less gory? Watch a romance or a comedy."

"Romance or comedies, or worse, combined as a rom-com? I'd rather watch a horror, thanks! At least you know what you're getting, none of this false pretence of a happily ever after."

"They can't all be that bad."

"Tell me a decent one, one that isn't icky. Tell me one that is genuinely funny, or truly romantic, where you know the characters will be happy and together in the future," she challenges as she folds her arms across her chest.

I lean against the bar, thinking of films I've watched. "*50 First Dates*," I suggest.

"Please, she has Stockholm syndrome, she just doesn't know it."

"*10 Things I Hate About You.*"

"She'll become a different person at college and forget all about him. What is he bringing to the table? Plus, she's too high-maintenance. He won't be able to keep up when there is nobody bankrolling his fake dates."

"*13 Going on 30.*"

"Are you literally just naming films with numbers in the title?"

"Okay, *Knocked Up.*"

"It'll never last. Poor kid will grow up listening to the parents constantly complaining."

"*While You Were Sleeping.*"

"Far too awkward, to know your wife loved your brother first, surely? Not only that but somebody who lied about being their fiancée?"

"*The Notebook.*"

She rolls her eyes. "Do not get me started on that one! People told me I would cry at that film as it was so romantic, but I didn't find it romantic at all," she continues. I want to laugh at the expression she has on her face. Her comment about crying at a film makes another title pop into my head, and I'm sure I'm going to beat her challenge with it.

"*Marley & Me,*" I suggest. She doesn't answer straight away like she is mulling over the film in her head.

"I'm not sure it fits the genre, but I'll allow it, only because it has a cute dog in it," she concedes.

"I am sure there are others if I think about it long enough."

"You have a good knowledge of romcoms. Is your girlfriend into them?" Beatrice asks. "Or boyfriend?"

"No girlfriend currently," I tell her. My last relationship had gone up in flames a few months ago. Jemima and I were never going to have lasted long term. She was part of my old lifestyle, not willing to give up the behaviours I'd worked so hard to leave behind. Whatever I'd felt for her, self-preservation won in the end. "My mother is a big fan of romance and comedy films. I used to watch them with her, under duress, obviously."

"Obviously."

"Besides, you say you don't like them, but you knew all the ones I mentioned. Maybe I'm not the only one who watches the films under duress," I point out, and she grins at me.

"Hey, Matt, are you actually going to help out tonight?" Isaac calls as he comes into the bar area. He stares at me and Beatrice.

"Sorry, Isaac, I was just giving Beatrice some pointers about how to tackle cleaning the toilets tomorrow." I grin.

"New girl on toilet duties? Excellent!"

"Come on, we'll get sorted and then I can take you home," I say to Beatrice. She nods and heads towards the kitchen area. I pass Isaac as I follow her, and he pulls me back by my arm.

"What's with you and her?" he asks.

"Nothing. She's my roommate's sister. She's just moved in with us, and she needed a job. Sounded like a win-win for us all." I shrug.

He grins at me like he doesn't believe a word I've said but then he follows me into the kitchen so we can finish cleaning up. I try to ignore the fact that my little exchange with Beatrice has been the most fun I've had in ages.

Beatrice: Now

The next time I open my eyes, it's easier to feel like I've surfaced. The room is brighter, and I can hear the hustle and bustle of somebody else in the room. I look over to them and see that it is a nurse.

"Good morning. How are we feeling today?" he asks me.

"Okay, I guess, just…not sure why I am in the hospital," I admit. I am still drawing a blank about yesterday.

"You were in an accident on the ice."

"Ice?"

"Yeah, last night was very cold; there was a lot of black ice."

"It's May." I laugh.

The nurse looks at me. "It's January."

"No, yesterday was 15th May," I tell him, firmly. "Do you know where my phone is?"

"It will be in the drawer," he replies though he looks concerned.

I reach into the drawer and find my phone, waking the screen. "What the hell?" I mutter to myself as I see the date and time on the display.

"I am just going to get your doctor," he says. He swiftly exits the room, leaving me wondering what joke he is trying to play.

I scroll through my contacts to call Ryan, but I can't find him. I frown, typing his number into the keypad of my phone. As I key in the digits, my phone suggests a contact, but instead of Ryan, it says 'Spawn of Satan'. As I read the name I've apparently changed his contact details to, I get a rush of resentment in my body, not the rush of affection I usually feel when I call him.

What the hell?

I move to my message apps, looking through my messages. The latest ones on my phone are with Ben, my parents and Jas, but there is nothing with Ryan. All my messages are dated January, and I don't understand why.

I switch back to my contacts, dialling Ben. "Ben, please help me. I don't know what is happening," I cry down the phone line once he answers.

"I'm here at the hospital, Beatrice. I just went for a coffee. We're on our way back to you now. I'll be there in a minute, stay calm."

Ben's voice is soothing, and he stays on the line with me, talking and trying to keep me calm, but I don't feel any less agitated, not until I can hear his footsteps coming down the hallway, his voice getting closer as I can hear him in the hall as well as through the phone.

He comes into the room, with his roommate Matt behind him. They're both carrying the types of cups that are from vending machines, and I can smell the coffee. They both look like crap, and it is clear they haven't slept recently. They are both wearing crumpled clothing.

"What are you doing here?" I look at Matt. He looks surprised.

"You don't remember?" he asks me.

I shake my head. "I apparently don't remember a lot of things. They are trying to tell me that it's January. Somebody must have changed the date on my phone, but who would do that?" My voice is loud, and if it weren't for the fact that I'm hooked up to an IV drip for hydration, I'd be out of bed and pacing the floor because I'm now fully agitated. Whatever is going on, it isn't funny.

"What month do you think it is?" Ben looks concerned.

"Why do people keep asking me the month? I know the date! It's 16th May. Yesterday was 15th May. I was planning for Cole's presentation. We were getting everything finished in the office as we are travelling today and… I…" I start but stop talking when I realise that I can't recall what I did after work.

"Beatrice, it is 31st January." Ben sits in the chair next to my bed.

"No, it isn't."

"You didn't do anything for Cole yesterday, you don't work for him. You haven't worked with him since early June."

"I…"

"You've been working for Matt since June. He was with you after your shift last night when you had the fall."

"I work for Matt? Where?"

"In a bar, in town. You've been mostly working behind the bar. You don't remember any of it?" Matt asks me. He has a look of disbelief on his face.

I frown at him. "I don't understand," I say again. Even I am getting frustrated with this sentence.

Before either Ben or Matt can speak again, a doctor comes into the room. "Hello, Beatrice. I'm Dr Edwards." She smiles as she introduces herself. She looks across at Ben. "Hello, Dr Schofield."

"I'm Beatrice's brother. She's a bit confused."

"And who are you?" Dr Edwards looks at Matt.

"I'm…"

"Our roommate."

"My boss, apparently," I say at the same time as Matt attempts to speak and Ben tries to clarify the situation.

"Okay, well, I will talk to Beatrice alone." Dr Edwards sounds firm. Ben and Matt don't argue. They both leave the room.

I look at the doctor. "Please tell me what is going on," I plead. She smiles and sits down in the chair next to my bed. I relax, confident she will tell me this is all a joke.

"We think it is focal retrograde amnesia," Dr Edwards says to us all, much later in the day. Since my conversation with the nurse this morning, I've been through a barrage of tests. I feel like I've been prodded and poked, run through a variety of machines, and been quizzed on a multitude of topics.

At some point, one of the nurses had shown me the things that I had in my possession last night, but I don't recognise the ring I was wearing or the delicate necklace. I don't even recognise the clothes that were in my drawer. I'm convinced they're not mine and want to call this new nurse a liar, but Matt tells me she is right, they were the clothes I was wearing to work last night.

After all the tests, it is clear I can remember absolutely everything from my history, with the exception of the past eight months which is completely gone, like I've taped over part of a recording, leaving the start and the end.

Ben has been filling me in on some things he thinks I should know, but everything keeps taking me by surprise and making me feel worse. It feels weird that I can tell Ben that he used to make me be his scrub nurse when he was playing doctor when we were kids, that the memories are so vivid I can recall him telling me off for handing him the toy thermometer incorrectly, but I am drawing blanks on anything he is telling me about recent events. I'm shocked by the news that I have apparently moved into his house, which he'd told me when I queried why he'd called Matt our roommate earlier in the day.

Everything he tells me feels like a body blow, but there is a small part of me that reminds me that this could be much worse. I remember more than I have forgotten. I try to focus on that throughout the day, but it is not a big comfort and doesn't stop me from trying to search my mind for answers.

I'm tired and struggling to focus on what the doctor is saying to me. Matt is sitting at the far end of the room, looking tired and grumpy.

"Are you sure?" Ben stutters. Even after all the testing, he still looks like he can't believe that this is happening.

"What does that mean?" I cut in, as it is clear from Ben's face that he knows what this means, but I don't.

"Your bump to the head has affected your memory, but it seems like it is only affecting memories from the last few months," Ben says in a gentle tone.

"Oh God, this isn't like *50 First Dates* is it, I'm not going to wake up tomorrow and have forgotten what happened, and you're going to have to keep telling me?" I blurt out, and I hear Matt give a little huff, like laughter, from across the room. I glare over at him. He shrugs and looks away.

"No, Beatrice, it doesn't look like it's impacting your ability to retain new memories," Dr Edwards smiles at me. "You can recall being in the hospital last night," she reminds me.

"Yes, I remember…" I begin, but I stop and frown.

"What do you remember?" Matt asks.

I shake my head. I don't want to talk about it. I remember somebody in my room. I remember somebody was holding my hand. I know I heard somebody crying. Who was that?

"Are you okay?" Ben reaches for my hand.

"Will my memory come back?" I look at the doctor and then at Ben.

"It's too soon to tell." Dr Edwards is the one who replies.

"Will they come back in one go, or just little bits at a time?"

"Beatrice, you will need to be patient. The brain is an incredibly complex thing, but the one thing it will not do is go by the pace you want to go at. If you are going to recover your memories, it will be at your brain's pace, not how much you are pushing. Your neurologist will talk to you more when you have further appointments, but I am advising you to be gentle and patient. You need to be prepared that you might never recall those memories you have lost."

"Never?" Matt asks.

"It's impossible to say. It is one of those time-will-tell moments." Dr Edwards looks sympathetic.

"When can I go home?" I sigh. I don't remember moving in with Ben and Matt, but maybe being home will give me a rush of memories that I am so eager to get back.

"Physically, you're well enough to go home…" Dr Edwards starts. I sense there she is going to add a 'but' to her sentence. I'm refusing to give her an opportunity to raise it.

"If I am physically okay, I would like to go home," I say firmly.

Later, Ben and Matt let me into the house. I'd had to argue with both the doctor and Ben about leaving the hospital though they eventually relent with the agreement that I'll be having follow-up appointments with the neurologists. I'm worn out and still confused.

As I step into the house, I don't get the rush of return of the memories I had hoped for, and I feel disappointed. Instead of the memories of the last few months returning to me, it's just older memories that I can think of, like how I'd visited Ben not long after our parents had sold their house when I had dropped off some things for him, and I'd stayed for tea.

"Your room is the second door on the right," Ben tells me as we stand in the hallway. Matt has made himself scarce in the kitchen. Ben looks like he is going to go up the stairs with me, but I wave him off and head to the room he had told me, wanting to be by myself. I'm grateful that I don't hear Ben's footsteps on the stairs behind me, that he's let me do this by myself. Maybe seeing my room will be the trigger I need.

I go up the stairs and push the door open, stepping into the room.

I don't recognise this room. It's full of my things, which reassures me that I am in the right place, but there are lots of things that feel foreign to me. It's like two people are sharing this room.

I go through the drawers, the wardrobe, the shelves, looking at everything in the room, cataloguing the things I don't recognise. I grab a notepad to write a list.

A red beret.

A bikini.

A ridiculously oversized teddy bear.

A red sequin dress, with long purple gloves and a red wig.

A cork board with ticket stubs pinned on it, to movies I don't remember seeing, and a stub to a festival that I don't remember attending.

Two sets of fairy lights, one wound around the mirror, the other around the headboard of the bed.

The cork to a bottle of expensive champagne, propped in a way that looks deliberate rather than something I forgot to throw away.

A shoebox full of paper origami.

Underwear from shops I wouldn't regularly buy from. The kind of underwear you put on when you want somebody to see it, the type you put on and intend for somebody else to take off.

I add to the list the ring they gave me in the hospital, the one they said I was wearing when I went in that night, and the necklace. They have both been tucked away in my pocket since.

I add to the list that Ryan's contact details have been updated to 'Spawn of Satan'.

I add that there is a password-protected folder on my phone that I don't know how to open, a folder that I do not recall the contents of. I'd discovered this when playing around on my phone in the car ride back with Ben and Matt, searching for more clues. I've tried all my usual passwords but the folder will not open. In what seems like a ridiculous joke, I'd apparently titled the folder 'memories'.

I stare at the list and wonder, who did I become in the last few months? What was I doing? Was I happy?

There must be somebody who knows the answers to these questions. It's clear from some of the things that I have discovered that there was somebody I was spending my time with, but there is nothing in my phone that suggests who this might be. There is no evidence in my recent messages with Jas that suggests I told her what I was doing though I have only skimmed a few so far. The only new contact in my phone is Matt, which Ben had told me in the car that he'd put into the phone for me when I had first moved in.

Whatever I was doing, I have clearly kept it all to myself.

There is a knock on the door and then Ben pops his head around.

"Have you had any epiphanies?" he asks. I haven't told him what I have been hoping for, but he knows me so well.

"No." I sigh.

"I am sure it will come back to you," he soothes. He comes into the room, pulling out the stool to the dressing table so he can sit down.

"It might not. The neurologist said I might always have a gap."

"We will work it out."

"Do you know why I quit my job?"

"I don't know. Mum and Dad told me not to ask you about it."

"Do they know? Did I tell them?"

"Not so far as I know. They thought you'd suffered from burnout. You looked fed up when you got here, so I didn't push it. The first few weeks you were here, you seemed so tired and worn out, but I thought if you had wanted to talk, you would do that, and you kept telling me not to baby you."

"What about Ryan?" I start to pace in my room.

"No, sorry, not got a clue."

"I didn't say anything?" I exclaim.

We had been together for two years. Did he do something terrible? Did I? I want to think I didn't, but as I can't remember most of the last year, maybe I did. The fact that I had changed his name in my phone suggests that I wasn't the one who did something terrible, but I can't imagine Ryan doing anything to warrant me apparently changing his name and blocking contact with him.

"I truly am a shitty brother." Ben looks sheepish for a moment, and then his face changes, like he is remembering something, and he clicks his fingers, excitedly. "Wait, I remember. I asked what happened, I said I thought the two of you were end-game. You told me to stay away from the slang, and told me that shit happens."

"That's it?"

"Yeah, I'm sorry that I don't have more answers for you."

"You're not a shitty brother, by the way. You've always been there for me. You let me move in, even if I didn't tell you why I needed to. You've been looking after me my whole life," I remind him.

"I just wish I could tell you the things you need to know right now."

"Well, why don't you start with some of the easier ones? Was Jas home for Christmas?"

"No, you told me she met a guy, and she was staying with them. You were worried that she might not come home when her overseas contract ended," Ben explains, and I nod because I had seen in the chat with Jas that she'd been telling me about the guy with the gorgeous eyes, the ones she said she wanted to look at forever.

"Did Mum and Dad come back for Christmas?"

"No, they were in Canada, they're still there. They haven't been back yet. I think they're planning on being back in the summer for a visit."

"Did you and I have Christmas together?"

"No, I worked a long shift on Christmas Eve and then went to Lily's. You said you were thinking of going to a friend's house, but I think you may have stayed here."

I think about the idea of staying at home for Christmas by myself, and I feel a pang of something in my chest. It isn't sadness or loneliness like I expect but…a longing, happiness, a feeling of perfect contentment. The feeling washing over me is enough to knock me off my feet, it's a powerful surge that came out of nowhere, and I sit down on my bed in shock. What the hell was that about? Ben must notice my reaction, as he moves to sit next to me on the bed. He looks like he can't decide whether to take my temperature or check my pulse, so I force myself to give him a small smile.

"I'm okay."

"Are you sure? What happened there? Did you remember something?"

"Promise not to laugh?"

"I'd never," Ben vows. I roll my eyes.

"I only lost the last few months. I can recall perfectly the times you laughed at me during my teenage years. I remember all the snide comments about my hairstyles and outfits."

"Okay, I wouldn't now…" he clarifies with a grin.

"It wasn't something I remembered with my head, but…with my heart," I tell him.

As soon as the words leave my mouth, I regret them, I expect him to laugh at me, to tell me that I am being silly. Instead, he gives me a little smile.

"Your brain will remember, eventually. If there is one thing I know about you, it's how persistently stubborn you can be but don't push it, if it will come, it'll come naturally. I'll help," he promises me, and for the first time since I woke up, I feel like I can solve this puzzle. Despite Dr Edwards telling me that I need to be patient and not push myself, I refuse to wait for my mind to catch up, I will find out what I have been doing in the last few months.

Beatrice: Then, June

Matt drives me home from the first shift at the bar. He seems to have had a complete change in personality today. He doesn't seem like the same annoyed person I met at my parents' party or the surly guy who let me into the house when Ben had been called into work, even the guarded guy who had arrived home from work last night. Instead, he's relaxed, funny and kind. He never made a comment about my over-reaction in the kitchen earlier when he had gotten too close to me, a reaction even I hadn't anticipated, and I'm grateful that he just let things go without asking me for reasons because I wouldn't have known how to even start in trying to explain.

"Do you want anything to eat?" he asks as he opens the front door when we arrive home. He lets me into the house first then locks the door behind him. The moment he mentions food, I feel like I haven't eaten in days. My stomach growls, loudly. He gives a little grin.

"No wonder you come home and eat. I ate on my break, somebody gave me a chicken salad, but it feels like it was a lifetime ago," I complain.

I follow him to the kitchen. I check the clock. It is almost one in the morning. I should really be getting to bed and trying to get some sleep, but I still feel out of my usual sleep cycles, especially after taking a long nap in the day before I had to get ready for work. My stomach isn't going to let me get to sleep, not until I've stopped the growling.

"God bless your brother," Matt says, reading a note that's been left on the kitchen side.

I read over his shoulder. *Hope your shift went well. There are burritos in the fridge, just microwave until hot. See you in the morning. Ben.*

"I messaged him earlier to say I was starting work with you," I explain as I reach into the fridge. Ben has cooked a batch of burritos; they're in a tub in the fridge, enough for tea tonight and breakfast for all of us tomorrow. I grab two of them like I've been thrown a lifeline and put them on a plate to microwave.

"I am going to assume from this gift of burritos that Ben isn't going to kill me for offering you a job that entails late nights." Matt takes the burritos from me, putting them in the microwave and starting it.

"He can take a chill pill. He works crazy hours, nights and weekends, he doesn't have a leg to stand on when trying to tell me to take it easy."

"He's just protective of the people he cares about." Matt's voice is neutral, much better than he had sounded last night when talking about Ben.

"Drives you crazy too, right?" I grin at him. Matt doesn't answer. He focuses on the microwave, watching as the timer counts down. He opens the door and puts my burrito on another plate for me, handing it to me.

"Here you go," he says.

I take a bite of mine, giving an involuntary moan as the flavours hit me. Ben's made breakfast burritos but with a spicy chorizo for the sausage, and I'm sure this is the best thing I've ever eaten. How the two of us know how to cook is a mystery, as neither of our parents is blessed in the arts of the kitchen department.

I glance over at Matt. "Aren't you going to eat?"

"I am going to go eat in my room. I'll see you tomorrow." He leaves the kitchen and heads towards the stairs.

"Goodnight," I call.

I finish my burrito, tidy up and then head upstairs to bed. I can see the light is on in Matt's bedroom from the gap underneath the door. Ben's room is dark. I head to my room, hoping that after a long night working, I'll get a full night's sleep.

An hour later, I'm back downstairs in the living room. I'd tossed and turned until I had given up.

"*Scream 3?*" a voice comes from the doorway. I turn and see Matt. He's standing there, holding his plate from earlier.

"What are you still doing up?" I ask.

"I could ask the same of you. Do you ever sleep? What's your excuse tonight?"

"I'm just trying to settle into the new room. It's too bright with the light on, but it's too dark without."

"Alright, Goldilocks," he says with a wide grin on his face. "So the answer is to come downstairs and watch scary movies? Put on a romance, judging our earlier conversation, you'll be so bored you'll be asleep in minutes."

"I'll fall asleep in a bit." I give a little shrug. "Do you want to watch with me?"

He walks away towards the kitchen and then returns a moment later. He sits on the chair, getting comfortable. We lapse into silence, watching the film on the screen.

I wake in the morning, on the sofa, a blanket wrapped around me.

"Morning, sleepy head. Is there something wrong with your bed?" Ben teases. He's sat in the chair that Matt had been sitting in to watch the film last night. I can't remember how much of the film I had seen before I fell asleep, but I feel like I have had a few solid hours of sleep.

"My bed is fine. I just crashed out watching some television," I reply. I sit up on the sofa and stretch.

"Do you want a burrito?"

"God, yes, they're amazing."

"Thank Lily next time you see her; she showed me how to make them."

"When is Lily here next?" I ask as I get up from the sofa and head towards the kitchen. He follows me.

"In a couple of weekends, we both have a few days off, I can't wait," he replies. "She's going to come here for a few days," Ben continues.

"Do you want one?" I gesture at the burritos that I've taken out of the fridge. He shakes his head, and I put one of the burritos in the microwave, setting the timer. "I'm looking forward to seeing Lily. I feel like I haven't seen her for ages."

"Well, you've been busy," he says, lightly. "You look a little better today."

"That's the power of these magic burritos." I smile. "Is Matt up?"

"He's gone out. He said he'll be back before your shift to take you to work."

"Okay."

"Are you sure it isn't too much? It is long hours," Ben asks after a pause. I glare at him. The microwave pings, and I take the burrito out. I check the time on the clock.

"I am going to eat my burrito and get ready for work. Are you working today?"

"I start nights tomorrow, for a week. See, not too bad living with your brother, we're like ships passing in the night." He grins.

"Keep up a steady supply of the burritos, and we'll be fine." I grin back.

"Hey, new girl, you're back!" Isaac greets me as Matt and I walk into the bar together later that day. Isaac reaches across the bar as I approach, giving me a high-five.

"I don't scare easily." I smile. "I heard there were toilets to clean."

"Not until you've washed a million glasses," he replies with a laugh.

Matt and I both cross over to stand behind the bar. The bar looks quiet, but it's only just gone three, and Matt had explained yesterday that this is often the lull between the lunch crowd and the party crowd.

"Have you been slacking off, Isaac?" Matt nudges him.

"No, boss man, blame the day staff. I only just started. The kitchen looks like a disaster zone."

"I'll get started." I head into the kitchen.

Isaac wasn't joking when he said there were a million glasses in the kitchen waiting to be cleaned. This is all a far cry from my previous job. I used to be a personal assistant to one of the company directors; I spent my days thriving under pressure; every day felt different and fast-paced, with unexpected curve balls and tasks to juggle. This is repetitive work, but I found yesterday I can throw myself into the work, keeping my hands and my mind busy. It's a remedy to the previous couple of weeks, where there had been no work, no distraction from my mind and constant overthinking.

"Do you want a hand?" Isaac asks as he comes into the kitchen a little while later.

"No, it's okay, I'm all good here."

"It's pretty quiet at the moment."

"Aren't they the famous last words?"

"I prefer it when it's busy. Matt does too as it means more money in his pocket. You know he's the boss, right?"

"Yeah, he told me he manages the place," I reply, putting a few glasses back in the right place.

"No, I mean, he is the boss. He co-owns this place. Some relative of his owns it, and Matt has a 10% stake, he eventually plans to buy the whole place." Isaac starts to put some of the clean glasses away with me.

"I didn't know that. I don't know Matt very well, just through my brother."

"Is that his roommate?"

"Yeah, Ben. He and Matt have been roommates for a while, I just moved in with them. Life went a bit sideways," I explain.

"Matt's pretty good at hiring people where life went sideways. What was your poison?" Isaac stares at me.

"Yo, Isaac, it's picking up out here, are you coming?" Matt yells from the bar area. Isaac gives me a shrug and heads back outside to the main area of the bar. I return to the glasses, throwing myself into the job.

Later, I take a seat at the bar, sitting opposite Matt as he wipes the bar down. I've washed more glasses than I can count, I've cleaned tables, mopped floors, cleaned the bathrooms and have a headache from the music that was playing earlier in the night. All the other staff members have gone home, it's just me and Matt as I wait for him to finish, so we can go home.

"Do you need a hand?" I ask him. He shakes his head.

"No, it's all good."

"Isaac said something earlier," I comment.

"Isaac has a big mouth." Matt throws the cloth towards the sink. He reaches under the bar for something and then he moves around to the same side of the bar as me, taking a seat next to me. He puts a piece of paper onto the bar. "What did he say?" Matt wonders. He busies himself with the piece of paper, folding it in half.

"He said you own some of this bar."

"I do. I thought Ben might have told you before." He folds the paper again.

"Who is the other owner?"

"My great-uncle. He's owned the bar for years. Antony wants to sell at some point, I couldn't get the capital to buy him outright, but he agreed to sell me a stake, and I'm working on the rest," Matt explains. He keeps moving the paper and folding it.

"That's great. This bar is awesome, it's a great atmosphere. I hope you are proud of this place."

"Yeah, I am."

"Isaac said you're good at hiring people whose life went sideways, and he asked me what my poison was. Do you know what he meant?" I watch him folding the paper in another direction. He glances at me, and then returns his gaze to the paper.

"I'm going to assume that Ben has told you that I had a problem with gambling?"

"He mentioned it." I shrug.

It's the same response he had given me yesterday when I asked him if Ben had told him about my heart surgery. Over the years that he has lived with Matt, Ben has mentioned Matt a few times, mostly when we would have dinner with our parents and talk about what was going off in our lives. He'd mentioned that Matt had a troubled past but that he had been working hard to get his life back on track. I hadn't paid too much attention, as at the time, Matt was just somebody in the abstract, with nothing directly to do with me.

"I got myself into a lot of trouble when I was younger. I started playing cards and roulette at a young age, old enough to gamble, but young enough to be naïve about what I was doing. At first, I felt like it was just a hobby, something that I'd do with a group of friends to have some fun, but at some point, it became more. It took over me, it became my sole focus, the only thing I wanted to do. It grew to something I thought about all the time rather than something I did to cut loose at a weekend.

"It became something I was doing every day. I couldn't pull myself away from chasing the next good hand, the next high from the roll of the dice or the thrill of the spin of the wheel. I gambled everything that I had. My girlfriend at the time, Jemima, was also in the lifestyle, and it was destructive between us. We lived together, but we both started losing track of where we were spending our money as it was all about the games.

"About four years ago, I lost every penny I had. I knew I'd fucked up, that it was no longer a fun activity but something consuming me. I moved back in with my family for a while, I went to gambling support groups, fell off the wagon a few times and got straight, but eventually, I decided I needed a clean break from the whole environment. All the old haunts, the old friends, it was just too much to be around constantly."

"Is that how you ended up here?"

"Yep. Antony offered me a job here, so I moved here. I stayed with Antony for a year, working and keeping my nose clean. I saved some money, and then I ended up moving into one of his rental houses, with Ben. Antony doesn't spend time at the bar now, so it keeps me busy and out of mischief.

"I feel like I have been lucky, I had support from my family, and from Antony, I got a second chance to make something good of my life, and I wanted to do something to help others. With Antony's agreement, I hire a lot of recovered addicts, gamblers mostly. In the bar, we don't allow any betting, we don't watch any sports games here. We keep each other on track."

"That's a really good thing you're doing."

"Isaac probably thinks you're a recovering addict of some sort. You can put him right tomorrow." Matt glances up and gives me a little smile, but then he returns his attention back to his paper.

"What happened with the girlfriend?"

"She turned up about a year ago, she told me she missed me and wanted to have another go at things, but she was still gambling, and she didn't want to change. I couldn't deal with that. I've worked too hard to stay on the straight and narrow to let somebody pull me back into that lifestyle. She moved back home, last I heard, she's still gambling."

"You can't help everybody," I sigh.

"No, you can't, you just have to focus on the ones you can," he replies. He gives a final fold of the paper and then hands it over to me. He's made an origami butterfly.

"That's really beautiful." I look over the butterfly, turning it in my hands, it's flawless. I can't believe he's managed to make this in front of me, knowing the folds by memory.

"You ready to go home?"

"I am." I smile. He gets up from the bar, giving a final check downstairs, flicking off lights as he goes. I follow him out of the building, watching as he locks up, and I slip the little butterfly into the pocket of my trousers.

We arrive home, Matt opens the door for me, and we head towards the kitchen, like an instinct. There is a pizza box on the side, our names written in marker pen on the top of the box in Ben's handwriting. Matt opens the box, and I grab a slice before he does. Like last night, I'm ravenous, even though I'd had a plate of chips on a break. I don't bother to reheat the pizza, and it tastes amazing.

"Want another slice?" Matt pushes the box towards me, but I shake my head.

"I'm going to try to get some sleep." I finish the crust of the pizza. "Goodnight, Matt." I walk towards the stairs. I head upstairs to the bathroom, brushing my teeth and washing my face. I go into my bedroom, and a minute later there is a soft knock on the door. I open it to find Matt standing there.

"Hey," he says; his voice is quiet, as he glances towards Ben's bedroom door like he doesn't want to wake him. "I have something for you," he whispers.

"That's a proper dodgy line." I giggle.

"Cool your jets, Goldilocks. You said it was too bright in the room if you keep the lights on, but too dark if you keep them off. Maybe this will be the 'just right' you've been looking for."

He passes me two little boxes. Inside each box is a set of indoor fairy lights. I take them from him, and for a moment I am not sure how to respond.

"Thank you, this is lovely."

"No problem. I saw them in town and thought I'd pick them up. Hopefully, they help."

"Goodnight, Matt," I say, softly.

"Goodnight, Beatrice." He walks towards his bedroom, stepping inside and shutting the door behind him.

I close my own door, flicking the lights on. I take one of the sets of fairy lights out of the box. This one is a delicate silver wire with little star-shaped lights on it. I wind the wire around the mirror that is hanging on the wall.

I open the other box, this one is also a delicate silver wire, but it has little flowers for the lights instead. I wind it around the headboard of my bed. I switch on the set of lights that is on my bed and then switch off the main light. The lights are twinkling above the headboard, giving a little light in the bedroom. It's light, but not too bright.

I take my shirt and bra off, pulling a tee on to sleep in. I take off my trousers, but before I put them in the wash pile, I take the little origami butterfly out of the pocket and put it on top of the chest of drawers. Then I climb into bed, curling up under the covers, looking at the patterns the light casts on the ceiling as I drift off to sleep.

Matt: Then, July

"Jesus, it's hot," Beatrice complains. She's fanning herself with an envelope that she's picked up from the stack that arrived in the post this morning. The rest of the post, she's dumped on the counter to sort through. It's only eleven, but it's ridiculously hot already. July is looking like we're going to have a decent summer this year.

"It's going to be busy tonight. It always is when it's sunny like this," I tell her.

"I assume it is normal times tonight?"

"Normal times," I confirm. We always work the same shift. It's easier for me to take her there and back. Beatrice puts down the envelope, so she can pull her hair into a tighter ponytail, winding the hair around and making a bun, her eyes closed, and a dreamy look on her face. I look away.

It's been three weeks since she moved in with Ben and me. In the last three weeks, I have learned so much about her.

She is stubborn as hell and the only person I know who can run circles around Ben.

Her best friend is on a year-long secondment in another country, and Beatrice phones her twice a week without fail though she always seems melancholy and wistful when she finishes the call.

She keeps track of her parents' travels on a map. They're currently travelling along the Pan-America Highway, and Beatrice puts little flags into the map when they tell her they have stopped somewhere, and she plans on giving them the map when they eventually return home.

She makes the best dinners when she isn't working, between her cooking and Ben's, who appears not to want to be outdone by his sister and has upped his cooking game, I haven't been so well fed since I left home.

She hogs the bathroom on a day off, spending what seems like hours in the bath.

She reads whenever she gets the chance. She likes thrillers and mystery stories, and surprisingly for somebody who hates the idea of a romance film, poetry.

She still watches horror movies though I don't find her in the living room late at night now.

She rubs her thumb when she is nervous, an action I'm not sure she is aware of, sometimes making her thumb look red and sore.

She tenses up every time somebody gets too close to her and then acts brightly like she's trying to pretend that it didn't happen.

She has her ex-boyfriend stored in her mobile as 'The Spawn of Satan' and scowls whenever he messages to tell her to pick up more post. She deletes each message when she gets one, and I've never seen her respond.

She drives me to distraction, every single day. She's got under my skin, and she has no idea. Every day, I remind myself, she's Ben's sister, my roommate. She's off-limits. Despite this daily reminder, I think of her a lot.

"Lily's here on Sunday," Beatrice reminds me, pulling me out of my thinking.

"Yeah, Ben looked like he was going to die of excitement this morning." I laugh.

"He's going to be insufferable." She giggles. "Oh, hey, more post for you." She slides a small envelope across to me, shifting the rest into a pile for Ben. I open the envelope and tip out the ring that I'd purchased. "Oh, pretty," she says, looking at the ring in my palm. It's only something cheap, an anti-anxiety ring.

"Here." I slide it across the counter towards her. "I thought it might help."

I watch as she makes that same move with her index finger, pulling it over the top of her thumb and rubbing at the same spot.

"This is for me?"

"You don't have to wear it, just thought it might save the skin on your thumb," I say. She pulls the ring onto her thumb, running her index finger over the beads on the band of the ring that moves.

"This is really sweet of you, thank you. Kinda goes a little way as repayment for cleaning toilets at work." She gives a little giggle.

"I pay you for that," I point out.

"Thank you, Matt." She leans over the counter, giving me a quick kiss on the cheek. "Fancy grabbing some lunch on the way to work?" she asks. I nod a response, as I don't trust myself to respond verbally. She leaves me in the kitchen. *Get a grip, Matt.* I tell myself. *Ben's sister*, I remind myself, for what feels like the hundredth time.

As usual, the heat outside has the bar packed solid. It seems like everybody is here tonight, all demanding pitchers of cocktails. In the past week, Beatrice has started working behind the bar with me when it's busy, serving customer after customer their drinks. She's fast and efficient and tends to get a flock of male customers waiting in her queue.

Tonight is so busy that Isaac, Kelly, Millie, and Tom are all behind the bar with us. There's not a lot of space, but at least the customers are getting served and everybody seems happy. I try to keep an eye on the rest of the team from the end of the bar where I am serving. I'm just finishing up a round of Porn Star Martinis for a rowdy bunch of women when I hear a commotion on the other side of the bar. There's a guy leaning across the bar, yelling at Kelly.

There is a spilt glass on the bar. I take the payment from the woman who had ordered the drinks and then push my way through the bar towards Kelly to see if I can diffuse the situation, but I can see Beatrice has already intervened. She's leaned over the bar to talk to the guy, who seems to be shouting back at her. She pulls away.

"You have yourself a lovely evening!" Beatrice exclaims to the guy, handing him a fresh drink.

The guy looks confused. He clearly doesn't know how to respond to her overly polite voice or the friendly smile on her face. He looks startled, the wind taken out of his sails, and he backs away from the bar, leaving his drink. He heads towards his group of friends. After a moment, they all get up and leave the bar. Kelly gives Beatrice a high-five as I eventually manage to make my way towards them.

"You are my hero!" Kelly laughs.

"Kill them with kindness, usually works." Beatrice chuckles.

"What happened?" I ask as I stand next to them.

"Guy over-reacted. He spilled his drink and blamed me, he got a little aggressive, but Beatrice sorted it out," Kelly explains.

"Take a break," I suggest. Kelly looks over at the queue. "Go on. We'll manage," I assure her. She slips out from behind the bar, heading towards the kitchen area for a break. I look at Beatrice. "Are you okay?" I ask her.

"Fine. Get back to work." She nudges me, so I head back to my section of the bar, but I can't stop looking over in her direction to be sure everything is okay.

The rest of the evening is hectic but without incident. The crowd starts to die down about an hour before closing, so I let a few of the team members go home early, leaving Beatrice, Isaac and I to wind things down.

After we closed the doors to the last customers, the three of us set around cleaning up. Beatrice tackles the tables whilst I clean the bar and Isaac cleans the glasses in the kitchen. Once Beatrice has taken the last tray of glasses through to Isaac, she helps me with the bar.

"I said we'd help Isaac with the glasses when we're done in here," Beatrice tells me.

"Thanks for everything this evening. You have a knack for diffusing a situation. You should give classes to the rest of the staff; I could get rid of the security team," I tease.

She winks. "Not sure if you could afford my teachings."

"That guy earlier had no idea what to say to you. He was looking at you like he had no idea what to do." I laugh.

"Most people don't know what to do with me." She laughs with me. She leans up against the bar opposite me, and I look her up and down, feeling heady. If she were anybody else, I would be teasing her, joking that I know exactly what we could do if she wanted to, and the words are on the tip of my tongue, almost bubbling over my lips, but I shouldn't. It's Beatrice. It would be a line that could change things between us and could alter this friendship we have been building.

Instead, I grin. "That's what happens when you deal with boys instead of men."

"Oh, men like you, you mean?" She snorts, and my reluctance to tease her, to cross a line, is gone.

"Beatrice, you wouldn't be able to handle me," I tease, throwing a tea towel towards her.

"Maybe you're the one that couldn't handle me," she quips as she catches it.

"Don't let your mouth write a cheque that your ass can't cash." I throw back at her.

"I can cover all my cheques, thank you very much." She smirks.

We stare at each other, and there is a frisson in the air. I can feel the tension between us. She stares at me with her brown eyes, her eyes seeming to search my facial expression for something I'm not brave enough to say. Her lips are parted slightly, and I feel like I've been electrocuted. My heart feels like it's beating a little too fast, and I wonder if she feels the same thing I am feeling, or whether this is all in my head.

"Hey, Matt, I'm drowning under these glasses, you almost done?" Isaac shouts from the kitchen area. Great fucking timing, as usual.

The tension between us dissipates, and she throws the tea towel back towards me.

"Stop slacking, Matt." She heads towards the kitchen to help Isaac. I take a moment before I follow, muttering to myself that I need to get a grip.

I spend Sunday out of the house. Lily, Ben, and Beatrice have been spending the day together, and despite being invited to be with them, I had made myself scarce. I want to clear my head because Beatrice appears to be filling my brain, and it's driving me crazy.

I return home in the evening and get changed, ready for a date I've arranged with a woman I've been chatting to. I head back downstairs to say goodbye. Ben and Lily are curled up together on the sofa, a bowl of popcorn between them. Beatrice sits on the armchair, a small tub of ice cream in her hand.

They must have paused the film on the television as I came down the stairs. I can tell it is Lily's choice as the screen is frozen on the opening credits of a weepy romance film. I meet Beatrice's gaze, and she rolls her eyes, mouthing the words 'I was outvoted'.

"Are you joining us, Matt? We ordered takeaway earlier, but there is enough left over if you're hungry." Lily looks over at me. She's a sweetheart.

"I would, but I have a date," I reply.

Beatrice smirks at me. "Pretty sure at this time of night, it's a booty call, not a date."

"It's not that late," I protest.

"Good to see you're getting back out there," Ben comments. "What's her name?"

"Ella. She's a waitress at a restaurant in town, and if I don't get going now, I will be late. See you guys later."

"Have fun!" Lily calls as I turn to leave.

"Good luck!" Ben says.

"Don't forget the condoms!" Beatrice calls at the same time.

I stop walking and lean back around the doorframe. "Enjoy the film. I have heard it's a real heartbreaker." I grin at her. She scowls. I resist the urge to laugh, and I head out of the door, to get to my date. I push the thoughts of Beatrice from my mind.

I meet Ella outside the restaurant where she works. We met on a dating site and have been exchanging messages for a couple of weeks, long before Beatrice arrived, but this is the first time we've agreed to meet in person. Ella is shorter than I thought she would be from her profile information, but as cute as she was in her pictures. Her hair has been dyed and cut since her last profile picture, instead of the dark hair she has in her profile, she's now a bright blonde, cut into a short pixie cut. She gives her hair a self-conscious touch as I walk up to her, smiling and greeting her.

"I'm not quite used to being blonde and short-haired yet," she explains.

"It suits you," I say though she looked better before. She doesn't quite pull off the brightness of her hair colour.

"Thank you. So are we still on for a drink?" she asks.

I nod, and we walk towards the cocktail bar we had discussed when exchanging messages last night. It's only a few buildings down from the restaurant she works at. The bar we've planned to go to is usually quiet, not like my bar which is often noisy and people shout for attention. I prefer the hustle and bustle of my bar, but at least we'll be able to hear each other on our date at the cocktail bar she has picked.

"How was your shift?" I make polite conversation as we walk.

"It was fine. I'm not going to miss working in hospitality though. I start a new job next week, no more serving people and crazy late nights. Why anybody wants to work in that industry is beyond me." She smiles.

"It's definitely not an easy job," I agree. I know I have told her what I do for a living and what I plan to do with the bar.

"Have you been working today?" she asks as I open the door to the cocktail bar for her. We walk in together and head towards the bar.

"No, not today. I have Sundays off. What would you like to drink?" I offer her a menu from the side of the bar.

"A Cosmopolitan, please."

"Go grab a table. I'll be over in a minute."

Ella heads towards one of the tables near the window, and I order her Cosmopolitan and myself a glass of whisky. I look over at Ella whilst waiting for the drinks. She's sat texting on her phone and fussing with her hair. I take my own phone from my pocket. I want to send a message to Beatrice, to ask her whether she is enjoying the film, but I hesitate. I put my phone away, collect the drinks, and head over towards Ella, who glances up from her phone and smiles at me as I cross over the bar towards her.

"Do you want to come up for a coffee?" Ella pulls me closer to her. We are outside of her block of flats. It isn't late, our date has been nice, but I've decided to call the evening short, telling Ella I can walk her home. She's reading more into my offer.

I look down at Ella. She's staring up at me, a small smile on her face. She stands on her tiptoes, leaning closer towards me. This would be the perfect opportunity for a kiss, and she's nice, but all I can think about is Beatrice.

"Maybe next time," I reply. I lean and kiss her on the cheek. "Goodnight, Ella."

"Next time," she replies. I wait as she lets herself in her building. I head towards home, walking instead of catching the bus or a taxi, hoping to clear my head before I get home.

I let myself into the house, it's dark and quiet. I walk past the living room to head to the kitchen for a glass of water, but I see a small glow of light from the living room as I pass. I look around the doorway, seeing Beatrice curled up on the sofa, listening to an iPod through some headphones, scrolling the screen for a different track.

I step into the living room, my shadow crossing over her as I walk, and she jumps, startled, pulling the headphones from her ears.

"Jesus Christ, you have to stop doing that!" she exclaims.

"I thought you said you could give Ghostface a run for his money. You would be easy pickings. I'm convinced you wouldn't last the first scene." I laugh. "What are you doing down here, I thought you were sleeping better?"

"I am. I just..." she starts. "They're not as quiet as they think they are," she finishes.

At that moment, I hear a series of bumps from upstairs. It's the unmistakable sound of a headboard thudding against the wall. Beatrice shudders.

I laugh. "Come on." I offer my hand to pull her up from the sofa. Once she is standing, I nip into the kitchen and grab two ciders from the fridge. I return to

Beatrice and lead her to the back of the house, opening the back door to the garden. We make our way to the end of the garden, sitting on the garden furniture.

"I love them to pieces, but Jesus, I'm scarred for life." She shakes herself like she's trying to get the sound out of her head. I hand her a bottle of cider. "So how was the booty call?"

"It was a date, thank you very much, not a booty call."

"You know the way to check whether it is a booty call is whether you did any man-scaping before this alleged date."

"Man-scaping?" I laugh.

"Yeah, if you prepped, it's a booty call."

"So, if you shave or wax your legs, it's preparation for something?" I laugh at her logic.

"Okay, shaving legs doesn't count, as there are other reasons for that. A doctor's appointments, shorts weather, and such. I just know, if I am putting on fancy underwear for a date, I have an intention behind it. Personally, if I'm putting stockings on for a date, I'm fully anticipating somebody else peeling them off."

Jesus, this conversation is making me feel uncomfortable.

"It wasn't a booty call. I am a gentleman." I find myself scowling.

"Are you seeing her again?"

"Maybe," I reply, but I'm not sure I will. "I don't know. She came across differently tonight than she had over our messages."

"How so?"

"A little condescending, like everybody is beneath her. I doubt she would understand if I told her about my past."

"The gambling? Don't make a big thing out of it. It's not who you are now, just a small part of what makes you who you are, not all of you. Show her who you really are. You're very sweet when you get past that prickly exterior of yours."

"Prickly?" I huff.

"Yeah, you are to start off with." She shrugs and takes a sip of her cider.

"In my defence, you're very intimidating. You're all smiley but asking very probing questions. People have upheld better under torture than being questioned by you."

"Tosser," she mutters but gives me a small smile.

"What about you? Any plans for getting back on the dating scene? What are you looking for?" I ask.

"Somebody who is upfront about who they really are, so there are no surprises. Somebody who stands by you when you need it," she replies after a long silence.

"What happened between you and your ex?" I wonder. She shakes her head. It is clearly a question too far.

"So, if this girl isn't the right one, what next? Who are you looking for?" She throws the focus back onto me.

For a second, I'm concerned that the 'I am looking for you' I hear in my head is something I've said aloud. As she doesn't have a horrified expression on her face, I breathe a sigh of relief.

"How long do you think they'll be at it?" I nod towards the house, changing the subject.

"Oh, I am in no rush to get back inside. It's nice out here." She smiles. She leans back, looking up at the stars. The back of the house is dark and secluded, so the only light is from the stars above and the small sliver of the moon.

"Beautiful," I agree. We sit talking in the garden until the early hours of the morning, only going back inside as the dawn breaks, and not once during the night do I regret my decision to come home.

Beatrice: Now

Mum calls the next afternoon. It's early in the morning for them, and I can hear Dad making breakfast in the background.

"Beatrice!" Mum has a way of making it sound like she is singing my name.

"Hi, Mum," I say to her, being grateful that she's phoned instead of video calling me.

The sound of my mother's voice and the sound of Dad swearing to himself as he makes breakfast fill me with nostalgia, and I take a moment to compose myself. I have called them overprotective and smothering in the past, but what would I give right now to be with them, to have Mum pull me close for a hug, for Dad to ruffle my hair and tell me his trademark comfort sentences like 'it'll all come out in the wash, pet'.

"Have you thought any more about what I asked?" Mum queries, and I feel my master plan of not telling my parents I have been in hospital could unravel immediately.

I have begged Ben not to tell our parents what has happened. He had reluctantly agreed last night after much pleading on my side. Now, as Mum is talking, I'm wondering how long I can pull the wool over her eyes. She's like a master detective, a super sleuth. She is the type of person who, if you don't respond at the right speed, instantly knows that something is wrong, even if you told her everything was fine. I'm not going to survive this conversation if I don't step carefully.

"Remind me, Mother, which one of the many things you have asked me about, do you currently mean." I attempt a laugh. "You have to at least put me in the right ballpark," I tease.

"Alright, cheeky madam, I was talking about the idea of you coming to stay with us for a while. I know you have your little job, and I know you seem happier, but we would love to have you. We're here for the next few weeks. You could hop on a flight and meet up with us."

There is a clattering in the background as Dad drops something and curses loudly.

"Is that just so you can have somebody else cook for you?" I tease. My mother is not known for her culinary skills. Neither is my dad, but he had planned to cook more whilst they're travelling. Ben and I had teased them when they had told us this, asking whether their travel plans were just an elaborate diet plan instead.

"Well, I wouldn't object to having you here and cooking, but I would love you here even if you didn't lift a finger. I miss you."

"I miss you too, both of you."

"Besides, you must be lonely there. Ben is always working, and Jas isn't home yet. Come stay with us until Jas is home. I can look after you."

"I don't need looking after," I remind her, gently. I may not remember the last few months, but I know my independence is something ingrained in me, something we have fought about a lot in the past. It isn't her fault, and I try not to be too hard on her when we have these arguments. I am sure that every time she looks at me, she sees me in a hospital bed, and she just wants to protect me from anything else.

It must have been hard for her. I can't imagine what she went through when I was sick, all the times she has worried that I will end up back in the hospital, but I am well. I am healthy. I may currently be hazy in the memory department, but I am still here.

"Come anyway. You always said you wanted to travel."

"Yes…" I begin. I want to finish with a reminder that I wanted to travel alone, not with my parents, but I don't want to hurt her feelings. My reluctance to finish my sentence is misinterpreted.

"Yes, you'll come?"

"No! Besides, Jas is home next week. I want to catch up with her," I remind her. I know this because, on the calendar app on my phone, I have a reminder set for in a week's time, title reading: 'the bestie is back'.

"You could come afterwards. What is holding you there?"

"Are you sure you're just not homesick?" I tease, just so I can avoid answering her question.

"No, we are having a blast! What is it they say, hashtag van life?"

"Please tell me you haven't signed up for social media," I groan.

I hadn't seen any profile for my parents when I scrolled through my remaining social media profile last night, looking for more clues. The only new pages I follow are apparently the bar I work at, and some model that I don't remember knowing about.

"No, but that is a bloody good idea. What do you think, Tommy? Shall we create a social media profile and document our travels?" Mum calls to Dad, and I hear him tell her to get lost.

"I think maybe you should stay off social media. Dad would get banned for excessive swearing, or you'd accidentally stream yourself doing something stupid, like bickering about how you cook bacon." I laugh.

"You could come and manage our account! Hashtag van life daughter."

"Use the hash-tag in a sentence again, and I will disown you."

"Just think about it." Mum grumbles. To change the topic, I ask Mum how they're finding Canada. She tells me about the places they have been recently (beautiful, breathtaking), the people they have met (wonderful, new friends for life), and the food they've eaten (miles better than your dad can rustle up in here).

We end the call with me promising I will think about their offer for me to join them for a bit, and they tell me to let Ben know they'll call him tomorrow.

Once my parents are off the line, I sit alone in my room for a bit. Ben's gone for a long shift today and Matt appears to be out, so I've spent most of the day alone. I look at the things in my room, the mystery items I have acquired in the months I don't remember. I pull out the necklace and the ring they gave me in the hospital. They're beautiful. The ring doesn't look expensive; it's made of sterling silver with crisscrossing bands and little beads that are on the middle band that can be moved around.

It looks to be an anti-anxiety ring; the type people can wear and use as a distraction. The necklace, on the other hand, looks expensive. It's white gold, a thin, delicate chain, and at the bottom, a circular band the size of a fifty-pence piece. On one side, the band is embedded with white stones, and on the other, it is engraved with the line from a poem, 'you are my sun, my moon, and all my stars'. It's exquisite. I put the necklace on, and the edge of the circular band falls to just above the top of my surgery scar.

As I close the clasp of the chain, I get the same feeling in my body that I felt when I had been talking to Ben last night about Christmas. I sit down on the bed, the feeling is something that feels pure and right, and I wonder how I came to own this necklace. It doesn't seem like something I would have purchased for myself, definitely not with it being engraved, even though I love the poem the line is from. I can't find a single memory in my brain about this necklace, but I know it is something important to me.

I put the ring on, it fits onto my thumb. Like instinct, my index finger goes across the top of my thumb, spinning the circles on the middle band. I wonder how many times I have worn this. How many times have I moved my finger in that action, playing with the ring? Did I buy it for myself? What is it that made me so anxious that I wear a ring as a distraction?

I keep both pieces of jewellery on, the necklace tucked away and hidden under my top, and I head downstairs to the living room. I flick on the television and launch Netflix. Ben had told me he had set me a profile up when I had first moved in. He had joked last night that it was because he didn't want to get stuck with recommendations based on my terrible viewing history, but in my list of recommendations, all I see are titles for horror films. I appear to have watched a load of them. I select *Scream* to re-watch.

I hear the front door open. A moment later, Matt stops at the living room door. He looks at the television.

"Classic."

"It is. I remember the first time I watched this. I was sure Drew Barrymore was going to be the main character, couldn't believe the first scenes." I smile at him, but he doesn't smile back. "Are you in for the night?"

"No, I have work in a bit," he replies, and he ventures into the living room, taking a seat on the opposite side of the sofa to me.

"Speaking of work…"

"Yes?"

"When do you want me back?" I ask him, and he looks a little startled.

"I wasn't sure you wanted to get back to work. You were telling Ben yesterday that you don't want people to know you've got amnesia."

"Correct."

"That's going to be difficult to hide at work. What about the other people you work with? You've had months with them, they all know you. You're not going to be able to bullshit your way through a shift with them, pretending to know who they are."

"I just don't want people to be all intrigued and sympathetic." I shoot back; annoyed at the suggestion I want to bullshit people.

"They wouldn't make you uncomfortable. They're a good bunch of people. You've been to parties with them, socialised with them, made friends with them."

"I have?"

"Yes. So, if you want to start work again, you'll need to be honest with them. I don't think it would be right to lie to them. That's not fair to them. If you want to keep this a secret still, then I'll keep you on sick pay for a bit."

"They're my only two choices?"

"They are my terms and conditions," he says with a shrug.

"Fine, I'll wait for a bit. Hopefully, I'll get my memory back quickly, and this will all go away, and you won't have to re-train me."

"Yes because it was so annoying last time." He sounds like he is joking, but his facial expression and tone don't match the words. He just ends up looking pissed off.

"Just a question… Are you a dick to everyone you speak to, or just me?" I ask him, and he gets an expression on his face that I can't read.

"What?"

"You're so closed off."

"Closed off?" he repeats.

"You have a very prickly exterior. You look perpetually pissed off," I elaborate.

"Good to know I've made such an impression in the, what, three days you remember talking to me," he mutters.

"Have you been like this the whole time I've lived here? I'm surprised you're still breathing and not buried under the patio."

"Confident of you to assume you could bury me." He shoots back, sounding like he is summoning all his bravado.

I shrug. "People underestimate me all the time. I'm pretty strong."

"I know," he says so quietly I almost miss it.

I look at him, surprised. "How do you know?"

"We take turns in doing push-up challenges before we start wrestling bears each morning. We bench press together in the gym," he replies, deadpan. I roll my eyes at him. Then he sighs. "Look, this is weird. I know you, and you don't really know me. It's awkward, and I don't really know what I'm supposed to say."

"So tell me all about Matt. What have I learned about Matt since I lived here? Fill me in on the details. What do I need to know?" I ask him, but he doesn't answer. Instead, he gets up from the sofa, heading towards the living room door.

When he gets there, he pauses. "To answer you earlier question, no, not you. I don't intend to sound like a dick. I'm sorry if that is your impression of me. I'm just going through something."

"Anything I can help with?" I ask, but he doesn't say another word, just disappears from the living room, leaving me alone.

Beatrice: Then, August

"Are you sure you're going to be okay by yourself?" Ben asks me.

It is early morning. His bag is packed and sat near the front door. We're having breakfast together before he heads to Lily's to pick her up for their week away in a log cabin. According to Lily, it's in the middle of nowhere, and they're both looking forward to the peace and quiet.

"I am not totally incapable of looking after myself." I roll my eyes. I poke at the rest of my Weetabix.

"I know, but I still don't like the idea of leaving you here alone."

"I'll be fine," I reply, firmly. I give him a bright smile. "I've got lots of TV to catch up on."

I've got a week off work, originally Jas was going to come home for a week for her summer holiday, but she's been snowed under with a work project and needs to stay. Jas had asked me whether I minded, especially as the decision was last-minute, and I'd told her it was fine, but now I am at a loose end. No work as a distraction. No Ben coming in and out of the house. No Matt distracting me as he's going away as well to see his family. Regardless of how adrift I feel, I'll be damned if my brother knows and worries about me.

"Okay, you know you can call me at any point, right?" He finishes his breakfast and puts the bowl into the sink.

"Get going, otherwise you'll get stuck in the traffic." I finish my own breakfast, put my bowl into the sink and then push Ben towards the front door.

"If there are any issues, do you promise to give me a call?" He picks up his bag, but he still looks troubled.

"Who do I call to say I have an overprotective brother who won't get the heck out of the house?" I pull a face.

He laughs and kisses me on the cheek. "I'll see you in a week."

"Text to let me know you got there safely. Say hi to Lily for me." I wave at him and watch as he walks down the driveway to his car. I watch as he drives off and then I shut the front door. I sit in the living room, flicking the television on and watch the breakfast news.

"Has Ben left?" Matt asks as he comes into the living room with a plate of toast, taking a seat on the sofa next to me.

"Yep. What time are you setting off?"

"Not long. What time is your friend coming?"

"She isn't. I thought I'd told you?" I look over at him.

"No, you didn't tell me that."

"I'm surprised Ben didn't tell you last night," I comment. He and Matt were out last night for drinks.

"He was too busy talking about Lily. I think a tornado could have come through the bar, and he wouldn't have noticed." Matt grins.

"Ha, sounds like Ben when he's got Lily on the brain."

"So, if your friend isn't coming, are you going to be here alone? Have you thought about flying to see your parents?"

"No, the flights are expensive. Besides, I want them to enjoy their time alone."

"What about catching up with other friends?"

"Other friends, no. Aside from Jas, they were mostly people from my old job. We don't keep in touch," I explain. I try not to feel a pinch of pain, but it happens anyway, and I fiddle with the ring he gave me. "Don't worry, I'll keep myself entertained, besides, I am sure Ben's installed nanny cams to keep an eye on me," I joke.

"No, sorry, not happening." Matt shakes his head.

"I was joking about the cameras."

"I meant it's not right for you to stop alone. That's not fair."

"Well, I'm not sure what to tell you." I laugh.

He is quiet for a minute. "You could come with me."

"I'm sorry, what?"

"Well, what else are you going to do? There's a spare room at my mum's, even with both my brothers being home. She won't mind."

"I can't gatecrash your family catch-up." I roll my eyes.

"You can't call it crashing if I have invited you," he says with a firm voice.

I hesitate for a moment. There is no reason why I shouldn't stay here by myself. This is my home. Regardless of how miserable I'd felt when I had been moving in, I wouldn't want to be anywhere else right now. I love this place, but staying here without the noise of Ben and Matt is something new, and I'm not sure I want the time to myself.

Six hours later, Matt is showing me to a bedroom in his mum's house. He puts my small suitcase on the bed for me.

"My mother will be home in about an hour. I'll introduce you when she's here."

"Are you sure she doesn't mind me crashing your holiday?" I fret.

Now I'm here, I feel suddenly nervous. It hadn't taken long for him to convince me to come along with him, but now, I feel like an imposter.

"I'm sure. She's working in the daytime this week, but she'll be around in the evenings, so it will be family dinners and the like. My brothers will be arriving in a bit as well," Matt tells me.

"Toby and Sam, right? You're the baby of the family, yes?"

"Less of the baby, thanks. Yes, Toby and Sam. Toby's wife is Polly, and Sam's fiancé is Andy. You'll like them. Right, I'm going to unpack. Get yourself settled."

He leaves the room, shutting the door behind him. I check my phone. Ben's messaged to say that he has arrived at his holiday home with Lily but tells me his phone signal is patchy. He gives me the landline number of the main lodge, for emergencies. I text him back the most exasperated emoji I can find on my phone. I want to message him a reminder that I'm a fully functioning adult, but given I've hijacked Matt's holiday rather than be by myself, I'm not sure I am on solid ground in that argument, so I switch off my phone instead, making myself busy putting my things away.

"So you're Beatrice. It is nice to meet you." Matt's mother, Alice, pulls me in for a big hug when we're introduced later that evening. I've already met Matt's two brothers and their partners, who are now all in the garden getting a barbecue going for tea. "Excuse the dog, he's a little friendly." Alice laughs, as a Springer Spaniel makes excited circles around my legs. Alice lets me out of the hug so that I don't get tripped over by the dog.

"Oh my, you are so cute! What's your name?" I fuss over the dog.

"That's Del-Boy. Rodney is on his way. They come to work with me every day, all the patients love them, and they adore the attention." Alice smiles. She reminds me of Matt, like him she is tall, dark-haired, and she has a smile that lights up her whole face.

"Del-Boy and Rodney?" I can't help but laugh.

"They replaced Batman and Robin." Matt laughs from across the kitchen. The second dog walks into the kitchen, and I bend to fuss them both.

"Thank you for having me here." I look up at Alice.

"Not a problem, I'm looking forward to grilling you later on what Matt's been getting up to."

"I will happily tell you all his secrets." I glance over at Matt who looks like he is about to protest, so I give him a quick wink. "Maybe towards the end of the week, in private, as I'm relying on him to drive me home."

"Hurry up with the burger buns, Matt!" One of his brothers shouts from the garden.

"Come on, Mum, hope you're ready for tea." Matt grabs the burger buns, walking towards Alice. He gives her a kiss on the cheek and then we head out into the garden for tea.

I wake to the sunlight streaming through the curtains. It is early in the morning. I can already tell it's going to be a scorcher of a day. Last night, we'd stayed up until late in the back garden, eating the barbecue food, drinking and laughing, telling jokes and stories. I'd laughed so hard at the stories that Matt's brothers had told me about the exploits they'd had growing up, some of which appeared to be new information for Alice who looked scandalised.

I stretch and get out of bed, pulling on a pair of shorts to make myself look a little more presentable for breakfast given I have no idea how many of Matt's family will be up.

I potter to the kitchen, finding Matt sitting at the breakfast bar. He is dressed in a short-sleeved tee shirt and shorts.

"Morning." He smiles, looking suspiciously pleased about something.

"Morning. Is it just us?"

"Yeah, Toby and Polly have gone for a bike ride, and they are then going to the beach. Sam and Andy are there already. We thought we would meet up and spend the day at the beach if you're up for it." He taps a cool box that is stored next to his feet. "Lunch is all ready."

"The beach sounds fun. Have you been up long? You should have woken me."

"I popped out to get stuff for today. You mentioned you don't have a swimsuit."

"Correct. But it's okay. I will just wear shorts and a tee if I go in the water."

"Ah, see, this is where my supply run comes in." Matt grins. He reaches behind the cool box for something. He hands me a bag, and I open it to look inside. It's a bikini. I shake my head.

"Not going to happen."

"Look, I know you tend to hide yourself away, but it is a lovely day, time to get some vitamin D."

"But…"

"Nobody is going to stare at your scar, not when I am going to wear these." He reaches into a second bag, and he pulls out the loudest, most ridiculous-looking swimming trunks I have ever seen. They're so florescent that they're hurting my eyes, and I start to laugh at the sight of them. "If you don't think they are distracting enough, I can wear these."

He pulls out a pair of tiny Speedos from the bag that I know instantly would look obscene on him. He swings them around on his finger and then puts them on the side. "Or, if that doesn't make you feel comfortable, I have this option," he concludes, and he pulls out a mankini. He waves it in front of me. It takes me a full minute to stop laughing. When I compose myself, he is looking at me, expectantly.

"If I wear the bikini, but don't get the courage to take off my tee, do you promise you won't judge me?"

"Absolutely."

"Okay. Give me a minute to change and then have breakfast. Oh, and you should wear the first set. You'll get arrested in the other two for public exposure." I grin. I head towards my bedroom.

"Aw, Beatrice, I man-scaped for this!" he calls after me.

The funny thing is I believe he might have done.

I go back to the en-suite of the bedroom I'm staying in and have a quick shower, wrapping myself in a towel and then going back into my room to look at the bikini. What he has picked out for me is nice. There is a pair of high waist bottoms and a halter next top, both in a dark emerald colour. I take my towel off, pulling the bottoms on and then the top. I look at myself in the mirror.

I don't often reveal my chest. It isn't that I am ashamed of my scar, far from it. Over the years I've learned to make peace with the scar, it's a memory of something I went through. What bothers me is that people react when they see it, and that makes me uncomfortable.

I had some issues with my recovery from surgery, and it left me with a hypertrophic scar, so instead of my scar fading as the surgeon had initially thought, it's visible and raised in places rather than flat. People tend to stare, and they're not as discrete as they think they are when they do. Adults are the worst for the gawking and staring.

My scar runs the whole way of my sternum. I feel like everything is on display in this bikini. I grab a tee and pair of denim cut-offs from my wardrobe to put on over my bikini and then head back into the kitchen to have breakfast. Matt has changed from his shorts to his swim trunks.

"You had a good guess of my size for the bikini," I say. I reach for some cereal.

"That's because you're always leaving your underwear to dry on the radiators for me to pick up," he jokes. More than a few times, I've seen him look horrified as a pair of pants or bra gets knocked off the radiator as he walks through the house. "Eat up and then we can get going."

By the time we arrive at the beach, both Matt's siblings and partners are already there. They've set up some windbreakers and mats, creating our own little section of the beach.

"Woah, man! That is some camouflage you have going on there." Toby grins. He points at Matt's ridiculous shorts. Sam shields his eyes.

"I'm blind!" he exclaims.

"Where the hell did you find those?" Andy laughs. He's rubbing sunscreen onto Sam's back but he stops so he can also pretend to shield his eyes.

"At least we will be able to find you in the crowds." Polly giggles.

"I think they suit him," I say, loyally, though they are ridiculous.

"Thank you, Beatrice, at least somebody else has good taste." Matt puts down the cool box, and pulls off his tee shirt, putting it into the rucksack he's got with him. He kicks off his trainers and then takes a seat on one of the mats. I take off my sandals and sit next to him, keeping my shorts and tee on.

"Are you coming for a swim?" Polly asks us both. She takes off her tee shirt, underneath she is wearing a skimpy red bikini. She looks fantastic, like a runway model. Sam, Toby and Andy all stand up to join her.

"In a min," Matt replies. The four of them walk towards the sea. Matt doesn't look like he is in a rush to go anywhere. He throws the car key into the cool box and settles back on the mat. We sit in silence for a few minutes.

"Come on then," I say, eventually. I stand up and take my shorts off. He props himself on one arm, looking at me as I hesitate on my tee.

"The world isn't going to stop turning, you know. If people are looking at you, it's not the scar, trust me. It's your knockout body."

"Hardly knockout." I roll my eyes. "Polly is a knockout."

"Well, she is a model." Matt shrugs "But you give her a run for her money."

"She's an actual model?"

"Yeah, that's how they met. Toby is a photographer. Cliché relationship, the photographer and his muse." He laughs as he sits himself up. I sigh, pulling my tee off and throwing it onto the mat. Immediately, I want to put it back on again, but the heat of the sun on my bare skin feels nice.

"Are you going to sit there all day? Are you a chicken?" I tease, trying to sound confident.

He gets up. "Chicken, Beatrice?" He tries to sound menacing. He looks like he is about to pounce, so I take a step back, turn around, and start a jog towards the sea. I'm almost at the water when Matt appears from behind me, scooping me up and throwing me over his shoulder. He carries me the rest of the way into the water.

"Put me down." I laugh, by now I can tell he's getting into deeper water as my feet are wet from the waves.

"Put you down? You sure?" With that, he goes to throw me into the water. I hold onto him, pulling him with me, the two of us falling together under the wave. The water is warmer than I expected, and when we resurface, we're both laughing.

"I'm going to have to tell your mother one of your secrets tonight to repay you for that," I warn him.

"Seems fair." He laughs as he shakes some of the water from his hair. "Come on."

He points over to where his family are swimming, a little further out, so we swim out to join them. The warmth of the sea, the heat of the sun on my body, it's glorious, and I'm so glad I decided to come away.

We swim and mess around in the sea for what seems like hours. Afterwards, we head back to the mats that they'd set up earlier, wrapping up in the towels, drying off and then sitting to eat the lunch from the cool box. Polly borrows Matt's phone and takes pictures of us all. She'd been telling me about her job, so I give her the most over-dramatic pose I can make for my picture.

After lunch, we slather ourselves in more suncream and then sunbathe, and I nod off for a while, enjoying the warmth of the sun. Matt nudges me awake later. Whilst I was dozing, the guys had set up an area for a game of beach volleyball. He asks if I want to join them.

Matt calls himself as team captain before either of his brothers can, and there is a disagreement between Sam and Toby as to who gets to be the other captain. A few of Sam's friends have joined us, and we are soon in teams of six. Matt and I are teamed up with Toby, Polly and two friends of Sam's called Daniel and David. Sam and Andy are on the other team with some more friends, Lou, Daisy, Aiden and Luka.

The game gets aggressive quickly, and at one point, Matt and I both run for the ball at the same time, bashing into one another. We end up on the sand together, him half atop of me, his face in the sand. I laugh a little.

"Are you okay?" He lifts his head and turns to look at me. There's sand on the side of his face.

"Yes, I think my boobs took most of the impact," I joke.

"Sorry." He stands and then offers me a hand to pull me up from the sand. "Are you okay to carry on?"

"Yep, all good." I reach up and brush the sand from his face.

"Are we back at it?" Aiden claps his hands together to rush us along. Matt shoots the volleyball over the net towards him. He gives me another glance to check on me.

"Head in the game, Matt, I'm playing to win!" I remind him. He shakes his head and laughs, returning to the game.

Later, Matt's family head off home, leaving the two of us on the beach. They've packed up the items we'd had with us, putting them in Matt's car. Sam and Andy are taking Alice out for dinner tonight, and Toby and Polly are meeting up with some friends for drinks. We keep one of the mats with us to sit on together. I stay on the beach whilst Matt goes to one of the beachfront stores, returning with a tray of fish and chips for me, and chips and a battered sausage for him.

We sit on the beach in silence to eat the food. The chips are hot, salty and soaked in vinegar; they're absolutely perfect.

"This is amazing." I lick some of the grease from the fish from my fingers.

"It's my favourite chip shop. I always come here when I am home."

"Thank you. I've had a wonderful day. Your family is awesome."

"Yeah, they're pretty great." Matt smiles. "I am glad you're enjoying yourself."

"I'll pay you back for the bikini; just let me know how much it cost you."

"Don't worry about it. I wasn't sure you would wear it or if you would be offended."

"I wasn't offended. Nervous that people would be making comments all day," I admit. Matt points towards the centre of my chest which is now covered up with my tee.

"That is a battle you won. Don't let anybody ever make you feel like it's something you should cover up."

"Why are you so nice to me?" I ask, nudging against him.

"Am I nice enough that you will let me have some of your fish?"

"Nope, sorry, I'm not sharing a fish this amazing." I laugh, but I cut off a piece of my fish to give him, and he gives me a piece of his sausage. We stay on the beach, watching the sunset.

Matt: Then, August

"So are you and Beatrice…?" Mum starts over breakfast, halfway through our stay. I pass her the coffee I've made her then take a seat at the breakfast bar.

"We are just friends," I reply.

"I was going to ask if you were up for playing the murder mystery game tonight, but good to know where your mind is at." Mum laughs. She feigns a look of innocence at the trap she's walked me into.

"We're on for the game," I reply. Mum gives me a look, the one I consider to be her trademark therapist-thinking look. Head ever so slightly bent to the right, one eyebrow slightly raised, lips pursed together. "What?"

"You seem to really like her."

"I do. She's a good friend."

"You seem to like her as more than a friend," Mum comments.

"She's my best friend's sister." I give a small laugh, like what she's saying is the most absurd thing to have been said, ever.

"She seems to like you."

"I don't think so," I say, shortly. I'm confident that Beatrice doesn't see me as anything other than her roommate, her brother's friend. "I'm sure she'd be looking for something more and better than what I have to offer," I add.

"I do wish you'd stop being so hard on yourself, Matt." Mum reaches across the breakfast bar to give my hand a squeeze. "At some point, you must stop punishing yourself for mistakes you made. You've turned your life around. You took responsibility, and you've done the hard work to move past that, you need to find a way to forgive yourself," she reminds me, gently.

Mum withdraws her hand and then drinks some of her coffee, staring at me over her cup as I contemplate what she has said. It doesn't do anything to take away the way I feel about what happened. I know my gambling could have all been so much worse than it was because I managed to stop before things were irreversible. I know people who had borrowed and stolen, changed their finances behind their loved ones' backs, gambled far more than they could repay and staked things they shouldn't on the spin of a wheel or a turn of a card. But, just because I hadn't got to the point where debt collectors were turning up at the front door, it doesn't make me feel any better.

I'd lost control of my life then. Turning up on my mum's doorstep, penniless, desperate for help, desperate for somebody to help me stop, that's something I won't ever forget. The shame of that first night back in my childhood home, where I'd sat and confessed to Mum just how much I was gambling, how much betting had seeped into my life, how much money I had lost, it'll always be part of me, along with the fear that I could relapse.

"You don't need to give me any free therapy. Save it for your patients." I smile. We have this conversation often. It's always laced with a bitter aftertaste for me.

"What are you and Beatrice doing today?" Mum asks.

I hear footsteps coming down the hallway towards the kitchen. I know it is Beatrice as both of my brothers are already up and out of the house. Toby and Sam have always been early risers.

"I'm taking her to the fair and then we're just going to chill here," I explain.

Beatrice comes into the kitchen. "Good morning." Beatrice smiles at both of us.

She turns her attention to the dogs. They had been sitting patiently next to my mother, ready to go to work but now they are jumping up like energetic puppies around her. She crouches down to fuss them, and for a moment I can't work out why she looks different. Then I realise, along with her denim shorts, she's wearing a v-neck top, looking very different to her usual high-necked tops. We'd done a bit of shopping yesterday, and I assume she'd picked up this top then, given it's not her usual style.

She looks sensational. Her long hair is piled on top of her head in a messy bun, strands of it falling out of the bun around her face. She has a beaming smile on her face as she plays with the dogs, asking them who is a good boy.

"Morning, Beatrice." Mum smiles. She's still fussing the dogs when Mum looks at me, a smug, knowing look on her face, like she knows exactly how far Beatrice has me thrown, every single time I see her.

"Coffee?" I ask Beatrice. She nods, so I make myself busy to make her one. Mum gives a little laugh.

"Right, I am off to work. Have a good day, both of you. Come on Rodney, Del-Boy." She stands, calling the dogs. They follow her obediently towards the front door. Beatrice and I call our goodbyes; then she and the dogs are gone, leaving just the two of us.

Beatrice sits at the breakfast bar, in the seat next to the one I'd been sitting in. I make her a coffee and then sit back down. She gives a little contented sigh after the first sip.

"Get some breakfast; we'll set off in about half an hour," I suggest. I give her a smile, and then head out of the kitchen, to get my head back on track.

The fair I take Beatrice to is a travelling fair, the type that is set up in a location for a week or two and then moves on. It's set up in a large field in the town and is popular with all the locals and holiday tourists alike. Even getting there early, the place is crowded.

Beatrice insists on riding the big wheel first, pulling me along to the ride and joining the queue. We make idle chit-chat as we wait though I keep looking up at the big wheel, feeling apprehensive. Heights really aren't my thing. We make it to the front of the queue, make our payment and then get strapped into the most rickety-feeling big wheel in the world.

"I feel like health and safety did not sign off on this contraption," I mutter as the ride starts. The wheel turns a little and then stops again to let another set of riders off and another set on in their place. It repeats this pattern until we are at the top of the wheel where we stop again.

"It's a beautiful view," Beatrice comments. She's looking out in the distance, towards the sea, sighing in contentment. "You were so lucky growing up around this."

"I know." I drum my fingers on my legs, wondering when the ride is going to start again, as it feels like we have waited at the top much longer than any other time we'd stopped. The sooner the ride starts again, the sooner it stops swapping passengers over, the sooner our ride will finish. Beatrice looks over at me.

"Are you okay?" She sounds concerned.

"I'll be okay when the ride starts again."

"It'll start in a moment." Beatrice smiles, but it feels like minutes pass, and we're still not moving. She moves around in her seat, trying to look to the front of the ride, where people get on and off, to see what the delay is.

"Please don't." I let out a breath. When she moves, it sways the seat we're in. I have my eyes closed now though this makes it worse as in my mind, I imagine we're swinging more than we probably are. I just can't force myself to open my eyes to confirm that the movements are all in my mind.

"Sorry," she says, and she slips her hand on top of mine. "You shouldn't have come on if you don't like them," she scolds.

"I just don't like the stop-and-start of it," I admit.

"I never thought you would be scared of anything."

"Sorry to disappoint," I huff.

"No, don't be. Even a superhero has a fear. What other secret fears do you have?" She squeezes my hand. A distraction technique.

"Oh, lots. Mostly, I'm afraid of fucking up again."

"You won't," she replies simply like she has utter faith in me.

"I'm afraid to turn out like my father," I admit. "He used to treat my mum badly. I don't remember much about him, but I never want to end up like him."

"You're a good man, Matt, right down to your core. Nothing could change that," she says in a soft voice.

I force myself to open my eyes so I can look at her. She's staring at me, a tender smile on her face. Before I can say anything, the ride starts again, and I breathe a sigh of relief.

Once we're back on firm ground, I ask Beatrice where she wants to go next. She pulls me towards the arcade section, and we take turns trying to shoot down cans, knock coconuts from shelves and get balls into buckets or hoops. She's competitive, reminding me of when we'd played volleyball where she'd had a determined look on her face throughout. Between us, we get a small stash of small teddy bears and other prizes, bagged up to take home. I pay for a third chance at the game where the grand prize is a giant teddy bear, and Beatrice squeals in delight when I get the final ball into the bucket, winning the game. The guy behind the counter looks bored as he points towards the selection of bears to choose a prize from.

"Which one do you want?" I ask Beatrice.

"Me?"

"Yeah, I don't have much need for an oversized teddy bear. I feel it would ruin my booty-call abilities when people see it." I roll my eyes.

She chuckles. "I thought you were a gentleman."

"I am a gentleman, which is why I'm graciously giving you the hard-earned prize." I smile. She selects the dog-shaped one, and the guy hands it to her.

"Can I take him to the car?" Beatrice asks once she is holding it. The teddy is almost as big as she is.

"I'll do it." I go to take it off her, but she shakes her head.

"No way am I letting you take Trigger anywhere. Give me the keys. You can get in the queue for candyfloss."

"Trigger?" I laugh at her choice of name, from *Only Fools and Horses*, like Del-Boy and Rodney.

"Trigger always made me laugh. My granddad loved Trigger." She holds her hand out for the key, so I give it to her.

"I'll meet you next to the candyfloss," I say.

I watch her walk off in the direction of the car park, carrying the teddy bear and the bag of other prizes, and then I join the queue for the candyfloss. I've been in the queue for a few minutes when somebody comes up behind me, putting their hands over my eyes.

"That was quick," I comment. I turn around, but it isn't Beatrice stood behind me. Jemima gives me a big smile.

"Matt Haliwell, I have missed you."

"Hello, Jemima," I reply. I haven't seen her since the day we'd broken up, the day I'd told her we were no good for each other, and she had to leave.

"Did you miss me too?" She runs her hands down my chest, stopping at my waist. I take a step back. Truthfully, I haven't thought about Jemima in a long while. "Are you home for long, maybe we could go out for a drink together, for old time's sake?"

"I don't think so."

"Any night you like. It would be great to catch up." Despite the distance I put between us by stepping back, she reaches to touch me again. I've nowhere further I can step, not without backing into the guy in front of me in the queue.

"No, Jemima…"

"Are you busy tonight?" She pulls on my arm. I pull it free from her grasp. Then I feel a hand on my other arm, and Beatrice is next to me.

"Hey, baby," she says the same greeting, in that same breathy tone, as she had the first night at the bar when there had been a few women who wouldn't leave. She does exactly the same thing with her hand, running it down my arm, reaching my hand and giving it a squeeze. She looks at me with a knowing smile on her face. I give her a small squeeze on her hand in return.

"Beatrice, this is Jemima."

"It is nice to meet you, Jemima." Beatrice gives a big smile. Jemima looks Beatrice up and down, her stare lingering too long on Beatrice's chest. Beatrice notices immediately. I want to shield her away from Jemima and her stupid gawking. Beatrice gives a small laugh. "Oh, this?" She gestures to her scar. "Animal attack." She sounds solemn, and I want to laugh at the expression on Jemima's face.

"Beatrice is a circus entertainer," I say. I spot the little tug of a suppressed grin on Beatrice's face.

"Really?" Jemima stutters.

Beatrice nods earnestly. "Oh, yes, I'm very entertaining when I am wrestling the bears. Matt likes to join in."

"That's how we met. I saw Beatrice wrestling bears, and I joined in," I tell Jemima.

"One minute, we were wrestling bears; then, we spent all night wrestling each other." Beatrice makes the last part of her sentence sound so suggestive like something explicit must have taken place, and I start to laugh. By now, I've reached the front of the queue, so I order a bag of candyfloss for Beatrice. I look at Jemima.

"You have yourself a lovely evening!" I say to Jemima, and I lead Beatrice away from the stall. We head to the other side of the fair, sitting on a spare bench.

"Sorry if I overstepped. You looked like you wanted out of the conversation, I was following instructions."

"I did. Thank you."

"You stole my line, about the lovely evening." Beatrice nudges me.

"I'm sorry she was rude." I open the bag of candyfloss, take some and then give the bag to her. "It must get tiresome, dealing with people like that."

"When I got sick and had my operation, my mother was the one who took a lot of time off work to look after me. She'd help me shower, get me dressed, all that stuff. Every time she saw my wound, she'd wince. I could see it on her face, every single time. I know she associates it with something I suffered through, something she would have gone through in my place if she could have.

"When I was better, I started covering up to save her feelings, and it became a habit because I saw how other people reacted. People who love me associate it with me being sick, a reminder of a time that I nearly died. Strangers who don't know the story behind it stare, trying to figure it out. But you were right with what you said at the beach, I do see it as a reminder of a battle I won, and maybe it's time others saw it like that too," she says. We are quiet for a moment.

"Animal attack, were you trying to kill me?" I break the silence and start laughing.

"Circus entertainer?" She snorts. It takes the both of us a moment to stop laughing.

"Just so you know, your ability to keep a straight face whilst lying your pants off is going to come in really handy tonight."

"I'm very intrigued about this game of your mother's."

"Come on, finish your candyfloss. I reckon I can survive another go on the big wheel." I smile at her, and she gives me a big smile in return.

"Okay, so, everybody can take what is useful from the box, and we will be back here in five minutes to make a start." Mum smiles at us all, later that evening.

On top of the kitchen side, she's placed the boxes full of costumes and dressing-up accessories. Over the years, she's added many items to the boxes. Each time we gather home, Mum has ordered a new murder mystery game for us to play, a format that consists of back stories for characters we're all assigned, a storyline for a murder mystery for us to solve as the game progresses.

I thought Beatrice might find the game stupid, I know over the years I've had times where I've wished my mum preferred something more traditional, but I've grown to enjoy the games as I've gotten older. Beatrice looks like she's having the time of her life as she reads her character description and back story.

Tonight, the character assigned to me is the international spy. I pick a few accessories out of the box to take with me, back to my room to get ready. Beatrice grabs a few things too and heads off to her room to change. The rest of the family are still going through the boxes to pick out accessories and pieces of clothing to wear for the game.

I change in my room, adding a jacket from my wardrobe given there are still some of my clothes here from when I lived at home, including the jacket I'd worn to Toby's wedding. In my pockets, I put the accessories I'd selected. I gel and slick my hair back, putting on the glasses with fake lenses on. I head back downstairs, passing Toby and Polly on the way, as they head up to change. I see Beatrice coming out of her room. She's wearing her pair of black cropped trousers, a white top, and a black beret from the accessories box. She's put on black eyeliner which she has smudged around her eyes, and a bright red lipstick.

"You look so cute in that beret," I tell her.

"Very French, no?" she says in an exaggerated French accent.

"Are you going to keep that up all night?" I ask.

"*Oui, bien, sur c'est une belle langue.*"

"I didn't know you speak French." I am surprised.

"Only French. Do you?"

"No, not French."

"*Je pense que tu es la personne la plus incroyable que j'ai jamais rencontrée.*" She takes a step towards me, and I curse that I learned Spanish instead of French.

"*Estás en mi mente todo el tiempo,*" I reply in Spanish. She gives me a curious expression, and I know she doesn't understand what I have said.

"Come on kids, the game awaits!" Mum calls from the living room. Beatrice and I grin at each other, ready to throw ourselves into the murder mystery game.

"I am sure there was some cheating going on in that game," I grumble to Beatrice after the game. She gives me a grin.

"We should get some people together and play that at home. It was awesome!" she exclaims. She's been smiling all night, dropping in French sayings as part of her character.

"Mum has loads of versions, she buys a new one each year, sometimes more than one. I'll borrow some," I promise.

"Good night, you two," Andy calls from the doorway. Sam is stood beside him, and he gives us a little wave as we call back our goodnights before they head upstairs to their room.

Beatrice gets up. "I should go to bed."

"Me too," I reply as I walk with her to the bedroom that she is staying in. She pauses at the door, looking at me.

"*J'aimerais pouvoir vous dire ce que vous représentez pour moi, mais j'ai peur.*" She sighs.

"You know I don't have a clue what you have just said?" I feel like I've missed something important.

"Maybe one day I'll tell you in English. Goodnight Matt," she says, kissing me on the cheek, and then opening the door to her room. She steps inside and shuts the door behind her.

I lean against the hallway, sighing to myself. She is like an itch to be scratched, deep under my skin, but even if she wanted it too, I know if I give in, I will scratch forever and drive myself insane. I sigh again and head up the stairs towards my own room, where I know I will toss and turn for hours, and if I do manage to fall asleep, she will be in my dreams.

Beatrice: Now

A week passes. I still don't remember anything, despite how hard I am trying. I haven't gone back to work yet. I still can't make sense of the items in my room. It feels like there is a cloud over the house. Ben's pensive. Matt's sulky. I'm frustrated. I've barely left the house since the day I got home from the hospital. I've started getting headaches which are annoying and not helping my mood.

The only bright spot is that Jas is finally home from her secondment and Ben is picking her up from the airport for me. In the last week, I've re-read every email and message exchanged between me and Jas over the year she has been away, starting with the messages that cover time I remember, messages where I told her how much I was missing my parents, what they were getting up to, where they were travelling, messages where I'd talked about what I was getting up to at work, how I'd had dinner with Cole and his family, where Anna had apologised for the fact she knew Cole had asked me to pick up his dry cleaning. I read the emails I'd sent about dates with Ryan, what I was planning for his birthday in July, and I had reopened the links she'd sent me as jokes, links to the sexiest boutique hotels in the UK and links to a few sex dungeons that she had captioned with 'spice up his birthday'.

I then moved on to the ones that I couldn't recall writing or receiving. Me telling her that I was no longer working for Cole. Me telling her that Ryan and I were over. Those are short messages, and I give no further information. There is a gap in the emails, but I cross-reference to our call history, and I can see that for two weeks solid; we'd called each other every day, and then the emails resume; the calls drop to twice a week.

I tell her in the emails how I'm working in a bar and how I love the environment. I tell her that Ben and Lily are very loud when they're together, and she sends me a link for noise-cancelling headphones and suggests I see a therapist for trauma. There are hundreds of messages between us, long chats and memes, questions from me asking her about the guy she had met, the one with the beautiful eyes. Links to holiday destinations for a trip we are apparently planning in summer. BuzzFeed articles that we have found funny, quizzes I'd done and sent her to tell her that apparently, my answers have determined I am missing love, with a lol written after it.

Quizzes she'd taken that proclaimed she was most like Cinderella as a princess, where she'd captioned it 'please, bitch, you know I'm 100% Merida'. Book recommendations we'd sent each other, saying we thought the other might like it. She'd sent me pictures of food she'd ordered in restaurants. I'd sent her a recipe for breakfast burritos, telling her they were life-changing.

There is nothing in them that tells me what I have been doing, but I feel like I know enough now to carry on with Jas like nothing has happened, as I've told Ben I still don't want anybody other than him and Matt knowing I've lost some memories, this decision still being the barrier for me going back to work. Jas has been too busy packing and preparing to come home to call, so I have been able to keep my secret from her given we had only communicated recently with brief texts.

"We're here!" Ben calls from the doorway, arriving back from the airport with Jas. He makes himself scarce in the kitchen.

I feel a wave of joy. I've missed my best friend so much. Jas comes into the living room, and she greets me with a huge hug, one that has us falling backwards on the sofa, laughing in excitement.

I hold her tightly. I can't believe that it's apparently been a year since I have seen her. We used to see each other every few days. We've been friends since we met at college, both of us opting for the experience of going to college and meeting new people rather than attending sixth forms connected to our schools.

We'd met in our first class, the two of us both giggling at an unfortunate typo in a handout, our eyes meeting and recognising a kindred spirit. She's been my best friend since. Jas is like a ball of energy, always full of happiness and fun. Her mother is French, her father is English, and she's never minded helping me improve my French, taking me from passable GCSE level to fluent.

Over the years, she has been my sidekick to so much, my confidant in everything. Throughout college, I dragged her to cooking classes, to theatre club, to poetry readings and re-releases of obscure horror movies. In turn, Jas dragged me to dance classes, to exercise classes and to the spa for pamper days. She was the one I cried to when the guy I really liked had been visibly horrified by my scar when he had taken my top off during what had been a lovely kissing session in his bedroom, causing me to put it right back on again and leave his house in a panic. She had been the one to tell me I was beautiful, and that he didn't deserve to see another inch of my skin.

I was the one she came to when she caught her boyfriend kissing another girl. I was the one who reminded her that he wasn't worth her time, that in five years' time, she'd probably be running the world, and he would still be unable to decide what his favourite ice cream flavour was.

How I've survived the year without her, apparently a year where I lost three things I'd considered important to me, my boyfriend, my home, my work with Cole, it's something I cannot fathom. All I know is that I am delighted to have her here, squeezing me tight.

"I have missed you, oodles and oodles!" Jas exclaims as we right ourselves on the sofa. "I won't be offended if you didn't miss me as much, given for you it hasn't been long."

"Bloody Ben," I mutter.

"Come on, he told me your plan not to tell anybody, but how do you think that was going to work with me?"

"I read through every message we'd sent each other in the last year as preparation," I tell her with a laugh.

"Well, my first burning topic is what the hell happened between you and Ryan. How were you going to get out of that? I know it's not in the messages." Jas ruffles my hair affectionately.

"I was kinda hoping I could get you to tell me," I admit.

"I would have told you if you had told me. You said you wanted to tell me face to face, and you refused to talk about it further."

"I'm surprised you didn't hound me for information."

"I did! You're very stubborn. Besides, you sounded so distressed every time I asked, and I felt like I was making it worse by bringing it up. I was so relieved when you said you were moving in with Ben. I thought you at least would have somebody looking after you, even if you couldn't admit you needed it."

Jas bites her bottom lip. "I am so sorry I wasn't here when you needed me. I phoned you a lot and once you cried for, like, ten minutes straight. It was killing me knowing you were going through something. I wanted nothing more than to hop on a plane and come home, so I could give you a big hug. You kept telling me no."

"Was I a ridiculous mess?" I wonder.

"Actually, no. Not after a while, anyway. You seemed happier. When we chatted, your voice seemed brighter. I could tell that there was still something that bothered you, but it didn't seem to be consuming you if that makes sense. You seemed happier, and I stopped chasing the subject because I didn't want to reopen the wound."

"What's happening between you and Alessandro?" I ask her about the man with the beautiful eyes, and she practically melts on the sofa.

"He's my soul mate. I love him. You'll love him, I know you will. He's coming for a visit next month, going to stay for a month, and we will see how things go. I can't wait for you to meet him."

"Where is he going to stay?" I wonder, as Jas had been living with her parents before her secondment, and they don't strike me as the type of laidback parents who would let her boyfriend stay. Jas gives me a little smile.

"I got a big bump in salary this year, so whilst I've been planning to come back, I've got myself a little place. I'll be completing the purchase soon. It's only somewhere small because I am young and essentially penniless after all. It has two bedrooms. You could move in with me if you like."

"And ruin your love nest and reunion with Mr Wonderful Eyes?" I tease her.

"I'd buy you some noise-cancelling headphones," she vows. I only know what she is referring to from the emails I've caught up on, so there is no real emotion behind my reaction. She smiles. "At least that's one thing you can be happy you have forgotten about."

"Yeah, I just wonder what else. Why am I blocking so much?" I lean against her. "I'm actually a little frightened that I am blocking out something I did that was bad," I admit.

"Like what?"

"Whatever it was that ended me and Ryan."

"What makes you think it was something you did?" she challenges. I don't reply. "Do you want me to talk to Ryan? I didn't before because you told me not to, but I will if you need me to talk to him now."

"God, no. Please don't." I shoot back immediately. I don't know why, but the idea of contacting Ryan, or anybody else from my past, makes me feel sick in my stomach. There is a silence between us, and Jas recognises it is time to change the topic.

"So are you going to show me around the 'getting my shit together' house or not?" she asks. I smile. I don't remember calling this place that. It wasn't in the emails, it must have been in a call, and it sounds like something I would have said. I stand up from the sofa, and we head up to my room, going inside. She looks around the room.

"I think Ben must have painted it before I moved in unless the previous guy was a fan of the pastels." I sit on the bed. She spots the box of origami that I'd left on the chest of drawers, and she picks it up, looking through it.

"These are so pretty. Do you think you made these?"

"I don't know. I don't think so. I didn't tell you in any emails I was doing it, and it seems like something I would have told you because you would have made some sort of joke that I should take up basket weaving instead."

"Sounds like me. Maybe you just wanted to do something for yourself, without me critiquing?" she wonders.

"I don't know."

"Hey," she says, after a moment of looking at them. "This swan has something written on it."

I know from when I looked at them all that there are a couple of swan-shaped origami, including two beautiful 3D ones that when stood together, their beaks touch and their necks curve gracefully to form the outline of a heart. The one Jas has in her hands is more simple, straightforward and sure enough, under the wing of the swan, there is some writing. She hands it over to me.

I pull up the wing gently so that I don't damage it.

"I fear no fate, for you are my fate, my sweet." I read the tiny writing under the wing of the swan.

"Is that by E. E. Cummings?" Jas asks. I nod a response. It's one of my favourites, along with the poem that is etched on my necklace. I look through the rest of the origami, picking up the little frog. I unfold it a little to look at the writing.

"Til the sun grows cold, and the stars grow old."

"Do they all have some writing on them?" Jas wonders. She looks through the box with me. Now Jas has pointed it out, I can see that some have been carefully unfolded before. On most, like the frog, I have to carefully unfold a section to see the writing that has been hidden. They're a mix of poetry lines I recognise, and some are in a language I don't know. I write them into a translation app, they're originally in Spanish.

Once translated, one reads, 'A little bit more, every single day'.

Another reads, 'Every inch of my heart beats for you'.

A third reads, 'You are the greatest treasure'.

A fourth, 'For you, I'd risk everything'.

"This is not my handwriting," I point out to Jas. "And I don't know Spanish," I add. She frowns.

"These don't look like something you would have brought yourself, and if you didn't make them, maybe…" Her voice trails off.

"Ryan didn't give me these." Of that, I am certain. He never understood why I love poetry, and when we went on holiday to Spain, it was clear his version of Spanish was just speaking key English words loudly and slowly. I'd teased him relentlessly about it on holiday, and he had grumbled that we weren't all blessed with the ability to speak another language.

"So…" Jas starts. I look at her.

"I know I am going to sound completely bonkers, but did I give you any indication that I was seeing anybody recently?"

"No, you didn't. I'm sorry, Beatrice, I don't know how to give you the answer you want. You're very private when you want to be," she reminds me. It's true, something she has complained about before, like how I didn't tell her for weeks my parents had decided they were selling up to go travelling as I was busy processing my feelings before I could speak about it.

"I think I might have been. I don't know. I just…maybe I did, maybe it fizzled out," I sigh.

"Well, if you were, it sounds pretty intense." She gestures to the origami and at the writing we have found.

"Maybe my heart was broken. Maybe I'm better off not remembering." I slide the little figures back into the shoebox. A little butterfly remains, I touch it, but instead of putting it away, I leave it on the chest of drawers. The butterfly is the simplest of the collection, it isn't made with colourful paper like the others, just plain white paper, but I like it the most. As I touch it, I get the same feeling I got when I'd thought about Christmas and when I had put the necklace on. It's a warmth through my whole body. I put the lid on the shoebox and kick it under the bed.

"Are you okay?" Jas asks, and her brow is furrowed with concern.

"Come on, do you want to go for a drink?" I ask.

"Dude, we've a whole year of missed drinking together to catch up on. I thought you'd never ask. Come on!" She pulls me by my arm and together we walk down the stairs. I call my goodbyes to Ben. As we walk down the hallway, the front door opens, and Matt walks in.

"Hey," I say to him.

"Hi," he replies, but he doesn't look at me properly. "Are you off out?"

"We're going for a drink. I'm going to take my addled brain for a change of scenery."

"Are you sure you should be drinking after a head injury?" he asks, a weird expression on his face, and I'm surprised that he seems concerned.

"For somebody who runs a bar, you seem oblivious to there being such a thing as non-alcoholic cocktails. Anyway, see you later." I smile at him. He gives a curt nod and heads upstairs, his feet thudding on the stairs.

"Still as grumpy as at the party, I see." Jas rolls her eyes. "I don't know what his problem is. Does he always look so thoroughly pissed off?"

"Come on. Drinks are on me." I change the subject. "Unless I changed my pin in the last few months, in which case, we're stuck." I laugh.

"Any bloody excuse so that I pay for everything." Jas starts laughing, and we head outside, with me feeling lighter than I have in days.

Beatrice: Then, September

September remains gloriously sunny, and the bar is packed every night. Everybody seems like they're out celebrating something, and every customer we have had this week has seemed full of life and happiness. Their happiness is infectious. Despite this being a million miles away from my previous job, I love every minute at the bar.

Tonight, Matt and I are on an earlier finish than usual. Usually, we're here until late, we always stay and do closing, but we're finishing at eight tonight, Isaac and Kelly doing their first closing up together. I'm already planning a long hot bath when I get home. Ben's on nights and Matt's got a date, so I know I can have the bathroom to myself, nobody knocking on the door or complaining they need to get in there.

The bar is busy, with people on dates and parties, people celebrating life and having fun. Matt's been doing paperwork in the little office, catching up on things he says he has neglected, though he keeps coming to check on us.

I check the clock. I've half an hour before the end of my shift, and I can almost smell the scent of the bath bomb that I've got stashed in my bedroom ready for tonight. There is a lull in customers at the bar, so I make myself busy tidying up after my last serve. Out of the corner of my eye, I notice a man and woman together at a table, and something about their body language is off. He's leaning in towards her, one of his hands on her wrist, she's leaning slightly away.

I watch them for a moment, she pulls her arm back, and he reaches for her again. Grabs her wrist. Moves closer to her.

I look around, feeling my heart rate has increased. Something isn't right between them. I want to go over, I want to ask her if she is okay, but something about the guy stops me. I've dealt with annoyed customers at the bar before, but usually, there is the bar between us as a barrier. Going over to their table would feel like exposure, but I can't leave it alone. I look around. Kelly is just at the office door.

"Can you get Matt?" I ask her. She gives me a concerned look and then goes to the office. A moment later, Matt is by my side. I knew he would be.

"I… Something is not right with that couple over there. She's trying to get him off her, and he doesn't look like he is taking no for an answer," I explain, but my voice is high-pitched and my words are fast-paced.

"Who paid for their drinks?"

"She did," I say, confused. I remember serving them earlier. He nods, then heads towards the table. He leans closer to the woman, speaking to her, gesturing towards the bar. A moment later, they arrive at the bar together, and they go into the office, the door open. The man sits at the table, tapping his foot and looking at his watch.

Five minutes pass, and I'm still watching the guy out of the corner of my eye. He's getting more agitated, and I can feel that my pulse is still racing. Matt comes back to the bar, without the woman. He's got his keys in his hands.

"Come on, end of shift," he says. I check the clock, there is still time left on my shift. "Kelly will cover for the gap. Come on." He takes me gently by the elbow, guiding me towards the door of the bar. Once we are outside, we head towards where Matt's car is parked.

"What happened with the woman?" I ask as we get closer to the car.

"I told her in front of him that there had been a problem with her payment, and that she needed to come with me to sort it out. In the office, she told me that she's on a first date with somebody she met on a dating site, and he's aggressive and too familiar. I let her out the back door and put her in a taxi. Isaac knows what happened, he'll keep an eye on the guy in case he kicks off, but most likely he'll just go home alone." He opens the car for me, and I get in. He looks at me. "It happens more than you like to think it does, but if we see it, we do our best to stop it."

"Thank you," I say quietly. It's the first time I've seen something like that at the bar.

"Can you tell me why you freaked out so much? You're as white as a sheet." He starts the car. He drives in the direction of home. "Beatrice, talk to me," he says once we are halfway home, and I still haven't spoken a word. I shake my head because I don't think I can make myself speak right now.

We drive the rest of the way in silence. He opens the front door.

"Beatrice. Talk to me. Please," he says with a sigh.

He closes the door behind him, and we walk into the living room together, flicking the lights on. I stand next to the cabinet, and he stands at the doorframe. I want to tell him, but at the same time, my bones are screaming at me to be quiet that I shouldn't say anything because the last time I talked about this, nothing went my way and I lost everything.

I can tell that Matt is concerned about my reaction. I take a big breath.

"I started working at my previous company a few years ago. There were two owners of the company, and they needed a PA to help them run the day-to-day things and manage their diaries, all that kind of stuff. The two guys, they're cousins, Taylor and Cole. I spent a lot of time with Cole, he was always very friendly. Then, something changed.

"The first few times anything happened; I assumed I was imagining it. It started with little things, simple things, like a hand on my shoulder, resting there a little too long. Or it was a chair moved closer to me than the available space required, a leg pressed up against mine. Sometimes it was a lean over my body to open the car door for me, his skin on mine. I made excuses for them all. He's just being friendly. There wasn't enough room. He's just being a nice guy.

"I'd worked for Cole for years, I knew his wife. I knew his four children. There was no way that he was doing anything untoward, he was my boss, a family man, a good guy. He had taken me under his wing when I started. I trusted him. I must be imagining things, right?"

I look over at Matt. He's stood, suddenly rigid, staring at me. He doesn't say anything, so I continue.

"I started trying to make things more certain, kept a bit of distance between us, and things seemed to settle down, so I wrote it all off as misunderstandings. The company got busy; their work took off; and it was longer hours and more work. They hired another PA and split the role I had in two. The other PA worked exclusively for Taylor, and I worked exclusively for Cole. It meant I spent more time with him and more travel, but I wasn't worried because I decided I had overthought things before that I had made things seem much worse in my head than they were.

"Everything seemed fine between us, and I felt bad that I had thought him capable of being like that with anybody. One night, we needed to stay away ahead of a pitch. We got to the hotel, and they claimed my booking wasn't on their system. Cole offered me his room. He had booked a suite, and he said I could stay on the couch.

"The rest of the hotel was booked, and I knew I should have gone and found another hotel to stay in, but we needed to work on some final pieces for his pitch, and I thought we would be working late. It seemed more logical for me to stay rather than travel to another hotel in the early hours of the morning. I thought it was okay. This was Cole, the guy who had been so nice to me. I trusted him," I repeat.

I take another deep breath, and wipe my hands on my skirt, as they feel clammy now that I have started talking. Matt still hasn't said anything. He keeps staring at me, letting me talk.

"We worked on the pitch. He called for room service. He ordered a bottle of wine. As the evening wore on, I was getting tired. The pitch was done, and I started dropping hints so that he would go to bed, so I could go to sleep, but instead, he sat on the couch next to me, way too close.

"The next thing I knew, he had me pinned down on the sofa. His hands were all over my body. I tried to push him away, telling him he'd had too much wine and wasn't thinking clearly. I told him he was forgetting who we were.

"He was trying to kiss me, I kept trying to push him away, but he wouldn't stop. He was saying things like it was okay, that his wife wouldn't care, that the way he felt for me couldn't be wrong. He was so strong, and I was frightened that I wouldn't be able to get him to stop."

I stop for a moment, my voice breaking as I feel the fear I had felt when Cole had me pinned on the couch and when he had been impossibly strong, with hands in places on my body I didn't want him to touch. My throat is suddenly tight. My hands are shaking.

"I managed to get out from under him, and I grabbed my handbag from the table and made a run for the door. Cole grabbed me and pushed me against the wall. He told me I wasn't going anywhere until I was calmer. He said nothing had happened and told me to go to bed. I pushed him away and went to leave, and he laughed, telling me nobody would believe me, and that if I spoke about it, he would ruin my life.

"I left and found another hotel to stay in. I had left my coat, my case, and my work things. All I had was my phone and purse. I was up all night, thinking about what happened and all the things I had done wrong. I should have been firmer with him. I should never have agreed to stay in his suite. I should never have had a glass of wine. I wanted to phone Ryan, so I could tell him what had happened, but I couldn't bring myself to do it over the phone, and I was worried he might ask me why I had made certain decisions, why I thought it was okay to sit drinking wine with my boss in his hotel suite, so I didn't call him. In the morning, I went back to the hotel to get my things.

"Cole acted like nothing had happened. He asked me how my night had been, and he never mentioned a thing, it was like I hadn't been in his room at all. He was pretending it hadn't happened, but there was no way I could rationalise it away, write it off as another misunderstanding. So, when we finished the pitch and travelled home, I went straight to Taylor. I told him everything that had happened."

Matt is still silent, but I can feel the weight of his stare as I continue to explain.

"Taylor told me that I was making a serious allegation, and he asked me to consider if my version of the story was accurate and truthful. I told him that it was, but then he handed me a piece of paper. It was an explicit email, from my work address to Cole, sent late in the hours of the night in the hotel. I'd left my work tablet in Cole's room, something he'd seen me unlock so many times it would have been easy for him to open and send to himself. Taylor asked me, 'What is Cole supposed to think when you're so desperate in this email?'

"He said he and Cole were willing to put things to one side, that I'd clearly had a moment of behaving rashly. Taylor told me that if I apologised, we could all carry on like it hadn't happened. He said I should take the rest of the week off, so I could think about my actions, and he didn't want to talk further. I went home and waited for Ryan. I was going to tell him about all the times I felt Cole had been pushing the boundaries, and what had happened that night.

"He came home late. Before I could speak, he told me that he had gone to meet me from work, to surprise me, and he had bumped into Cole. Cole had told him we slept together, that I had been the one to initiate things and said I'd snuck into his room and waited for him. Cole told Ryan he had given into temptation, and he felt dreadful that he felt he should confess to Ryan because he didn't think I would do the honourable thing."

I pause again, as I'm back to how it felt when I'd stood in the living room with Ryan, listening to him explain what he'd been told, seeing on his face how much he believed what Cole had said.

"I tried telling him the truth, but Ryan was angry, and he wouldn't listen. He kept saying that I had broken his trust, that I was twisting the truth to save my skin. He reminded me about all the times he had mentioned me spending lots of time at work where I'd laughed and said it was my job. He said it was clear that I had been after Cole all that time. I kept telling him it wasn't true, but he said he didn't know who I was anymore, that I wasn't the girl he had loved, he would never be able to trust me again, and our relationship was over.

"I knew he was right, but not for the reasons he thought. He thought he couldn't trust me to be faithful. I knew I couldn't stay with somebody who didn't believe me over the lies of somebody they barely knew. I stayed in the spare room for a few days, I didn't go anywhere. I went from being shell-shocked to being angry. How could Cole get away with this?

"He had ruined my job and my relationship, destroyed me like he said he would. Neither things were salvageable, and I was so angry. I just wanted him to feel the smallest bit of pain that I felt, so I did the only thing I could think of. I went to his house to tell his wife."

I stop again. Matt still hasn't moved.

"Anna called me a wannabe home-wrecker, a slut, and she slapped me. She screamed at me, saying she knew I had tried to seduce her husband. Anna asked me how I had the audacity to turn up at her house. She didn't want to hear a word I had to say. So I knew I was done.

"I had tried to tell three people. Cole had told these three people three different stories. To Taylor, I was somebody who had come onto Cole, provoking him with emails, chasing him and then lying when I didn't get my own way. To Ryan, I was somebody who had made the first move and chased Cole until he gave in. To Anna, I was a home-wrecker, chasing a happily married man, desperately trying to get him to give in and lashing out with lies when he wouldn't. There was no doubt in the minds of these people that it was me at fault, that I was the one in the wrong.

"So I quit my job. I couldn't go back there. I didn't even go in to clear my desk. I stopped trying to get Ryan to see my side of the story. I couldn't bear to even look at him any more knowing he thought more of another person's opinion than my truth. Three people and they all believe him over me. My word was worth nothing."

Now, I'm crying, huge, loud sobs. I haven't spoken to anybody about this since the day I cleared my things from Ryan's house. As I had left, he had grabbed my arm. I had wondered if this was the moment he would apologise, to tell me he believed me, that he loved me, that he was sorry. Instead, he held onto my thumb, using it to twist my arm behind my back, and then he called me a bitch and a whore, telling me my family would be disappointed in me if they knew what I had done. So instead of telling Ben, like I should have that first night, I'd kept it to myself since, and now I've let the words out again, all that is left is pain, sadness and anger.

Matt clears his throat. "I believe you." It's a simple statement, but it means everything. It feels like the floodgates have opened, and I cry even harder. He takes a step forward, closer to me, and he reaches for my hand. "I believe you, Beatrice," he says, more firmly. "That shouldn't have happened to you. I am so sorry."

With that, I fall against him, my head on his broad chest. I sob against him, and after a moment, he puts his arms around me, holding me as I cry.

"I'm sorry. I'm going to ruin your shirt." I wipe my eyes, but I don't want to step out of his embrace. I feel warm and safe in his arms.

"You should have told Ben," Matt says. "There isn't a doubt in my mind about whether he would side with you. He would be right beside you. He would believe you."

"I was ashamed."

"Of what? That you had some asshole of a boss who thought he was entitled to take something you didn't want to give? Some asshole who refused to take no for an answer then treated you like shit when you called him out on his behaviour? Some asshole that forced himself on you, and did shitty things to try to save his own reputation?"

"All of it. For letting it happen."

"You didn't let anything happen. This was all him."

"Women, we're told from an early age to mind ourselves, to watch what we wear, to be cautious about where we go, to watch our drinks, to be mindful of our surroundings. We're told to watch our behaviour, told not to lead people on. We're taught how to behave so we don't get hurt, and if we do get hurt, we're asked what we did, what we said, what we were wearing, what we did to give the wrong impression, to send the wrong signals. I let my guard down with the wrong person, I ignored the signs, and I put myself in that position. I should have known better."

"Bullshit. Beatrice, you are not at fault. It's not up to you to modify your behaviour for the sake of some men. There isn't a single thing you could have done that would have stopped what happened. If it didn't happen in that hotel room that night, it would likely have happened somewhere else because that's what men like that do.

"An asshole is always going to act like an asshole. What happened was not your fault. You did nothing wrong, it was all him," Matt tells me, his voice firm. "Ben would say the same thing."

"Please don't tell Ben," I plead. "I will tell him one day, just…not yet."

"It's not my story to tell. I won't tell anybody," he vows. I don't doubt the sincerity in his voice.

"Thank you. I'm sorry for offloading on you. I'm sorry for getting your shirt wet when you've got a date to get to." I pull away from his embrace.

"I don't have a date. I cancelled earlier." He shakes his head. "It wasn't going to work out with her."

"Why not?"

"I have someone else on my mind," he says as he frowns. "I need to get my head clear."

"Head, heart, or somewhere further south?" I tease. I want to clear the air from my heavy past. Teasing him seems like the right way to go. He gives me a grin, acknowledging that I've closed the topic of what happened with Cole.

"Maybe it's all three."

"Well, she sounds like a hell of a woman if she's affecting you in all the major areas." My tone is still teasing, but he looks like he wants the conversation to be over, that it is no longer light-hearted banter.

"Yeah," he says, and he has a frustrated look on his face.

"So what's the problem?" I probe.

"It's complicated."

"Isn't it always?"

"Not like this."

"Tell me about it, maybe I can help you make sense of things."

"Anyway, in the absence of a date…" he replies, and it is clear he isn't going to let me find out any more about this mystery woman. "We could watch a film, if you don't have plans."

"No plans for me. What film were you thinking?"

"I got us *A Nightmare on Elm Street*."

"Oh, sure! Though who is going to watch over us if we have nightmares about Freddy when we sleep?" I grin at him. I've never seen the film before, but I know the storyline.

"I'll keep you safe." He smiles.

"I know you will," I reply quietly. Of all the things I know in the world that Matt would keep me safe is high up on the things I know to be irrevocably true. "I'll keep you safe, too," I tell him, and I hope he knows just how much I mean it.

Matt: Then, September

I shouldn't be here. This is crazy. Despite the fact I have been telling myself for the last fifteen minutes that this is a moment of insanity, a series of questionable choices, I haven't been able to convince myself to get up and leave.

I've been seething with anger since last week when Beatrice broke down and told me what had happened to her and how she ended up moving in with us. She rationalised later that night that it hadn't been too bad, that things could have been worse, like she was trying to convince herself that because he hadn't done more, what had happened was insignificant.

She'd told me that she was working up the courage to go back to the office to collect her things, the one thing she wanted being an engraved token that Ben had given her years ago, something she'd always kept nearby when she was working. The fact that she hadn't gathered the courage to go and get something that meant so much for her obviously bothered her, and she had changed the subject, making it clear she didn't want to talk any more about Cole.

We'd spent the rest of the week working and watching films together late at night, and we hadn't spoken about things since, but I understood everything about her so much more now. The fiddling of her hands when she's restless. The times she'll step back when somebody is too close to her. He did that to her. He caused those reactions in her.

Last night, on her last shift for the week, a guy in the bar had been a little over-familiar with her, and I'd seen the flicker of fear over her face before she had rebounded to react. I hate that her ex-boss has made her feel like this. I hate that there have been no repercussions, no retribution, no justice. The anger had boiled through me all last night, where I'd tossed and turned in bed, getting more frustrated as each hour had passed.

Today, Beatrice and Ben had made plans for the day before Ben's going to Lily's tonight, and as I'm not working today, they'd invited me to spend the day with them, but I'd declined. Instead, I'd felt aimless all day, until I found myself outside of the building where Beatrice had worked. As soon as I arrived outside of the building, I realised that this was inevitable. From the moment she told me, fate was going to position me here. It's inevitable, but stupid. Really fucking stupid.

"I'm so sorry for your wait, Mr Haliwell. Cole is ready for you now, please follow me." The PA smiles at me. He'd been surprised to see me arrive in the office building at the end of the working day, claiming I had a meeting with Cole, insisting that it had been on the books for weeks, that it needed to be today for the meeting to take place.

The PA opens the door to the office, letting me inside.

"Mr Haliwell, thank you for waiting. I'm so sorry for the mix-up."

Cole gets up from the desk to come and shake my hand. I grip his hand tightly as I shake, and then take a seat across from him. I look over at him. I wasn't sure what I had expected him to look like. He sits back behind the desk, movements of a man who is cock-sure of himself.

He's in his late thirties, blond-haired and pale-blue-eyed, wearing a pair of charcoal grey suit trousers with a shirt where his sleeves are pushed up like he's trying to present himself as somebody who is professional but cool and trendy. On his desk, positioned for visitors to see, is a picture of him with a ginger-haired woman, smiling widely for the camera with four young girls gathered around them. It looks like one of those choreographed photographs. They're all wearing whites and creams, beaming smiles for the camera. I wonder if they'd taken the photograph recently, whether this was before or after the wife's life was rocked by the accusations at her husband.

"Thank you for sparing the time," I say.

"I'm sorry that we seem to have lost the details for the appointment. We have had a few changes in staff, and I assume we've lost the information in the handover."

"Beatrice, right?" I ask. Cole looks surprised to hear her name. The colour seems to drain from his face, but he rallies himself quickly.

"Yes, Beatrice. Was she the one you made the appointment with?"

"No." I lean back in my chair. Cole looks unsettled.

"May I ask how you know Beatrice?"

"I know all about Beatrice." I fold my arms across my chest.

"I'm not sure what you're intending to get out of this meeting, Mr Haliwell."

"I want you to admit what you did to her."

"I think it would be best if you left." Cole stands up.

"I'm not going anywhere." I remain seated. Cole reaches for his phone, picking up the receiver and dialling to connect to another line.

"Taylor, can you spare me a minute?" he asks, and then he puts the phone back down. He sits back in his seat, staring at me. The door opens, and in strides another man. He stands at the desk next to his cousin.

"How can I help?" he asks, staring at Cole and then at me, then back again.

"You're Taylor, right?"

"Yes, I'm Taylor. What can I help you with?"

"He wants to talk about Beatrice." Cole cuts in.

"Beatrice?" Now Taylor is the one looking surprised.

"You let her down. She came to you, she confided in you about what had happened, and you didn't listen to what she had to say." I snap at him.

"I don't know who you are, but I think you should leave."

"She trusted you to help her and support her. She came to you at her most vulnerable, and you treated her like shit," I continue. I'm so angry at them, Cole, for what he did, Taylor for being irresponsible as a boss. I'd never treat any of my team like that.

"I don't know what you think happened, but…"

"You're lucky she doesn't sue you," I point out. At this, Taylor looks startled.

"She quit."

"You didn't give her much of an option, did you? Instead of conducting a proper investigation into what she told you, you told her to consider if she was being truthful, making it clear you thought she was lying, trusting a fabricated email. You automatically sided with him. What option did she have when it was clear you were going to cover up for your cousin?" I snarl.

"I wasn't…" Taylor starts.

"I'm here for Beatrice's things," I cut in. "Get them, and I'll get out of your way."

"I'll be back in a minute," Taylor says, but he looks at Cole who nods before he leaves the room. He leaves the door open, but I get up from my seat and shut the door. Cole gives a small laugh; surer of himself because he knows Taylor still backs him. He stands up, pulling himself to his full height. He's a little taller than I am.

"I bet you thought you were going to be here like some big man. Coming in here like Beatrice's knight in shining armour, but you've got nothing. She has no proof. She doesn't have a leg to stand on. Nobody believed a word that she said. She can't prove shit," Cole snarls. "Get the fuck out of my office." He gives me a shove. I don't think; I turn and shove him back. He stumbles backwards until he backs into the wall. I hold him against the wall.

"You're wrong. I believe her. I can tell you're a piece of shit. You're just a disgusting bastard who is past his prime, desperately trying to exert dominance to make yourself feel like a man. How many women have you tried it on with, how many times have women had to fight off your advances?

"Or was it just Beatrice? All the lies you have told since, do they eat away at you? Or do you believe them, that you're some innocent person in this?" I hiss.

He pushes against me, but I hold him firm against the wall, my forearm against his chest. I can feel the anger ingrained in my bones. "How do you feel, fighting to get away from somebody who is stronger than you, somebody determined not to let you go? It doesn't feel good, does it? Any time you think you can try it on with a woman who clearly doesn't want anything from you, I hope you think of this moment, how it feels right now when you can't fight your way out from under me. If there is even the smallest hint that you're doing to somebody else what you did to Beatrice, I'll find a way to ruin your perfect fucking life. I will make it my mission to ruin everything for you," I snarl. I release the hold I have against his chest, and he seems to rally himself.

"Tell Beatrice I miss her around here." He smirks. I pull my arm back, fist clenched, ready to punch him. Son of a bitch. I swing for him, but at the last moment, flex my arm, hitting the plasterboard wall at the side of him.

The pain of my fist connecting to the plaster radiates down my arm, but I know it's better than smacking him in the face, no matter how much satisfaction I would get out of wiping that smug smile from his face. "You're crazy. I could have you arrested," he stutters.

"You touched me first. I reacted in self-defence. It would be my word against yours, and you can't prove shit," I snap, repeating his words. I move away from him, leaving him standing against the wall. "If you go to the police, I'd have to tell them why I was here, I'd have to tell them about Beatrice.

"I'm sure that's something you don't want to open yourself up to. I'm sure your wife would be thrilled to have the whole sordid topic discussed again." I give him a smile. I know there is no way he is going to go to the police. I walk past his desk, stopping to pick up the photograph that he has on display, the one that proclaims to the world that he is a good person. "Nice family you have there.

It's a shame your kids have such an asshole for a father, and your wife has you as a pathetic excuse for a husband."

I drop the picture back onto the desk and stalk out of his office. I walk into the main area of the office, just as Taylor comes out of another room with a box in his hands.

"These are the things that Beatrice had on her desk," he says.

I grab the box from him. I rummage past the water bottles and the packets of painkillers, the cereal bars all the usual crap that people keep in their drawers until I find the item Beatrice had spoken about. A silver medallion, etched with the words: *'To Beatrice, the world's most okayest sister. Love always, Ben, the world's most okayest brother'*. I take it out of the box, putting it into my shirt pocket. I shove the rest of the box at Taylor.

"You did wrong by her. Do better."

I storm out of the office building without another word.

Once I am outside, everything feels like it's overwhelming me. My heart is pounding in my chest, my knuckles are throbbing and shame rushes through my body. I'm ashamed of what I've just done because I've spent years trying to keep myself on track, contained, desperate not to turn into somebody like my father, and I've crossed a line, completely lost my cool, but I know I'd do it all again, for her.

I want a drink. I want to lose myself. I think of Beatrice, and I turn to head home, head towards Beatrice, she is like a beacon, guiding me back to the light.

I walk in the front door. The house is quiet. Ben's car is gone, so I assume he has left for Lily's. It's only six, but I pour myself a large whisky. The first sip burns my throat, distracting me from the pain in my knuckles. I can see I have split the skin open on my middle knuckle, and it hurts like a son of a bitch.

Beatrice comes down the stairs and into the kitchen.

"Hey, how was your day?" she asks. "Have you eaten?"

"No," I say, but it's a struggle. She glances at the glass of whisky.

"Is everything okay?" She seems surprised to see me drinking.

"Fine," I reply. She walks closer to me, spotting the damage to my hand, the split skin, the bruise that is forming and the blood oozing from the damaged skin. She reaches for my hand, gently taking it into hers, so she can take a closer look.

"What happened?"

"It's nothing," I reply. She sighs, releases my hand and walks out of the kitchen. She returns a minute later, a bottle of TCP, some cotton pads, and a packaged bandage in her hands. She takes my uninjured hand and pulls me towards the living room, guiding me to the sofa. I sit where she wants, and she sits down next to me.

"Did you do this hitting somebody?" she asks, opening the bottle of TCP. She pours some onto the cotton pads. The scent of the antiseptic hits me.

"I hit a wall," I explain. She looks bemused.

"Intentionally?"

"It was less satisfying than smacking his teeth in, but also less likely to land me in jail," I mutter. She takes my hand in hers again, then dabs at my oozing knuckles with the cotton pad. I suck in a breath, swearing as she sweeps the antiseptic across the skin. She lifts my hand closer to her face, blowing across the knuckles. This is an entirely different sensation. My whole body tenses. She wipes my skin with some more TCP.

"Poor baby," she murmurs as I flinch. She reaches for the bandage, takes it out of the packaging, places the padded section over my knuckles, then winds the rest of the bandage around my hand and ties it to secure it. When she is finished, she kisses the top of the bandage.

"Thank you," I sigh. With my other hand, I reach into my shirt pocket, getting the token that I had collected from her office. I press it into her hand. She looks at it, and then she takes a sharp intake of breath, then her gaze is on me, a mixture of shock and apprehension.

"Cole?" she stutters. "You went there?"

"Yes."

"You hit him?"

"No, I told you. I hit his wall. I would have preferred to smack that smile off his smug face though," I mutter.

"You went and got this for me?" She sounds incredulous.

"For you, yes," I reply. She stares back at the token in her hand and then she clutches it like it is a talisman before putting it into her pocket.

"Thank you," she says. Her voice is thick.

"Any time." I give her a small smile, and she stares at me, holding my gaze. She inches towards me, sitting closer to me on the sofa.

"I mean, this is the most alpha male, craziest, stupidest moment of insanity that anybody has ever had for me. I should be reprimanding you for letting your temper get the best of you and telling you that I don't need anybody to fight my battles. But…" She stops talking and inches a little closer to me again, her eyes searching mine. "Thank you," she whispers again.

The air feels thick around us, and I am not sure I am breathing properly anymore. She's so close to me now that we are almost touching. I can smell her perfume, the scent of her shampoo. I can feel the heat of her skin, so close to mine. She gives me another look, and then she closes the last bit of distance between us, her lips on mine. She kisses me, softly at first, starting as a kiss on the corner of my mouth, like she is being tentative, but then she is all in, kissing me like there is nothing else in the world she wants to be doing.

This kiss is everything I imagined it would be, and miles more, like I could ever have contemplated how amazing her lips on mine would feel. For the second time today, all sanity leaves my body, and I pull her closer to me, kissing her back, hungry for more of her, though I know I should stop. This is Beatrice, there are a million reasons why I shouldn't be kissing her, but she is the only person in the world I have been dying to kiss, so I surrender for a moment, basking in the feelings running through my body, wanting nothing more than this. Her hand reaches to touch my face, and I feel a moment of clarity returning.

I need to stop this before we both regret our actions.

She moans slightly, and my fingers caress her cheek.

I desperately want to stay like this forever, as in this second I can imagine a whole lifetime with her, a lifetime of joy and happiness, laughter and love, pure bliss, but I know I am in danger of ruining everything we have built between us. There are so many reasons why this between us is a risky path.

I pull away from her, an action which feels infinitely more difficult than pulling myself away from a roulette table or a good hand at a game of cards.

"I'm sorry," I whisper, and I get up from the sofa, rushing up the stairs to my room. I shut the door behind me, leaning against it, trying to hold on to my sanity. Every fibre of my being is screaming at me to go back downstairs to be with her. I can't. I shouldn't. But I want nothing more than her.

Beatrice: Now

The day after Jas arrives back in the UK, she turns up on my doorstep at midday, a couple of bags in her hands and a big smile on her face.

"Twice in two days, I am blessed!" I grin at her. She steps into the house and puts her bags down on the floor, throwing her arms around me and giving me a kiss on my cheek.

"I needed a dose of Beatrice. I've a year to catch up on. I'm going to be bugging you at every opportunity," she tells me.

"I missed you, too," I tell her. Whilst I might not remember the whole year, I know I've missed her.

"I am not back at work until next Monday, so I am at your disposal. I thought we could have some lunch and a bit of a pamper session." She lets me out of the hug, picking up the bags again and marching through to the kitchen.

"Go ahead and make yourself at home," I tease, watching her unpack some food and putting it into the fridge and cupboards.

"Well, based on the bare shelves in the fridge and cupboards, are you sure you've been fed over the past few months? I'm surprised you haven't starved."

"You know I'm a perfectly capable hunter-gatherer, right?" I lean against the counter. "I just think we have been a little distracted this last week or so. Shopping hasn't been at the top of the agenda."

"I'm teasing. Who is home anyway?"

"Ben is at work. No idea about Matt. I guess he will be back later," I reply.

"Okay, well, upstairs. Come on." She grabs the other bag from the side and then pulls me by my hand to the staircase. Jas is a whirlwind, and it's always easy for me to get swept up in her enthusiasm.

We head to my room. She puts the bag down on my drawers, pulling items out. She's got with her some face masks, bottles of nail polish, a manicure kit, headbands and other items. She looks like she's just robbed a health and beauty counter.

"You've gone all out." I pick up one of the many bottles of nail polish to look at the name of the colour. "I love this colour." I show her the bottle I am holding, the blue with a hint of grey.

"Okay, go wash your face, we'll start with the face masks." Jas smiles.

I start to walk out of the bedroom and then I pause at the doorway. "You really are the best friend I could ever wish for," I tell her.

"Love you too, Bea." She smiles back at me. She's the only one who calls me Bea, and I feel a thump in my heart as I hear the nickname. I head to the bathroom and get myself ready for the pampering day that Jas has clearly planned, feeling grateful that she is home.

"Have you thought about signing up for a dating app?" Jas asks me. We're both wearing face masks, sitting on my bed.

"What makes you think I am in need of a dating app?" I laugh.

"Well, it has been a long time since you and Ryan broke up. Maybe it's time to put yourself back out there."

"I don't know," I reply. I feel anxious at the very idea of being with somebody right now. My whole body seems to reject the very notion.

"When was the last time you had sex?" she asks. Jas has always believed in having frank discussions on these topics. I'm surprised she didn't ask me more yesterday.

"Jas, I don't remember a single thing since the middle of May and surprisingly, my vagina has not been very helpful in telling me what I have been doing these last few months." I laugh. I am quiet for a moment. "I know I asked yesterday if I'd given any indication that I had been seeing somebody, but I do think I might have been."

"What makes you think that?"

"I have a load of new underwear."

"Maybe you were earning extra money on an x-rated site, and they were your uniform," she jokes. I start to laugh but then have a moment of panic because I genuinely have no idea if this could have happened. She laughs at my expression. "Jesus, I was joking. Bea, you wouldn't do that."

"Mock my life, why not?" I grumble.

"Are you sure you didn't get them when you were with Ryan?"

"Definitely not. For starters, it would have been a lot of fancy underwear to purchase in the last few weeks of our relationship. Secondly, I went through my online bank statements, and I can see when I spent the money in the shop."

"You are a bloody master detective, you know that, right?"

"You're telling me that if you lost some of your memory, you wouldn't do the same?"

"I'd ask you to do it for me, you're very thorough."

"I haven't finished going through the statements yet. I'm sure to find other things I can investigate in between the million tickets I appear to have purchased at the cinema," I tell her.

"I was looking at all your ticket stubs whilst you were in the bathroom. I think you have seen every release for the last few months, plus a bunch of special showings. Maybe your mystery man works at the cinema?"

"A mystery man who works at the cinema but makes me pay full price for our tickets? I sure know how to pick them," I joke.

"Do you miss Ryan?" she wonders.

"No. I don't know what happened between us, but I don't feel like I miss him. I know I loved him, and I know I told you I thought he was the one for me, but if that were the case, I'd be calling him, right? Like I said yesterday, I get a funny feeling when I think about him, or anybody else I used to be around. You, Ben, Lily, my parents, you're the only ones who don't give me a funny feeling…and Matt, I guess, though I'm not sure he likes me much."

"I wouldn't take it personally. I don't think he likes anybody much." She smiles at me. "I think it's time to wash the face masks off. Then I will go make our lunch, and I'll do your nails after," she tells me as she gets up from the bed. I follow her to the bathroom, so I can wash off my facemask as well.

"I need a haircut." I look at myself in the bathroom mirror after I've washed off my face mask. I've clearly let my hair grow over the last few months.

"Oh, no don't, it looks gorgeous. Let me braid it for you!" Jas looks excited.

"How come I feel like you've turned me into your little pet project this week?"

"Please?" she cajoles.

"Food first," I say. I know with Jas, it is easier for me to just give in.

After lunch, Jas sits me in the dining room so she can do my hair. I take off my necklace so she can brush my hair without snagging against it, putting the necklace on the dresser next to all the items she has laid out, a multitude of nail varnishes and hair accessories.

"French or Dutch?" she asks.

"Whatever you fancy doing," I reply, getting comfortable in my seat. She starts to braid my hair.

"I'm going to see the house tomorrow, to do some detailed measurements. Do you want to come with me?"

"I would love to. I'm so happy for you."

"I'm very excited. I've been looking at cutlery sets."

"Look at you, you're all grown up." I laugh.

"You can still come live with me, you know."

"I'm happy here. I think."

"Well, the offer will always be on the table for you." She makes her promise as she carries on braiding my hair.

"Is that so you'll always have the option of playing dress up?"

"Nails next, sweetie. Now, be quiet, so I can concentrate, otherwise you're going to end up with lopsided braids." She lapses into silence, concentrating on what she is doing, and I sit quietly, letting her work.

"Thank you for a lovely day," I say to Jas later in the afternoon. She's off for dinner with her parents, and I'm expecting Ben home later.

"You're welcome."

"I do love these nails. The colour is lovely." I look at my nails. The blue-grey colour makes me happy.

"Suits you," she says as she gathers the last of her things and heads to the door. "I'll come by at 10:00 tomorrow. Is that okay with you?"

"Perfect. Have a good evening and say hi to your parents for me." I smile. She gives me one last kiss and then she is gone, sauntering down the path towards her car.

I close the door and go to tidy up the kitchen. I put things back in the cupboard and see what Jas meant about bare shelves. I don't know whether we've been cooking much here. Since I got back from the hospital, I've tended to eat whatever Ben has ordered or come home with. I head upstairs to get my purse, a fleece and a scarf, and then I walk out of the house towards the direction of the shops so I can buy things for a nice tea for us all.

I can hear Ben and Matt talking as I walk back into the house a little later. I've two shopping bags full of ingredients for a few days of dinners I've planned. I'm looking forward to cooking, something quick and simple for tea tonight but a hot madras planned for tomorrow. Ben and Matt stop talking when I walk down the hall and Ben rushes towards me.

"Where have you been?" he exclaims.

"Shopping, obviously," I say, holding up the bags. "I thought I could make us all tea."

"I was worried about you. I didn't know where you were."

"I didn't realise I was under house arrest." I roll my eyes. I walk through to the kitchen to put the bags onto the side. Ben and Matt follow me into the kitchen. I take off my scarf, and I look pointedly at Ben, waiting for a response. He looks annoyed.

"You're not, but you should have left a note."

"At what point in the day do you need me to write a note, Ben? You've been out at work all day, if I popped out at lunch, should I have left a note to tell you where I was? How about the nights you'll be planning on staying with Lily, if I leave the house, should I leave a note then? Do you need a daily plan? Hourly updates?" I ask, lightly, unpacking the bags.

"I knew where you were today, I just didn't know where you were when I got home. I was worried." Ben tells me, and I can tell he is trying to keep his voice even. We've argued many times in the past about my family being overprotective.

"How did you know where I was today?" I ask. I stop unpacking the bags and stare at him. I hadn't known Jas was coming over. Ben has the decency to look contrite. "If you tell me you've been discussing with Jas the times that she has to babysit me, I swear to God I'll…"

"You'll what, Beatrice? Why can't you just accept that we care about you?"

"There is caring for me and then there is smothering!" I snap. "Why can't you accept that I don't need to be so protected all the goddamn time?" I pick up a jar of passata and put it into the cupboard, more forcefully than I intended.

"Careful," Ben chides, and it makes me feel more frustrated than I did before.

"Careful, Beatrice, you might hurt yourself. Careful, Beatrice, you might be overdoing it. Careful, Beatrice, you shouldn't exert yourself," I mock.

"How about careful, Beatrice, you might knock yourself out and get amnesia," he snaps.

"Come on Ben, that's…" Matt cuts in, but Ben holds his hand up to silence him.

"No, Matt, she needs to hear this."

"It was an accident. You're being too hard on her," Matt says firmly. I'm surprised he's standing up for me, but if the roles were reversed, I'd feel uncomfortable at the argument as well.

"My parents asked me to take care of her and look what has happened. I should have been doing a better job of…"

"She isn't to blame for what happened, nor are you, so you need to calm down," Matt cuts in.

"She is my responsibility!" Ben snaps back.

"For God's sake, Ben, I am not your responsibility. I don't need taking care of!" I exclaim.

Ben turns back to me. "Clearly, you do. Mum and Dad were right, they should have come home."

"When did they say they were going to come home?" I ask.

"Before you moved in here, they were going to come back to make sure you were okay. If they knew what was going on, they'd want to come home now. I am going to call them and…"

"If you dare tell Mum and Dad about my accident, I swear I will never speak to you again," I threaten, cutting off his sentence.

"Seriously?" Ben scoffs. He knows it's probably an empty threat because we've said this to each other throughout our childhood, but I need him to know I'm serious.

"Actually… I'll tell them it was you who broke that antique mirror." I throw at him, and he stares at me.

"You wouldn't." He sounds like he doesn't believe me.

It's been years since the two of us have held this secret. Ben had smashed a mirror not long after I'd had my operation. We'd been home alone, and he confessed he felt hopeless about what had happened to me. I'd been the one to suggest he threw stuff to feel better, and he'd ended up accidentally smashing the mirror. It was a family heirloom and my mother's favourite possession.

I will always remember the look on his face because he knew our parents would be furious. I'd taken the blame and said I'd smashed it, knowing my parents wouldn't yell at me because I was recovering from surgery. It's one of the things that helped Ben and I strengthen our relationship, from being siblings frustrated by each other to two who truly cared for one another, and who would stand up for one another and take the blame.

"Try me."

"You're being childish." He rolls his eyes.

"Yeah? How's this for childish? Make your own goddamn tea," I snap at him and then I stomp out of the kitchen, up to my bedroom. I feel like I'm a teenager all over again as I slam the door behind me and throw myself onto my bed. I switch my phone off because I know Ben will likely text Jas to tell her what has happened, and I don't want to talk to her right now.

I roll over and grab hold of the oversized teddy bear. I can't remember when I last slept with a teddy bear in my room, but this teddy gives me comfort, and I have slept with it on my bed since I got out of hospital. I hold onto the bear as I lie still on my bed, staring at the ceiling, watching the light fade as time passes.

I don't move until there is a knock on the door a little later. I go to open the door, ready to shout at Ben again, but it is Matt who is at my door, holding a plate with a burrito and a small tub of ice cream next to it. He holds the plate out for me. I take it from him, and he turns to walk away.

"Thank you," I call to him. I want to clarify that my thanks are not just for the food, but for trying to intervene in the kitchen, but I don't and hope he just knows.

"You're welcome, Beatrice. Goodnight," he replies, and he disappears into his room, leaving me alone. I go back to my bedroom, sitting on my bed so I can eat my burrito and ice cream. I take some painkillers because the crying has given me a big headache, and then I climb back into bed, holding the teddy bear, exhausted and frustrated.

I sleep fitfully. I'm never rested when I'm arguing with people. I know Ben loves me. I know he just worries about me, but it still makes me frustrated. I don't need sympathy or overprotection.

The house is quiet when I get up which is unsurprising given the time. I don't have long until Jas is supposed to arrive. I get up and shower. As I am washing with the shower gel, I realise I don't have my necklace on. I remember taking it off yesterday when Jas was brushing my hair.

I finish getting ready and head downstairs to find it. I get a rush of anxiousness when I see it isn't there where I left it. I start looking around in case it has been moved or knocked to the floor, feeling more anxious when it is clearly not here, and it's like I have lost something important all over again.

The knock on the front door stops me searching. I go to answer, finding Jas on the doorstep.

"I'm in trouble, aren't I?" Jas asks without waiting for me to greet her.

"I know your heart is in the right place, but I don't need to be mollycoddled. Especially from you, you know how much I hate it. You should know better," I reply.

"I'm very sorry. It won't happen again."

"Apology accepted." I open the door for her and head back to keep looking for my necklace, hoping that I have missed it in my previous search.

"I did text you last night," Jas says from behind me.

"I haven't seen your messages. I switched my phone off last night, and it is still off. I will look at any grovelling texts you sent me later," I tell her.

"I was texting before I knew you were upset with Ben. When I got home, I saw I'd accidentally swept this up with my things. Is this what you are looking for?" Jas asks. I turn to look at her, and she is holding my necklace.

Immediately, I burst into tears. "I thought I'd lost it." I manage between tears.

"Hey, come here." Jas soothes. She pulls me into a hug.

"I don't know where I got it, but I don't want to lose it," I explain. I'm not sure she hears everything given I am still crying.

"I'm sorry, I didn't realise you'd be so upset. If I knew, I'd have come back to give it to you last night." Jas lets me out of the hug and hands me the necklace. I put it on, fastening it. I look at her.

"Don't tell Ben about this," I plead. I'm pretty sure he'd want me certified if he knew I was crying over a necklace.

"I promise. Though in my defence, it wasn't like I've been telling Ben about your secret boyfriend who enjoys fancy bras and writes sweet love notes. I just agreed to tell him you were okay. Also, don't ever think I am babysitting you. You're my bestie. You're stuck with me." She smiles.

I give her a little smile and then I get my things ready. Before I leave the house, even though I know he'll know where I am, even though I am still mad at him, I leave a little note for Ben, telling him I am with Jas.

Jas and I spend the morning measuring the rooms, and then we go to mine to look over websites for potential furniture, and we make jokes about what she can do with her spare bedroom.

Jas leaves in the afternoon, and I set about making the tea I'd planned when I did the shopping. Despite the day being fairly laid back, I have another headache. I focus on making tea, but by the time Matt and Ben are home, I feel like my head might split in two.

I finish making tea, and we all sit in silence to eat. Ben and I are still not talking. It leaves an uncomfortable atmosphere in the room. I feel sorry for Matt. I wonder how many times he has had to referee between me and Ben.

Ben must know I am still mad at him as he doesn't offer to wash the pots. I start clearing the plates and Matt helps by putting things away. I'm nearing the end of washing the pans when I can't help but take an intake of breath when a shot of pain goes through my head.

"Everything okay?" Matt asks.

"Fine. Just a little headache. I've had a few since the accident. I'll be fine," I say shortly.

"I'll finish up in here," he suggests. I nod and head upstairs to take some more painkillers, hoping they'll work their magic and take the pain away. A minute later, there is a knock on my bedroom door. Ben stands in the hallway.

"How bad is your headache?" he asks. I would tell him off for listening to my conversation with Matt, but I'm too tired to fight.

"They're getting worse," I say, and for the second time today, I start to cry.

"Why didn't you tell me you were having headaches?" he asks like he doesn't already know that it's because I don't want to give another reason for people to treat me like I'm going to break. He sighs. "Come on, we should go get you checked out."

For once, I don't have the energy to fight him. I follow him down the stairs, walking past Matt who is loitering in the hallway. He gives us both a curt nod and then heads upstairs. I follow Ben out of the house and down the driveway towards his car.

"I'm sorry for being so stubborn," I say quietly as he drives away from the house. I'm holding onto my head, trying to stop the ache.

"You don't have to tell me everything that is going on, but maybe don't keep something like these headaches to yourself. It's not a weakness to ask for help, Beatrice," he chides. I'm too tired to argue, so instead, I tell him I think he is an awesome brother and that I'm sorry for being defensive. He apologises too, and we let this fight between us blow over, for now.

Beatrice: Then, September

I walk up the stairs towards Matt's bedroom door. I stand outside the door for a second. I can't hear any movement inside his room. I reach up to knock, but then the door opens, and he is standing in front of me. We stand in silence for a second, looking at each other, searching each other's expression for answers. Then he pulls me close towards him, cupping my face with his hands, and his lips are on mine again.

God, he can kiss. The first few kisses with somebody new are usually awkward, clashes of teeth, wondering why they're being so weird with their tongue, and trying to find the right pace to settle into, but Matt kisses me like he's been kissing me for years like it's the one thing he's worked to master. There is a synchronicity between us that feels like perfection. I don't know why I am surprised. Over the last few months, there have been multiple times I've been convinced that Matt was made especially for me.

His fingers are in my hair; my hands are on his side, pulling him closer. He breaks away from our kiss, but this time, instead of rushing away, he stays close to me, his face still close to mine, and one hand still on my cheek.

"We shouldn't," he whispers.

"Why not?" I challenge.

"We live together."

"There is a simple solution to that, I can move out," I whisper.

"I don't want that," he whispers back.

"I don't want that either. I love living here."

"I'm also your boss."

"I can quit."

"I don't want that," he says, and his thumb brushes against my cheek.

"I don't want to quit either."

"You've been hurt," he murmurs against my lips. At this, he sounds upset.

"You'd never hurt me." It feels like the truest, simplest fact that exists in the universe. This is nothing like the situation I had with Cole.

"I'm a gambling addict," he says, sounding wary and ashamed.

"We all have a past." I soothe and hold him tighter.

"You're Ben's sister. Ben would kill me." Matt concludes, but his lips graze against mine as he talks, and I feel myself go weak at the knees. "This is not a smart choice," he adds, but he still doesn't pull away.

"Screw being smart, some things defy logic," I reply. "You have been driving me crazy for a long time," I admit.

"You've been driving me crazy since the day I met you," he says, and he kisses the corner of my mouth, leaving me wanting more.

"If you want me, please don't stop again," I plead. I know if he were to pull away again, to close the door, I'd be devastated.

"Do you want to come in?" he asks. It's more than an invitation. This is a choice he is offering me, letting me be the one in charge of what happens next.

"Yes. Do you want me to come in?" I ask, kissing his bottom lip as I talk.

"I do." He gives a little growl, and he pushes the door wide open with his foot, and we step into his room. We make it to his bed, small steps we take together, our lips still on each other, and we land on his bed together.

"I want this. I want you," I tell him. I open the first few buttons of his shirt. I kiss his chest. He sighs in contentment.

I'm not sure if it is from my kiss or from my words. I finish opening his shirt buttons. I've seen him shirtless before, many times, but he still takes my breath away. He's got a beautiful, strong body, tanned from the week away where we'd spent a lot of time at the beach.

I trace my fingers across the muscle definition on his chest and stomach, something I had thought about doing during those days on the beach, something I feel confident enough to do now. "You really are gorgeous. Even those hideous swimming shorts couldn't take that away from you," I tell him with a smile. I kiss him down his stomach, to the edge of his trousers, and he takes a sharp intake of breath when my hand reaches for the zip of his trousers. He takes my hand. Kisses my fingers.

"I haven't had sex in a long time. I've been thinking about you for a long time." He sounds anxious. It dawns on me that he's worried he's not going to last long. I move to kiss him on his neck; he frees my hand, and I unzip his trousers.

There's another catch of his breath as I slip my hand into his boxers, taking him in my hand. I move the fabric, freeing him, stroking him with my hand. He screws his eyes up like he is trying to concentrate. He reaches to me with his uninjured hand, landing on my breast, his thumb skimming lightly across the nipple. I keep going, watching him until he screws his face up.

"Let's just call this pre-gaming, a warm-up to a much bigger event," I whisper in his ear, and he climaxes, warm on my hand, groaning.

"Jesus," he mutters. "I haven't been that fast since my first time. I'm sorry." He looks flustered. I reach across to his bedside table where I can see a packet of tissues, and I pass them to him so he can clean up, cleaning up myself as well.

"Don't apologise. It's kinda hot. I haven't even taken my clothes off yet or shown you my best moves." I grin. He gets up to discard the tissues, pulling his trousers the rest of the way down as he walks, and then he returns to me, pulling me up with one hand so I am sat up on the bed. He sits down next to me, turning his body towards me.

He reaches for my top, and I tense a little. Matt smiles at me, and together we pull my top over my head. He puts his hand between my breasts, his fingers splayed across my chest, his middle finger lining up against my scar. He pauses for a moment like he is feeling the beat of my heart.

"So strong," he whispers to me, and then he leans forward to kiss my neck. "You're so beautiful, Beatrice, so wonderful."

He keeps up a flurry of kisses on my neck, and he slips one arm behind me, so he can undo my bra clasp. He pulls the straps down my arms and then throws the bra to the floor. He puts a hand back on my breast, circling one nipple with the pad of his thumb. Now it's my turn to give a sharp intake of breath. He guides me to lie back on the bed, and then he lifts my hips, so he can pull down my shorts and underwear so that I am naked underneath him.

He kisses me everywhere like he is mapping my body; each kiss is a marker as to where he has been, land he has claimed. By the time he reaches my hips, I'm wriggling in anticipation. He moves a little higher up, his lips on the lower section of my torso, where he follows up a kiss with a suck of the skin in a way I know will leave a telltale love bite, and I flex my hips underneath him, hot with desire, knowing that I'll think of this moment every time I see it until it fades. My hands are in his hair, and I hear him ask me what I want.

"Everything. You. More. Now," I manage. I hear him rustling in the drawer beside his bed for a condom, and then he is back to me, and he slips a finger inside me, then another. I gasp out the words: please, more, now. He groans, and then he is pulling off his remaining clothes, pulling the condom out of the wrapper, rolling it down his cock. He pauses before he enters me, so I nod, pull him closer, and I bite near his collarbone as he enters me, gasping at the feel of him.

As soon as he starts moving in me, I'm struck by a thought, wondering why we haven't been doing this all along because this is fucking exquisite, the weight of him above me, the feel of his body on mine, in mine, it is perfection.

Nothing has ever felt this perfect. I writhe underneath him, staring up at him, and he stares back down at me, slowing his pace, so he can stroke my face, kiss me, then we twist around together, so I'm sat on him, his torso against mine, his arms around me, his hands on my hips, my fingers in his hair, my lips on his neck, moving in synchronicity, pushing each other to higher levels of bliss.

This time, when he climaxes, I come undone with him. It's a moment of pure ecstasy between us, clasped together, holding on like we're each other's grounding force, like we never want to let go. Panting, we lie down together on the bed.

After a moment, he cleans up, then pulls me close and kisses me on my shoulder.

"What now?" I ask the words that no guy who just slept with somebody wants to hear. The words tumbled from my mouth before I had a chance to engage my brain. He tenses a little. I feel it in the arm that is under my neck and curved to hold me across my chest. I prepare myself for him to say that this was a fun one-off, something for us to do to get over the urges we had been feeling, and to now pack it away as a one-off experience, never to be spoken about, never to be repeated.

"What do you want to happen now?" he asks instead. His breath is warm on my neck, and his lips connect to my skin in the smallest hint of a kiss.

"If you want to forget that this just happened, I will understand."

"Do you want to forget it?" He is still holding me close. He is giving me no indication that this was a mistake, a one-off, and I realise, again he is letting me guide him, he is letting me set the pace, set the tone.

"No."

"I don't want to forget about it, either," he replies.

"I know you have somebody you needed to get off your mind, but…" I start, and the little laugh he gives stops me from talking.

"Don't you see it, Bea? It's you. You're the one who has been on my mind."

I turn on the bed, facing him. I prop myself up on one arm. "Me? I am the head, heart and further south girl?"

"Oh, God, okay, let's first remind ourselves that you came up with that name, not me. But yes. You have been the one who has been in my head, driving me crazy. You've been in my head and everywhere else."

"Aw, Matt, you're so romantic," I tease, but there is a rush in my body as I understand just how much I have been affecting him. I thought I'd imagined things, wanted him to feel more for me than he did, and to know he does warms me.

"You want romance? You want flowers, expensive gifts, and weekend trips to Paris, chocolates and three-course dinners? You tell me what you want, Bea, and I'll do my best to give it to you." He seems suddenly urgent.

"I just want this, Matt," I tell him. I let my fingers run over the bandage on his hand. A memento of a stupid risk he had taken for me. "I just want you, just how you are."

"You have me."

"I have some conditions…"

"Oh, yes?"

"No more crazy actions." I tap lightly on the bandage.

He winces. "Done."

"In front of others, nothing changes. We don't tell people at work. We don't tell Ben anything. Not yet. I just want us to enjoy this, without scrutiny. Is that okay?"

"Yes, anything else?" He gives me a small smile.

"Just one… Whenever the opportunity and mood arise, I'm going to need you to do all of this again." I gesture at our naked bodies. "It's definitely something that I think should be non-negotiable," I tease. "You can call me demanding, but those are my terms and conditions."

"And there's me thinking you were going to ask for something difficult." He grins.

"Are there any conditions you want to raise with me, other than the ones I have mentioned?" I ask. He thinks for a moment.

"Okay, if you want to carry on as normal as if nothing has changed between us, then you're going to have to stop giving that little sigh of contentment you do sometimes when you take a first bite of something when you're hungry. Now

I know that you make that noise in other situations, it's going to make it hard for me to concentrate." He tries to keep a serious expression but fails.

"Well, I wouldn't want to make it hard for you." I grin. A flicker of desire runs across his face. "Where do I sign to accept the terms and conditions?"

"Anywhere you like." He smiles lazily. I reach across him to his bedside table, where it looks like he's dumped everything from his pockets after yesterday's shift at work. There is a marker pen on the table, and I pull the lid off. He lies still on the mattress, and I move down on the bed.

"I, Beatrice Schofield, promise never to make orgasmic noises when eating something heavenly and decadent. Henceforth, I shall restrain my orgasmic noises to any room where it is just me and you, at a volume of my choosing." I doodle a drawing of a bee on his lower abdomen, putting an x next to the picture. I hand the pen to him. He grins at me. I lie back on the bed, and he positions himself in the area he wants.

"I, Matt Haliwell, promise to forego all moments of insanity. I pledge to carry on as normal, so we can enjoy this without the pressure of scrutiny. I promise to do my best to cause those orgasmic noises whenever the opportunity and the mood arises because I love the sound. I promise to protect you, always, from whatever may arise," he vows, and he signs his name across my right hip bone.

He clicks the lid back onto the pen, tossing it to the floor, then lowers himself to kiss my hipbone where he has signed. All the joking now seems insignificant, put away, a thickness in the air. He looks up at me. He holds my gaze, and I can feel the rhythm of our breathing change.

"We have the opportunity," I say. "We have the mood." I flex my hips underneath him. I bite my lip in anticipation and give a little moan, and with that, Matt pulls himself back up the bed, his mouth is on mine.

"See, I could lose myself forever in that sound," he whispers.

"I lose myself in you," I whisper back, pulling him closer to my body, and we surrender ourselves to each other.

Matt: Then, September

"Are you still lost?" Beatrice asks. Her voice is teasing. We're in my bed, limbs tangled together, my heart still racing from our second time together.

"I think I'm going to be lost forever," I tell her, honestly. "I feel like I've been given everything I've been dreaming about for a long time."

"Yeah, since when?" she asks, intrigued, and she shifts on the bed slightly to look at me properly.

"You mean how long have I been pining after you?" I laugh.

"I was going to ask how long you've liked me, but if you want to go for a girly pining, who am I to argue." She grins.

"For me, from the moment you ran your fingers down my arm at the bar that night, and said that first, breathy, 'oh baby'. Then we came home, and you made that noise eating your burrito. I ended up in my bedroom, dumbstruck, knowing I was in deep trouble." I smile at her, thinking of how I'd felt when she'd touched me that night at the bar, how I'd felt like I'd been struck by lightning in the kitchen.

"Since then?" She seems surprised.

"Yes, since then."

"Why didn't you say anything?"

"Many reasons, really. Who you are, who I am, the friendship we've built, they're all big things I didn't want to risk, but the main reason I didn't do anything earlier was because I knew you needed time. That morning in the kitchen, you'd reacted so skittishly when I'd stood too close to you. I knew something had set you on edge. I've always liked you, but there was no way I felt like I should do anything if you were hurt."

"I needed a bit of time to heal," she admits. She's quiet for a moment. "This has been the first time I've been intimate since…" her voice trails off.

I pull her closer to me. "I hope…" I begin, but she cuts me off.

"It was perfect, Matt, really perfect. I meant it earlier, with my terms and conditions about whenever we have the opportunity and the mood. I've been worried that it would always be on my mind when the time came to be intimate with somebody, but…it wasn't, and I think that's because it was you. I know you'd never hurt me. I trust you. I… I like you."

"How long have you *liked* me?" I stress the word like she had earlier. "I had no clue you thought of me in any other way than a friend."

"A while, but somewhere between the fish and chips on the beach, and the big wheel ride, I knew there was more to what I was feeling. I knew I was hoping something would happen and knew you meant more to me than just being a friend."

"I got so much shit that week from my brothers." I laugh.

"Really?" She grins at me.

"Sam took me to one side after the first night and asked me why we weren't sharing a room. He thought we were just hiding a relationship, and he refused to believe that nothing was going on between us. Then he spent the rest of the week giving me shit for being a 'dumb ass chicken' in not telling you how I felt," I tell her.

"Polly asked me on the beach how long we had been together, and seemed very unconvinced by me saying we weren't together." Beatrice giggles. "Maybe we need to work harder on our deadpan facial expressions, otherwise Ben's going to be suspicious."

"He's back tomorrow. He and I are going out for drinks in the evening," I remind her.

"We have a few hours to be working on serious faces then."

"Maybe I should arrange a fake date. You can remind me to take my condoms," I tease.

"I was quite bitter with the idea of you going out and being with somebody else." She bites her lip.

"I know this is going to sound terrible, but I was thinking of you the whole night. I wanted to text you so many times that night to ask you questions like how you were enjoying the film."

"That film was bloody torture." She rolls her eyes. "Lily has no taste."

"I had to keep reminding myself that it would be rude to be texting you something I had seen that was funny, or ask you how you were getting on when I was supposed to be on a date. She deserved better, so I cut the date short and came home to have the best evening with you instead. Every time I've been trying to organise a date since I've not gone ahead with them because I've had you on my mind. That's what I said to you at my mum's house, in Spanish."

"Really?" She smiles. I nod.

"Are you going to tell me what you said in French?" I ask. I watch as a small blush comes on her cheeks.

"I said French is a beautiful language."

"You know that is not the two sentences I am referring to." I grin.

She's quiet for a moment. "I told you that I think you're the most amazing person I've ever met. Then I said…" she stops for a moment. She bites her lip, and I'm curious about what she has said.

"You don't have to tell me if you don't want to," I reassure her.

"I said I wished I could tell you what you meant to me, but that I was afraid," she says, and she looks away.

"Oh, Bea," I sigh. I pull her close to me. I wrap my arms around her. "You have nothing to be afraid of, I promise," I soothe. I kiss the top of her head. "I'd do anything to protect you. I won't hurt you."

"I know you won't," she says, her voice quiet. "Just, telling you would put what we had at risk. I was afraid to lose what we had by trying to change us. But I'm glad we took the risk, as I wouldn't change this for the world."

"Me either, Bea," I reply, still holding her tight, still amazed that I'm so goddamn lucky.

I am halfway between sleep and awake when I hear her walking back into the bedroom. She gets back into the bed, snaking an arm around me and giving a little contented sigh. At the feel of her touch, I'm fully awake. We've been awake most of the night, talking, kissing, and just marvelling at everything that is unfolding between us. I turn on the bed, facing her.

"Good morning." I kiss her forehead. "I was a little worried I'd dreamt this all. Where'd you go?"

"Bathroom. I didn't mean to wake you when I came back in."

"You can wake me anytime."

"Still no regrets?"

"The only regret I have from yesterday is that my hand is as sore as hell. Ben's going to give me so much shit about it tonight."

"I'm not done giving you shit about it." She grins, but then she looks concerned. "Do you want me to get you some painkillers? Maybe we should go get your hand checked out. I'm a mediocre caregiver."

"Pretty sure you're not supposed to blow on wounds," I tease though I get a jolt as I remember the sensations I'd got when she'd taken care of my hand.

"I put TCP on afterwards, I'm sure you're good." She grins.

"I'll double-check with Ben later; it would be an inconvenience if my hand were to fall off." I smirk.

"You know, I'm not used to waking up in bed with somebody and hearing them talk about my brother." She gives an exasperated look.

"What does Miss Schofield want to talk about instead?" I kiss along her collarbone. "Shall we talk about how I think you are wonderful? Shall we talk about how I think you are the most beautiful woman I've ever seen?" I kiss her neck. "Shall I tell you how you're the smartest, funniest, strongest woman I've ever met? Shall I tell you how your eyes remind me of hot chocolate?" I kiss her cheek.

"You have gorgeous eyes. They're a lovely blue-grey colour." She leans over to give a flutter of kisses against my eyelids.

"I'm not done with my compliments yet," I murmur. "I was just about to start on your lips."

"Stop talking Matt," she murmurs back, and she pushes me back down onto the bed, climbing on top of me, and all words disappear.

Afterwards, she draws over the faded bee she had drawn the night before, a mark for only her to see on me. I write a line from one of her favourite poems across the top of her thigh, and she jokes that we need a more permanent method of sharing notes. We spend the morning exploring each other's bodies.

Later, we go to work. I take it easy due to my hand, catching up in the office and on admin tasks rather than mixing drinks and serving people at the bar. Beatrice takes the lead at the bar, and we keep the night professional between us, keeping our distance until our early finish arrives.

We walk back to my car and as soon as we get there, I scoop her into my arms, kissing her, feeling like a man who has finally been given everything he desired. We kiss until she's telling me we need to go home. We arrive home, making it through the front door before we kiss again. I'm desperate for her, and she squirms in my arms in a way that makes me think she's desperate for me too, pulling me closer, giving a soft moan against my mouth when we break away from a kiss. I'm trying to calculate how long we have before Ben is due home, but then the hallway is lit up by his headlights as he pulls his car into the drive. Beatrice gives a little groan.

"Pretty sure it's illegal to get me this turned on and then disappear out for drinks," she grumbles.

"Pretty sure I'm going to be calling your brother a cock-blocker all night," I quip back, and she laughs.

"I have no objections to him cock-blocking whilst you're out tonight." She winks as she straightens herself up, I tuck my shirt back in, and we're sitting in the living room with the TV on by the time Ben walks into the house. There is a round of greetings between us.

"What are you doing tonight?" Ben asks Beatrice as I stand up as we'd planned to go out straight away.

"I am going to take over the bathroom without you two losers needing to get in there the minute I put my foot in the bath."

"Well, we will leave you in peace. I'm just going to change my shirt." Ben starts to leave the living room.

"Where are you two off to anyway?" Beatrice's question stops him.

"Just for a few beers," Ben replies.

"Matt was telling me you're going to be his wingman tonight. It's apparently a while since he got laid," Beatrice says. Ben looks shocked. At no point in our friendship have we ever acted as a wingman for each other. I'm convinced Ben has never acted as a wingman in his life. I look over at Beatrice, and she flashes me a cheeky grin before Ben turns around to look at us both.

"Well, sure, okay, if…" Ben starts.

"I don't need to get laid, thank you very much," I cut in. "I'll get changed and meet you down here in ten," I say to Ben. He nods and heads upstairs.

Beatrice stands and gets closer to me. "Mission accomplished." She gives a little bow like she's pleased with her performance. I want to laugh, but I know Ben's going to be quizzing me all night now about my love life. "Have fun tonight, just…not too much fun. I'll be thinking about you whilst I'm in the bath," she whispers and then she is gone from the room before I have a chance to tell her I'll be thinking about her all night long.

"How's Lily?" I ask Ben later. We're seated at the bar with two beers in front of us. I can't help but grin at his reaction as it's ridiculously wholesome. He always looks like he's unable to string a sentence together when he's thinking of her. I hope I do a better job at hiding my emotions whenever I talk about Beatrice; otherwise, I'll be breaking her terms and conditions a lot sooner than she's hoping.

"She's fine. We're in a really good place."

"I'm really pleased for you. You two deserve all the happiness possible," I tell him honestly because Ben is the best guy I know, and Lily's a sweetheart.

"There's a doctor at work, she's single. I think you'd get on. Do you want me to set you up?" Ben asks.

"No!" I laugh.

"Are you still looking for somebody?" Ben sounds curious. The last time we were out for drinks, we must have talked about everything bar women. It looks like he's now going to catch up on that topic with me.

"No. Yes. No." I flip between my answers. "I am fine taking care of my own love life, thanks. No meddling required from either Schofield." I smile.

"I am just following on from what Beatrice said earlier." He shrugs. As we'd left the house, Beatrice had shouted after me, asking if I had remembered my condoms.

"Beatrice likes to mess about. She thinks she's funny," I reply.

"She seems more like herself now," Ben muses. The first time we'd been for drinks after Beatrice had moved in, he'd told me how worried he was about her.

"She seems good," I agree.

"Maybe I should start looking for somebody to set her up with instead if you don't want my matchmaking skills." He smiles.

"You think you can find somebody good enough for your sister?" I try to sound light-hearted but the idea of him coming home one day, saying he has found somebody perfect for her makes me feel a little sick.

"Yeah, you're right." Ben laughs.

"Did you like Ryan?" I prod.

"He was alright, I guess." Ben shrugs. He doesn't often talk badly about people. "I'm kind of glad they're not together. There was nothing wrong with him, I guess.

"I know my parents had reservations given he is ten years older than she is, they always wondered what somebody in their early thirties wanted with somebody in their early twenties, but they accepted it in the end. I just... I guess I always worried that when it came down to it, he didn't seem to be the type of guy who would be there if the shit hit the fan." Ben explains, and I wonder if

Beatrice will ever tell him what happened, confirming his accurate assessment of Ryan's character. I only met Ryan once, but for him to treat Beatrice so appallingly, to refuse to listen to her, to believe somebody else over her, it disgusts me.

"Yeah, he seems like a dick," I reply, darkly. Ben looks at me, surprise on his face. I shrug, trying to look unbothered. "I mean, come on, that time I met him, he spent most of his time making the conversation about him and grabbing her ass," I point out.

Ben finishes his beer and gives a little shudder.

"Making me like Ryan even less now," he jokes. "Okay, so I'll be keeping my eye out for a non-ass-grabbing supportive guy for Beatrice, and I'll keep my eye out for somebody for you, too."

"I'll go get another round," I say, getting up from the table and heading to the bar, trying not to feel disappointed that Ben's never considered me as an option for his sister.

I'm at the bar when my phone buzzes with a text message. I open it to look at it and smile when I see it is from Beatrice. It asks if I can text freely, so I reply I am at the bar and ask what she wants. I order the beers and keep an eye on my phone, waiting for her new message to come through.

I know I joked before about Ben helping you find somebody to get you laid, but can I amend my terms and conditions? I know it's only been one night, and I don't want to seem like some unhinged stalker but... I don't want to sleep with anybody else, and I'd rather you didn't either. Is that okay? she's written.

I wonder how long she's been worried this evening that I might be searching for another woman, like anybody could capture my interest in the way she does. I type a message back, *the only person I want to be with is you. The one I want to talk to? You. The one I want to laugh with? You. The one I want to watch shit movies with? You. The one I want to share my bed with? You. It's always you, Bea. It's been you since the start. Is that okay?*

The bartender passes me my beers, and I pay for them whilst keeping an eye on my phone. I can see she is typing.

Yes. That's okay. Enjoy your drinks. Her reply makes me smile.

I'm going to get back to your brother now, now we're two beers in, he'll ask me what I have done to my hand.

She messages her response: *Tell him you dreamt you were fighting Freddy Kruger, and you woke up with the injury.*

I type back: *I'll give him an elaborate excuse and ask him if I'm about to get gangrene.*

Get lost, I know you enjoyed that, she replies.

More than you know. Enjoy your bath. See you tomorrow x.

I put my phone back in my pocket, grab the beers and head back to Ben. I pass him his beer. He looks at me. "So can I ask what the hell have you done to your hand?" he asks. I laugh and sit down across from him. "What's so funny?" he asks.

"You don't have to worry about it. It was a stupid thing, but nothing to worry about."

"I do worry about you. I want the best for you," he replies.

"I know you do. All is good, I promise," I tell him. I know he wants the best for me. I just wonder if he's going to feel the same when I eventually tell him I have fallen in love with his sister.

Beatrice: Now

"Is it still just us for tea? Where are Ben and Matt?" Jas asks as she arrives a few weeks after my accident. She hands me a bottle of wine as I let her in the door.

"Ben and Lily are away somewhere. Apparently, the stars aligned, and they somehow managed to get ten days off work at the same time. According to Ben, this is a miracle."

"What about Matt?" Jas sits herself down on the sofa.

"He went to his mum's apparently. He left a note for me and Ben, but I don't think Ben saw it before he left," I reply.

"Or Ben's so focused on getting to Lily, there could be a tornado, and he wouldn't notice." Jas grins. She's met Lily a few times before, I remember her telling me that they were a perfect couple, and often refers to them as Doctor and Doctor Happily Loved Up.

"Dinner won't be long," I tell her, taking a seat next to her and putting the wine bottle on the floor for now.

"So how is your investigation going? Recovered any nuggets of memory yet?" Jas wonders. She asks me this every time we speak. Given it is now March, I imagine she's now sick of asking, especially when my answers are always so disappointing.

"I have learned a few things this week, but nothing that has made me suddenly get an explosion of memories back."

"I thought your neurologist said…"

"He said not to force things. I'm not. I'm just writing down facts I have found out." I smile, trying not to sound frustrated. I had been waiting for the neurologist to give me a magic trick to make my memories pop back into my head, and I'd been disappointed when he had reminded me what Dr Edwards had said, that it might never happen.

"Come on then, tell me the facts."

"Okay, fact one, Lily and Ben broke up for a bit."

"No freaking way," Jas exclaims. "I'm opening the wine. This will need wine." She gets up, goes to the kitchen and returns with two glasses. I open the wine, pouring us both a glass. It's my first drink of alcohol since the accident.

"I don't know much more than that. Lily was the one who told me when she came for a weekend. She knows I don't remember things because Ben can't keep a secret to save his life though apparently I am still in the clear with the parents. Anyway, Lily had mentioned it, it happened before Christmas. She freaked out about the two of them living so far apart, always being long-distance, and apparently spent the next few days crying until she phoned him and asked him to take her back."

"Doctor and Doctor Happily Loved Up, I would never have thought it," Jas muses. She sips her wine. "Anything else?"

"I finished checking through my recent bank transactions. Before Christmas, I spent a healthy chunk of money at a jewellers who also specialise in engraving. I went and checked, they couldn't tell me what I had purchased, but they told me they don't sell the necklace I'm wearing. So I spent money on something else, and I don't think it was for me."

"Maybe you sent something to your parents?"

"Maybe. Ben says we'd agreed to do a belated Christmas though, so unless I've hidden it away somewhere, I don't have a clue."

"Did you work out your social media accounts?"

"I deleted one in January. Not just closed it, but requested the whole page to be deleted. It can't be recovered. Another one, I still have, and I apparently liked a lot of posts by a model called Polly. She's married to some photographer called Toby. I liked her announcement that she's having their first baby. I've never been that invested in somebody I don't know before."

I bite my bottom lip. I hesitate to tell Jas that I'd even messaged this Polly in December, writing *'I'm so happy for you both'*, and she'd replied with *'thanks Beatrice, I'm so happy I could burst'*! It might not be unusual for somebody like her to interact with fans, but I have no idea why I would be one.

"Can you see more details about the both of them?"

"Not really. They're just Polly and Toby on their social media pages. He has a website for photography, but it's literally along the lines of Photography by Toby. They don't live anywhere near here. They split their time between London and the South West coast of England."

"Anything else?" Jas asks. The timer on the oven beeps, so I go to the kitchen to dish up. I've made a chicken pie and herby potatoes. I dish up the dinner, putting our plates on the breakfast bar.

"Nothing else," I finally reply, taking my seat. "I don't know what else to try."

"Have you been into work?"

"No, Matt was adamant that I couldn't fake knowledge with the people there, so I have stayed away."

"Maybe you should go," she suggests after a mouthful of food.

"Maybe," I sigh though I'm not convinced. What Matt has said about going back makes sense. It would be clear I didn't know who anybody was, and then I would have to face questions.

"Are you still getting headaches?"

"Less so, now," I reply. I'm glad because the headaches in the first couple of weeks had been painful. The night Ben had overheard me telling Matt about them, we'd spent hours at the walk-in centre and then hours again in A&E. The doctor eventually told me it was just a symptom of being concussed, that they would ease and settle eventually. I suspect if the news had been any different, Ben would have been an overprotective pain. He has chilled out since our fight, but I know he still keeps an eye out on me.

"How are you feeling, generally?"

"Still out of sorts. I swing between being frustrated and being sad. I feel a little lost," I admit. I don't tell her how I wake in the middle of the night, upset by the feeling I am missing something, something I am unable to quantify what it is. Instead, feeling like I might cry if I speak another word, I focus on my dinner. There is a silence between us whilst we eat.

"Well, my dear friend, I can confirm you didn't forget your ability to cook a splendid dinner." Jas smiles. She holds her wine glass up, and I clink mine against it, the back of my mind thinking about whether I should go to the bar at some point in the week.

I switch the topic of conversation, asking her questions about her job and her new office, asking when she is getting the keys to her house, and when Alessandro will be flying to see her. Her face lights up as she talks, and it's clear she loves this guy she has met, and she tells me she is excited for me to finally meet him.

A few days later, Matt returns home. I'm sat in the living room reading when his key turns in the door.

"Hi. Is Ben home?" he asks.

"No, Ben is away with Lily. They've been away for about a week."

"What have you been doing by yourself?" He sits down on the chair in the living room. For a moment, I'm surprised. He rarely spends time with me by myself. I've tried talking to him, but if I push too hard, he gets up and walks out of the room. Ben tells me it is my imagination but that's because Matt only seems comfortable when we have Ben in the room as a buffer.

"I have been enjoying the peace and quiet," I reply, pointedly.

"Do you have plans for the afternoon?"

"Other than enjoying my book in peace and quiet, no." I sound sour.

"Would you like to go to the cinema? I saw an advert that a cinema is doing a re-run of *The Blair Witch Project*."

It is so out of the blue that I'm taken aback by his suggestion. It takes me a moment to answer him. "Seriously?"

"Yeah, it starts at three."

"Are you asking me on a date, Matt?" I tease, and he looks flustered.

"No, I just thought…" he starts, and I feel bad for teasing him, especially when he appears to be making an effort to be friendly to me.

"Relax, I'm joking. Yeah, sure, the cinema sounds fun."

"Okay, be ready for half one. It's a bit of a drive," he tells me. He gets up. "I'm going to unpack. I'll see you later. Enjoy the poetry," he says, and with that, he's gone. I look back at my book, open on my lap, and wonder how he knows I'm reading poetry.

"Ben told me your car was stolen, that must have been a pain," I comment on the drive to the cinema. He's been trying to make conversation, but it's felt a little awkward between us, so I'm trying to put in the effort and help clear the air between us. Apparently, talk of his stolen car is not a good topic, as I am sure I see a flash of pain across his expression like there is more to the story. Before I can comment, he recovers.

"The insurance company were pretty good. They sent me a settlement fee really quickly, and I got this at a good price."

"It's nice. Roomy," I say, and then I sigh. "Sorry, I have no idea why I've just described your car as roomy, what bloody adjective pick is that? How about…powerful? Sleek and sporty?" I offer.

He laughs. "I'd settle for reliable and secure."

"I had a sporty little convertible. Or rather, Ryan did. I love driving. I wonder why I haven't got myself a car. I guess I thought it would be a wasted expense if I was looking for my own place, eventually."

"Not much point in having a car when Ben and I would drive you everywhere."

"Really?" I laugh. "You're telling me I had you both at my beck and call?"

"Yes, Beatrice, I was at your beck and call." He sounds deadpan again like he did when he joked about wrestling bears.

"Alright, I was only joking."

"I would drive us to and from work," he says, and it sounds so logical given we had worked together.

I twist around in my seat to get a better look at him. "You know, this is technically my first car journey with you driving. Maybe we should play twenty questions? I can use the twenty questions to get to know you better," I suggest. He looks hesitant for a moment, and then he shrugs.

"Go on then."

"Okay, let's pretend that you've turned into a woman for a day. What would you do?"

"I would take a long hot bubble bath and leave all my underwear drying on the radiator." He fires back.

"I feel like you're trying to offend me." I laugh. "What's your family like?"

"There's Mum, me, and my two older brothers. Close-knit family. One sister-in-law, one future brother-in-law, and one niece or nephew on the way. I also have a few great aunts and uncles who are fun and good people," he replies, smoothly.

"What about your dad?" I ask.

"What a waste of a question when you only get twenty." He gives a small smile, but he keeps his eyes on the road ahead.

"Who are you closest to in your family?"

"Aside from Mum, I'd say the middle brother. Sam's very chill and less serious than the rest of us."

"What language do you wish you had learned?"

"French."

"Oh, I can speak French! Do you want me to teach you?"

"Wasted another question there, Beatrice." He laughs. "That's six down already."

"What was the last film that made you cry?"

"*Marley & Me*."

"How do you treat somebody who is annoying you?"

"I tell them with a big smile to have a lovely evening."

"No way, I do that too!" I exclaim. He glances at me, a small grin on his face.

"Who do you think taught me?"

"I taught you?" I ask, then I curse when I realise I've wasted another question.

"That's nine, by the way."

"Fine. What's the strangest way you have become friends with somebody?"

"I played twenty questions with somebody with amnesia," he quips.

I swat him on his knee. "Fine, you be like that. What's your biggest regret?"

"Gambling," he says quickly. I want to ask more questions, I remember Ben told me in passing that Matt had previously had an issue with gambling, but it feels like it would be more than twenty questions, and he might not want to talk about it.

"Okay, what one thing can't you live without?"

"Air, obviously."

"You do know that wasn't what I was aiming for, right?"

"You do know that was another question, right? You're at thirteen."

"Do you believe in true love?" I fire another question.

He is quiet for a moment. "Yes, true love exists," he replies.

"Who gave you your bracelet?" I ask. He is quiet, and I look at him. I can tell I have hit a nerve. For a second, I think he isn't going to answer me. He flexes his grip on the steering wheel and looks at the woven bracelet he wears on his right wrist.

"Somebody I care very deeply for." It feels like it takes him forever to reply.

"Are you with them?" I ask, curious. As far as I know, Matt isn't dating anybody.

He slows the car as we come up to some traffic at a set of red traffic lights and glances over at me. "It's complicated."

"You must have feelings if you're still wearing it." This is not a question.

"Yeah." He sighs as we wait. The lights change to green, and the cars in front start to move.

"Is it the head, heart, or somewhere further south?" I tease him. He looks taken aback, and he stalls the car.

"Fuck," he mutters, quickly restarting the car, trying to ignore the angry driver behind us who is blaring their horn. He starts to drive again.

"Well?" I prod.

"She's everything to me," he replies.

"Well, I hope things work out," I tell him honestly. He seems quite upset at whatever it is that is going on and for a moment his guard is down, looking vulnerable.

"Me too." His voice is tight. "I think you have two questions left."

"Maybe I'll save them for the ride home," I say because the game doesn't feel as fun anymore. I have a funny feeling wash through my body, and it unsettles me. I suddenly feel off-kilter. I settle back in my seat, staring out of the window, feeling like I have missed something. Matt doesn't speak for the rest of the drive.

Matt parks the car in the cinema car park, and then we head into the lobby. We're running late as we got caught up in some road works, but fortunately he had pre-booked our tickets, so arriving just before the film is due to start is not an issue. I wonder if he'll want to skip the concession stand and go straight for the film, but he joins the queue. I stand next to him, looking down the aisle for the queue he's stood us in.

"What?" he asks.

"You know this is the queue for only ice cream, right? Popcorn and drinks are in the next queue along."

"I know what queue I am in. What's a horror film without ice cream?" He shrugs.

I stand in the queue with him, and I wonder how many times over the last few months have we done this exact same thing, as I get the feeling that this isn't the first time. When he gets to the front of the queue and orders two sundaes, one for me with my favourite flavours, I'm no longer curious, I'm sure. We have done this before. I just don't know why he seems so reluctant to tell me.

Matt hands me my tub of ice cream. Our fingertips brush, and I feel a jolt.

"The ice cream," I murmur. I think of the night he came to my room after my fight with Ben. It's only now, seeing this ice cream, that my mind clicks. The day I had fought with Ben, I'd checked the freezer before I shopped. We didn't have any ice cream. Where had that come from?

"Yes?" Matt asks. For a moment, I feel like I am going crazy. I tell myself; Ben must have gone out to get me the ice cream. I force a smile.

"Looks yum," I answer him eventually.

"Come on, the film will be starting without us." He takes a step away from me. I follow him, and we find our screening, finding our seats.

I spend the whole film feeling oddly on edge, my skin tingling, my heart racing. Matt never once glances my way.

Beatrice: Then, October

September seems to disappear in an instant and October arrives, the weather changing, my feelings for Matt intensifying. It seems for the first week of October that Ben has been home every single minute of the day that we have been there. Lily was on nights, so even Ben's days off were spent at home rather than driving to sneak some time with her.

Matt and I resort to parking on empty country roads, kissing in his car for as long as we can, and tonight, I climb from my seat to his, sitting on his lap to kiss him, pressing my body against him.

He groans. "We're not having sex in the car," he says between kisses, but one of his hands is already up my top, his fingers under my bra, driving me crazy.

"I think we could…" I rotate my hips, and he groans again.

"You're making this very hard for me," he complains as I kiss behind his ear in the spot I know drives him wild. I kiss there whenever I have the opportunity.

"Oh, I am aware how hard this is for you." I laugh, shifting in his lap again, feeling a surge of desire running through me. But then I behave myself and get back in my seat. "I'm sorry. I just really want to be with you. This is driving me crazy."

"Then we would have to tell Ben, to stop sneaking around."

"No, I'm not ready. You're not ready for that either, are you?" I ask.

"I know I am risking my friendship with Ben to be with you, and your brother means a lot to me, but I'm willing to risk his anger, for you. So, if you want to tell him, we will. It was your term and condition," he reminds me.

"Not yet. I don't like keeping secrets from Ben, but I still want to enjoy this between us, just us. Even if the secrecy means I feel like I'm perpetually horny and at risk of pouncing on you." I reach for his hand. "And I want to fall asleep and wake up with you, I miss that, just so you know I'm not treating you like a piece of meat for sexual gratification, even if you are really good at giving me sexual gratification." I grin.

"That is very reassuring to know." His lips tug into a full smile, the favourite kind he gives. I'd swear he reserves this smile just for me. "Come on, home." He starts the engine, and we drive towards the house.

There is a dim light from under Ben's doorway, so Matt and I give each other a squeeze of the hand rather than risking anything else, and we both head towards our own rooms.

A minute later, my phone buzzes. I pick it up. On the screen is a message from Matt, telling me to turn the volume of my phone down. I turn the volume right down and send a message in confirmation, and then the alert comes up on my phone, telling me Matt wants to video chat. I accept with a smile on my face. I can see from the screen that Matt has propped his phone up against the pillow on the side of the bed I sleep on.

"Hey," he whispers. "I thought this might be the next best thing."

"This isn't your way of introducing phone sex, is it?" I whisper back. The image of him on my screen looks startled, and I snort. "Relax, I was joking. Though I'm not averse to the idea, just so you know. In fact, now I think about it, the more I think it is a fantastic idea, maybe the best idea you've ever had."

"You're terrible," he teases, his voice low.

"Let me get comfortable." I move Trigger the teddy onto the bed, putting my phone between his paws; then I take my clothes off and lie naked on the bed.

"Jesus," he murmurs. "I wasn't expecting this."

"You're naked as well," I point out.

"I've got boxers on," he replies.

"Well, take them off and join me in being naked." I smile.

"You are deplorable." He smirks, but I hear the rustle of bedcovers as he takes the rest of his clothes off.

"You could always just come in here, we could be very quiet," I whisper, my hands wandering across my body. I can see from the video screen that he is doing the same. I watch the change in his facial expression as he grips himself.

"Do you think you could be quiet?" he teases.

"Probably not. I'd have the best of intentions, but the minute you put your hands on my body, I stop thinking."

"Is that a good or bad thing?"

"It's a very good thing. The only thing that exists is you and me, and it is sensational, Matt. I wish you were in here with me right now. I wish you were about to slide into me. I really love it when you stop, halfway in, before going all the way in. You always look like you want to lose control, and it drives me wild." Now I've started, I can't stop talking. Matt, with a slightly ragged breath, joins in, telling me what he likes, and just like that, we find a new way to be together.

In the morning, I make us all breakfast. Matt and I aren't at work late tonight, we're both finishing at eight, but Ben is also off, and I know he is planning on cooking tea. I wish we'd told Ben that we were doing the close, as I'd happily take Matt somewhere for a few hours, just to be able to wrap myself around him, hold him close and feel the heat of his skin against mine.

The postman arrives, a bundle of letters for me that have all been automatically forwarded from Ryan's address, a service from the postal service that stops me getting annoyed messages from Ryan about collecting post. It's worth the fee. I put them all to one side.

"Morning," Ben says as he comes into the kitchen. "Still in for tea tonight?"

"Yeah, what are you cooking?"

"A Mexican feast. All of Matt's favourites, to celebrate another year of him not gambling," Ben explains.

"Another year?" I murmur, wondering why Matt hasn't told me. Another year he has succeeded. I hope he is proud.

"Yeah, I got into the habit of trying to do something nice on this date. Are you okay with Mexican?" he asks.

"Sure. Anything," I reply, stopping myself short of adding that it's anything for Matt.

I don't mention anything about the anniversary to Matt. I can tell a few people at work know as they congratulate Matt by slapping him on the shoulder. Kelly, who is almost one year free of gambling, tells him he is her inspiration. Matt takes it all in his stride. He doesn't bask in the congratulations like some would because that isn't who he is.

We go home and eat the dinner that Ben has made, and I let them take the lead in the conversation, watching their banter and joking, seeing once again just what good friends they are for one another. Matt seems to bring Ben out of his usual serious shell, and Ben cheers Matt on in things when he seems down. I hate the idea that I could be a catalyst for altering that friendship, and I know I'll do whatever I can to keep Ben in the dark, until Matt and I are sure of us. Then, I can only hope that Ben forgives me for being deceptive, and accepts Matt and me as a couple, regardless of the way he wants to protect me from everything.

Matt calls an early night after tea, Ben tells me he's going to bed early too as he has an early start in the morning. I tell them both to go to bed, and I do all the cleaning in the kitchen, staying up late so that the pots are all washed and put away, killing time until I am sure Ben is asleep. When I finally go upstairs, the light is off in Ben's room. Matt's light is still on. I don't knock.

I just let myself into his room. He's sat on his bed, wearing just his boxer shorts, reading through a book of poetry, one of mine that he'd asked to borrow. He looks at me, surprise on his face. I put my finger to my lips. I step lightly to the edge of his bed, pulling him to stand. Once he is stood, I kiss him.

"Can I give you a treat?" I kiss against his neck.

"You can give me anything," he whispers back. With that, I pull his shorts down, and he catches onto my plans. I push him lightly on the shoulders to sit him back down on the bed, and then I kneel in front of him, taking him in my mouth. He curses softly at the first feel of my mouth, arching his back slightly as he leans back on the bed.

I suck and play with him until he loses control and comes in my mouth, and as he does, he grips my hair in one hand. I swallow and enjoy the feel of his grip on my hair, love feeling how he loses control with me. I'm desperate to be able to climb on him and reach that pleasure together. Instead, I pull back, giving him a little smile.

"Congratulations on your anniversary," I whisper to him. He sits up, reaches down and slides a hand under my skirt, his fingers slipping under the side of my underwear, finding me slick with desire. He rubs his thumb on me, then his mouth is on my neck, kissing me, and I lose myself in the sensation, the whole of the week feeling like it was a long, drawn-out game of foreplay, and it isn't long until I lose myself completely, my body shuddering with the strength of my orgasm, and I have to bite down on Matt's shoulder to stop myself from crying out.

"God, how can I miss you so much when you're so close to me?" he asks, stroking my cheek.

"I'd give anything to stay here right now," I admit, moving up to kiss him. I really wish I could stay. Instead, after a moment in his arms, I stand. "I'll call you in a minute," I add, quietly. I leave him on the bed, go to the bathroom to get ready, and as soon as I am back in my room, I grab my phone to video call him.

Each call registers on my phone as the only call, as I've got into the habit of deleting my call and message history with him as I'd almost had a panic attack when Ben had picked up my phone in the week. I've even created a folder to store photographs of the two of us, privately, password-protected.

Matt answers the call, and tonight, we whisper to each other for hours; I fall asleep still on the call, telling him this is the next best thing.

The following day, Ben's out early like he had told us. I've plans to go to Matt's room as soon as I wake up, but he makes it to my room first. He places some origami figures he's made me on the chest of drawers, a small smile on his face. He moves Trigger from the bed, placing him on the bedside table, facing the wall.

"Poor Trigger." I giggle.

"There are things he doesn't need to see." Matt grins and then he gets into bed with me, making up for lost time.

Later, we eventually make it downstairs to eat before work. Ben has separated out the post that I had ignored from yesterday. Most of my post that have been forwarded is junk mail, and circulars from companies I haven't updated my address with. Usually, it is stuff that is pointless, but today, there is a letter that makes me stop, and I feel my hand shaking as I hold it in my hand.

"Are you okay?" Matt asks.

"This is from Cole and Taylor's company." I show him the envelope, the telltale logo at the top. Matt drops down the post he was opening. I open the envelope, pull out the printed letter and skim the text.

"What is it?" Matt sounds exactly like he had when I first met him, pissed off and grumpy like he can't believe the company has had the audacity to send me a letter.

"They want me to go in and meet with them on Friday," I murmur. "Actually, they want us to go in and meet them."

"What the fuck?"

"The letter is addressed to me, it's from Taylor, but he's added he would like to speak to 'the gentleman who visited their premises' as well. Oh, Jesus, you don't think they want to press charges against you, do they? That we'll get there and the police will be waiting to arrest you? You can't go. I won't tell them who you are. You're not getting into trouble because of me," I rant.

"Bea, you're not going by yourself. I will be there. If I get into trouble, it isn't your fault, it was my actions. As for calling me the gentleman, I already told them my name. It's written in their visitor book. M. Haliwell." He shrugs.

"You signed in with your real name?" I scold.

"I wasn't exactly thinking clearly. Besides, I wasn't intending to punch anything. I just…he's a smarmy mother fucker," Matt says, darkly. I snort.

"I'll go on Friday if it's okay to cover my shift."

"I'll ask Kelly. She's saving, so she can move out of her dad's. She'll probably appreciate the extra money. I'll ask Liam to cover my shift. I'll be there with you," Matt says, and I breathe a sigh of relief.

Friday afternoon, we find ourselves in the waiting room. The PA let us in, asked us to take a seat, and then they left. We've been sat waiting alone since. I don't recognise a single member of staff. It's like everybody I knew and was friends with, they've all been sent away, to stop me talking to them.

"I can't believe they're making us wait this long," I stutter to Matt. My palms feel sweaty. He takes my hand and gives it a squeeze.

"You don't have to stay. We can get up right now and leave or at any point during this meeting. The second you want to go, we'll go," he reassures me.

The door to one of the conference rooms opens, and Taylor steps out.

"Beatrice," he says. He doesn't look particularly welcoming, but Taylor's the more stoic of the two of them. "Please, both of you, come through."

Matt and I stand, and I feel like I can't take a single step forward. Matt puts his arm around me, steadying me. We walk together into the office. Taylor takes a seat at the top of the conference table, and I take a seat near to him, Matt at my side. I'm relieved that it is just the three of us in the room.

"How are you, Taylor?" I ask.

"I'm well, thank you, how are you?" Taylor asks.

It's a loaded question. I don't know how to respond. I want to tell him how he had made me feel. How I'd thought he would help me, but I'd been left devastated that he had ignored the issues I'd raised, automatically taking Cole's side. I want to tell him how I couldn't get out of bed for a week after it all happened.

I want to shout at him, telling him that his cousin had left me questioning every single interaction we'd had, looking for the fault in my actions. I want to tell him of the first few weeks when I couldn't sleep properly because when I felt like I was drifting into a deep sleep, I was jolted awake because I was scared of my guard being down, and I'd ended up sleeping with fairy lights on, like a child who is afraid of the dark and the monster under the bed. But…that's not how I feel now. I'm a little removed from it, and I know I wasn't at fault for what happened, so all I have now is the anger for the way I was treated, anger at him and at Cole, at Anna and at Ryan, simmering away in me.

"I am good, thank you for asking," I say politely.

"Spare her the false pleasantries. Why are we here?" Matt asks, his voice flat, getting us straight to the point.

"I asked you here so we could come to a settlement regarding the incident that took place between Beatrice and Cole," Taylor replies.

"You mean where your cousin forced himself upon Beatrice, and you didn't do anything to support her?"

"It wasn't handled in a way that aligns with this company ethos, we fell short," Taylor says, and I spot that Matt's words are hitting a nerve. I put my hand under the table and onto Matt's knee. He moves his hand onto the top of mine. Our fingers interlace.

"You called me in for an apology?" I ask.

"Yes, and we would like to avoid any reputational damage, so as a show of goodwill, we are looking to make a settlement with you. Our condition is that the two of you sign a non-disclosure agreement. We'd also like to check who else is involved in this narrative."

"Just Matt," I reply. "My ex-boyfriend had already had his ear bent by Cole, and believed Cole though it was surprisingly a different story to what Cole had told you, and different to what he told Anna." I shrug.

Taylor gives a slight wince but nods, and he slides a piece of paper across the desk to me. I skim through the wording and see that they are offering to pay twice what was my annual salary as a settlement fee. It's labelled as a redundancy payment. Attached to the back of the offer letter is an official-looking document, the non-disclosure agreement that he had mentioned.

"It's a very fair offer, Beatrice," Taylor adds.

"When do you need to know?"

"Ideally, by the end of next week." Taylor clears his throat, and he gets another piece of paper, passing it over to Matt. "This is your non-disclosure agreement. We won't pursue any further action against you if you'll sign that paperwork."

"You won't pursue any further action against me because you don't want any 'reputational damage' if it became public, as I'd be very clear about what type of person Cole is if this went further, so don't use that excuse to try to influence her decision," Matt replies, and he hands the paperwork to me without even looking at it. To Taylor, Matt probably comes across as being an arrogant asshole, but I know his gesture is a sign that he'll do what I want, that it is my decision what I do next, that I am the one in control.

I know this man of mine.

"We'll be in touch," I reply, standing, gathering the paperwork with me. I put it into the envelope and then into my bag. Matt and I walk towards the door to the conference room.

"Just so you know, I will be keeping a closer eye on Cole. Whatever happened, or didn't happen…" Taylor calls after me.

I stop and turn. "It did happen! Don't try to brush this away again. Cole attacked me. I asked him to stop. I told him no. I begged him to stop. I begged him to let me go. I think you know I am telling the truth so stop deluding yourself. He did it to me, exactly as I told you. I might not be able to prove this to the police, so I am begging you, don't ever let him do this to somebody else."

"I will keep an eye on his actions," Taylor promises. I don't say anything else. Matt follows me out of the conference room, and we leave the building in silence.

We don't talk as we make our way to his car. He starts to drive us away, and he lets me sit quietly for a while. I stare out the window, not concentrating on where we are going, my mind running in overdrive, reliving that night.

"Are you okay?" He brings me back to the present. I have no idea where we are, or how long I've zoned out for.

"It feels like silence money. There will be literal tape over my mouth if I sign that paperwork. I wouldn't ever be able to tell Ben what happened, or Jas."

"It's your decision, Bea. You have to do what you think is right for you."

"You don't think I'd be selling my soul?"

"No. I think whatever they're offering you, you view it as money out of their back pocket, a financial hit to them. It won't be what you deserve, but unless you want to file a complaint with the police, it'll be all you get. You're the one who needs to decide that you'd be okay not telling other people, that you'd be okay not seeing Cole properly punished. I'll be by your side if you decide you're going to report Cole, or I will sign whatever you want me to sign, but it's all your decision," Matt says.

I think about what it would be like to report Cole to the police. Would they be like Ryan, automatically believing fabricated evidence? When they ask questions about the events of that night, would they look at me kindly, or would there be scorn in their eyes about the choices I had made? Would they tell me they believed me?

How devastated would my family be if I told them?

Matt turns the car off the main road.

"Where are we going?" I ask, looking around.

"I thought after a shitty meeting, you might like something fun."

"Finally going to give in to having sex in the car?" I tease.

He laughs. "You'll kill me one day."

"Tell me you don't think about it," I challenge.

"I think about you every second of every day, and yes, I think about it," he replies. "I think about it way more than I should do, and in very graphic detail."

"That'll have to do," I reply. He turns the car off onto a side street, and then I see where he is driving us. "Man, you're the one killing me!" I exclaim as he parks in the car park of the animal shelter.

"You have to promise not to fall in love with any of them. We can't take any home, so don't get attached," he warns.

"I will make no such promise." I laugh, getting out of the car.

We head towards the shelter, and he pulls us in the direction of the dog section. We hold hands as we walk around, and I fall in love with every single dog we see, fussing over the ones that are allowed out on a walk and the paperwork in my bag is a distant memory.

Matt: Then, October

Beatrice signs the paperwork the following week. She'd taken her time to make her decision, going back and forth between feeling like the payment would be vindication, acknowledgement of what had happened to her, and fear that she was making a mistake. She asked me, before she signed, if I was okay to sign my paperwork too, and I had kissed her, telling her I would do whatever she wanted.

The cheque came through a week later, and we go to the bank together, so she can set up a new bank account to put the money into, saying she doesn't want to see it in her account and doesn't want to think about it until she's decided what she wants to do with the money. I offered to go with her because it seems that when it comes to anything to do with Cole and what happened to her, she wants somebody with her, even though I know it pains her to show any kind of weakness.

She hides her copy of her NDA and her new bank account set up in her room, taking the bottom drawer of her chest of drawers out, taping the paperwork to the bottom, telling me that she doesn't want to see it, that for now, she's drawing a line in the sand.

True to her word, Beatrice hasn't mentioned Cole, Taylor, Anna or Ryan again. I don't raise the topic, either. Instead, we spend as much time as we can with each other, enjoying it just being the two of us. We go for dates when we can get away without anybody noticing. I take her to the cinema, and we watch all the films we can, even the romantic comedies, and I laugh when she claims each one 'gave her the ick'.

I never remember the plots because I'm usually zoned out, lost in the sensation as she strokes my arm throughout the film. She always buys the same flavour of ice cream as a treat and tells me that popcorn is the worst cinema treat and should be outlawed. I know she pins her ticket stubs onto a noticeboard in her bedroom.

Through an offer at work, I get tickets to a festival, and we go together, dancing together, drinking lager, hands in each other's back pockets, free to enjoy our time together, knowing nobody knew who we were, no need to hide.

Every time we are alone in the house, we meet in my room, or hers, and we lose ourselves in each other, time and time again. I know I'm never going to get enough of her. I spend all my time thinking about the future I want to give her. I worry that I'm not good enough for her, that one day she'll see me the way I see myself, but any time I start to voice my fears, she seems to know what is on my mind, telling me she thinks I'm wonderful, telling me she couldn't imagine her life without me.

Every few days, I give her a new origami I've made. I started learning how to make them after I first stopped gambling when I needed something to do to keep my hands busy, a distraction from picking up a pack of cards or feeling the weight of poker chips in them. Over the years, I've become quite good, and when I make them for Beatrice, I write little messages in sections that are hidden away by the last folds. I don't think she knows the messages are there, each one contains a message about how I feel for her, how I think of her all the time, how she is everything and how much I fall for her, every single day. We haven't said 'I love you' yet, but I am sure she knows how I feel.

As time passes, it gets harder to hide our relationship at work. I'm terrible for looking at her a moment too long. Isaac notices one night, asking me again if I am sure she's just a friend. I tell him to get back to work, but I find it difficult to keep the smile from forming on my face.

At home, I'm terrified that Ben is going to discover what we are up to. He's my best friend, I know he wants the best for me, and he loves Beatrice to pieces and wants nothing but goodness for her, and I am not sure those two things will reconcile in his head. Beatrice would be the best for me, but I don't think Ben will easily accept the idea that I would be the best for her. Regardless of our friendship, I'm convinced Ben will disapprove. The secret we hold from Ben, it's something Beatrice and I talk about a lot, both trying to work out the best time and the best way to tell him.

It becomes clear that for now, neither of us is willing to make a move, suggest a change, content to carry on with the secrecy, both of us quietly afraid that the truth could mean the end of us.

"I think Isaac knows about us," I tell Beatrice. It's the evening of Halloween, we're not on shift, and Isaac has invited us to a party that he is throwing. We are the only people from work that he has invited, the rest of the guests are his friends. We've known about the invitation for a few weeks, and Beatrice has insisted that she has the costumes for both of us in hand. I still haven't seen what she has ordered for us. When Beatrice wants to keep a secret, she guards it like she's made an unbreakable vow.

"He likes to think everybody is shacking up. He told me that Kelly is seeing Nicole."

"They are seeing one another," I point out.

"Are they?" Beatrice sounds surprised.

"Yes, they have been seeing each other for a while, since before you and I started up. They're not particularly discrete about it. I found them kissing in the office a few weeks ago."

"Really, what did you say?" She laughs.

"Nothing. It was before their shift, and it isn't any of my business. Besides, it's not my place to keep track as to who is shacking up with who." I shrug. It isn't uncommon for the people at my workplace to be dating each other. There's always been a core set of staff and then a set of people where we have a higher turnover, always somebody new catching the eye.

"Have you ever shacked up with somebody from work?" She seems suddenly unsure of herself.

"Just you, Beatrice." I've never dated anybody who has worked for me before, Beatrice is my exception. She is my exception for everything.

"Okay."

"When I said that first night that I hadn't had sex in a long while, I meant it. I hadn't been with anybody since I broke up with Jemima, which was right before your parents' party."

"Was that why you were so grumpy that night because you had just broken up?"

"No, I knew it was the right decision. I was grumpy because Ben had insisted on dragging me to a party that I'd told him I didn't want to go to because he didn't think I could be trusted not to go do something stupid like head to a casino. He said, 'I don't want to leave you alone; come with me. You can finally meet my sister. You'll like her, she's awesome'. Then he spent the whole car journey telling me everything about you. Do you know the last thing he told me about you?"

"I'm going to guess it was something about how he always has to look after me?"

"No…the last thing he told me was your boyfriend's name." I laugh. She reaches for my hand, a smile on her face.

"Poor baby," she murmurs, and she kisses my hand like she had that first night. Then she spots the time on my watch. "Oh, time to get ready for the party!" With that, in excitement, she pulls me out of the kitchen. We head upstairs, to her bedroom, where reaches in and grabs a bag for me, shooing me to my own room.

I open the bag that Beatrice has put my costume in. I take out each item. There is a dress shirt. A charcoal and grey pinstriped suit. A fedora. Striped braces. A distinctive, art-deco silk tie.

As soon as I see the design of the tie, I start to smile. The costume she has for me is for Eddie Valiant, the detective in *Who Framed Roger Rabbit*. I can't believe she remembered a flippant comment I'd made about how, as a teen, I'd wanted to be a private detective, joking that I'd have happily investigated Jessica Rabbit. At that thought, I take an intake of breath, wondering if she's really going to dress as I think she might be.

I strip my clothes off and dress in the costume, and I go downstairs to wait for her. It takes a few minutes until I hear her door opening. I wait at the bottom of the stairs as she comes into view.

"Jesus Christ," I stutter.

She's wearing a long, red, glittery dress, on one side there is a slit that goes right up to her hip, and I can see she has added stockings under her dress. She's wearing a push-up bra that pushes her breasts high and tightly together. On each arm, she wears long, purple, silk gloves. Bright red lipstick is on her mouth, and she wears a long red wig which is styled to cover one of her eyes. She walks down the stairs, carrying a pair of glittery red shoes. She gets to the bottom of the stairs, drops her shoes on the floor, stands in front of me and pulls my tie.

"I'm not bad. I'm just drawn that way," she whispers in my ear, her voice deliberately breathy.

I pull her close to me. "You look sensational."

"Well, there is a lot of scaffolding and tape holding things up and in place and keeping some of my modesty. I've had to tape the dress to my thigh, just in case." She grins. She gives me a kiss on the cheek, pouting, and I can feel the lipstick she has left behind on my skin. "There, your costume is complete."

"We don't have to go to the party if you don't want to." I run my hand up the leg where her dress has the split. I feel the pattern at the band of the stockings she is wearing, and then further up, to the bare skin above. I can hear her breath as it hitches. I want her, desperately. She gives me that little moan she does.

"People are expecting us," she reminds me, but she sounds like she doesn't really care.

"Isaac won't mind. He's probably invited so many friends that he wouldn't notice we weren't there."

"Maybe we need a code sentence, just in case I am overcome with a desire to come home and have my wicked way with you."

"What were you thinking?" I ask, still feeling the bare skin at the very top of her thigh.

"Roger Rabbit," she says with a gasp.

"Okay, Roger Rabbit it is. Just so long as you know, I'm going to be counting down the time, all night, until we can return to this moment. I hope you are too."

She slips a hand down the waistband of my trousers, into my boxers. A small smile forms on her face when she finds just how ready I am for her.

"You'd better believe it, buster."

"Am I right in assuming that you're planning for me to peel those stockings off you later?" I ask. I feel thick-headed as she continues to stroke me. She smiles, like she's delighted that I have remembered something she said to me, ages ago, when she thought we didn't mean anything to one another. She pulls her dress up, the side she hasn't taped down, pulling it above her hip, and she unzips my trousers.

"Do you want me?" she whispers in my ear.

"Always."

"Please," she urges, moving her underwear to one side and pulling me towards her. "I need you."

She tugs at the braces that are stopping my trousers from falling and when she succeeds with her goal she wraps a leg around me, pulling me closer. All at once, we're a tangle of limbs, mouths on mouths, hands exploring, and I'm marvelling how I never imagined it could be this good until she kisses me in the spot that I like, and I lose the ability to think at all, lost in the sensation, lost in her.

We make it to the party, late. Isaac gives me a knowing grin when I make my way towards him to say hello, which is amusing as he's dressed as Sheldon from *Young Sheldon*, complete with a briefcase, checked shirt and bowtie.

"Don't tell me you're just friends because that lipstick on your face is telling a different story."

"Part of the costume! From where Jessica blows a kiss at Eddie…"

"Dude, it's just me. I won't tell anybody. Kiss her all night long. I won't say a word at work."

"We're just friends." I laugh.

"So you won't mind if I go over there and snog her face off all night?" he asks, and he seems to find the expression on my face hilarious. "Man, you have it so fucking bad. I've never seen you looking so whipped. Go get yourself and your lady a drink."

I get the two of us a drink and make my way back to Beatrice through the crowd. I tell her what Isaac has said, leaving the decision for her whether she wants to make our relationship public in front of him, but she gives me a little shake of her head.

"It wouldn't be right to tell somebody before I tell Ben."

"So let me tell him," I suggest.

"I have to be the one to tell Ben. Promise me, Matt, that you'll let me tell him." She sounds urgent.

"I promise," I say, and we finish our drinks, joining in with the rest of the people who are dancing, a jumble of costumes and themes.

"Holy crap, Matt! I didn't know you would be here!" A voice calls out later that evening. Beatrice and I had been dancing, but we pull away from each other.

"Oscar! Hi!" I reach to shake his hand, and he pulls me towards him and bumps my chest, the way he greets everybody.

"Roberta dragged me here. She knows the host. How do you know them?"

"I work with Isaac."

"Small world, right? Roberta knows him through the evening class she goes to." Oscar gives me a grin. "It's so good to see you. How's Ben? Is his sister still living with you?"

"He's good," I reply. I don't know how much Oscar and Ben stay in touch.

Oscar had only lived with us for a couple of months, and our shifts meant we were barely in the house at the same time, with Oscar working shifts as a paramedic. I know Ben and Oscar occasionally cross paths at work, but I think their conversations are usually work-related, handover of patients rather than catch-ups, but the last thing I need is for Oscar to say something to Ben about me being at a party with Beatrice. We're discrete at spending time with one another.

When Ben is off work, I only spend time with Beatrice when we are at work. We only go out together when Ben is at work or at Lily's. I turn and look at where Beatrice had stood, but she is no longer there. My phone buzzes. I look at it and see a message from Beatrice. It reads, 'Roger Rabbit. Tell him you have an emergency'. I fight the smile that is forming on my face.

"Everything okay?" Oscar asks.

"I'm so sorry, mate; I have an emergency to get to. You and Roberta, come by the bar this week. We'll catch up!"

"Will do. Say hi to Ben for me!" Oscar spots his girlfriend and gives me a nod before heading in her direction. I say goodbye to Isaac and then search for Beatrice, finding her in the front garden.

"You kinda looked like you wanted out of that conversation, but I thought my usual tactic wouldn't work." She smiles.

"You are very skilled in this area." I laugh.

"Oh, I'm skilled in lots of areas. We should go home, so I can show you," she teases, but I'm already pulling out my phone to call us a taxi to go home.

The house is dark when we arrive. We go upstairs, and she pulls me towards her bedroom. I prefer her bedroom.

"How do you feel about me, Matt?" she asks as we fall to the bed together.

I hold her close and stroke her face. I kiss her. "Don't you know?" I ask between kisses.

"I think so…but tell me, just in case I'm wrong," she whispers.

"Bea, I love you," I say, surprised that she doesn't know. She gives a little smile.

"You do?"

"I thought it was obvious. I am deeply in love with you. You're everything to me. I might not be the type of guy who says it all the time, but, yes, I love you."

"I love you too," she whispers back. "So much. I've never felt like this before."

"I don't want to lose you. It would be like losing part of me." I hold her closer.

"One is not half of two…" she starts.

"Two are halves of one," I finish. She smiles at me, that beautiful smile of hers, and then she kisses me, long and deeply.

"You'd never lose me," she promises. She rolls over on the bed and grabs the pen that she's kept on the windowsill. She pulls my shirt from my waistband, and she writes 'I'm yours, always' on my stomach. She hands me the pen.

"Bea, I've been writing you notes for ages. You just haven't found them yet," I tease. She takes a moment to think, and then she gasps.

"The origami!" She scrambles off the bed, to the drawer where she keeps them. She pulls out the first one that I had given her in her room, the swan. She gives it a glance over, spotting the section to lift to see what I have written. She reads it aloud. "I fear no fate, for you are my fate, my sweet."

"I read it in your poetry book. It is exactly how I feel about you," I say.

"For somebody who says they don't say 'I love you' very often, you sure know how to say it well."

"Just because I don't say it often, it doesn't mean I don't feel it, always. Those drawings and lines you write on my body might fade, but the way you make me feel, that's permanent. I'll feel this way for you, forever," I vow.

She throws herself into my arms. "And I love you, I love you," she says between kisses. It sounds like a song, like a promise.

"We are running the risk of getting really, really, cheesy right now, so, are you still up for me taking off those stockings?" I tease her.

"Surprised I'm still waiting, to be honest." She giggles. "Just, don't be disappointed when you get to my bra and remember that my boobs are, like, six sizes smaller than what they are in this outfit."

"Bea…" I start, kissing her neck. "Nothing about you could ever be a disappointment."

Beatrice: Now

April seems to arrive out of nowhere. People around me seem to love April. The clocks have changed, the nights are brighter, and everybody seems to have a spring in their step. Everybody but me, as I feel like I am under the darkest cloud and can't summon any of the hope that people usually get when spring is arriving. People spent the morning of the first making jokes, but I can't join in, or find anything amusing. My whole life seems to have descended into one long April Fool's Day joke, and I'm still hanging around, waiting for the punch line.

"Are you going to tell us what has been bugging you all day?" Ben asks as I make myself a cup of tea. He and Lily are dressed up, as they're staying at a fancy hotel with an exclusive restaurant tonight, a Christmas voucher from her parents that they've only just managed to find time together to enjoy.

I thought I'd done a decent job today with them hiding how frustrated I am, but obviously not well enough, as they have concerned looks on their faces.

"I'm fine." I force a smile.

"You've spent all day looking really weird." Ben pulls a face. I'm not sure if he's trying to mimic the facial expression I've apparently been wearing. "You kind of looked like we were torturing you on that walk."

"It might not make much sense," I sigh.

"Tell us. See if we can help." Lily offers.

"I just feel like I am supposed to be doing something important today. I don't know how to describe it. I just feel, in my bones, that today is important for some reason, I just don't know what it is," I explain. They give each other a concerned look. "I know it sounds crazy," I add.

"Surely somebody would have told you if you were supposed to be doing something?" Lily soothes.

"I know it's bonkers, I just know it's the truth. I am sure I am supposed to be somewhere. I'm so frustrated! How can I know that today is important, but not know why? I've felt it all day long, jittery, nervous," I try to explain how I've felt since I woke this morning. The feeling that I know I have missed something important, that there is something that requires my attention. I groan and put my cup of tea down on the side, more forcefully than I intended, swearing as the tea spills onto the side. I leave it and start to pace the room.

"Beatrice, I think you're just overwhelmed with everything that has been happening." Ben reaches out for my arm, but I pull away from him.

"What is happening, Ben? I don't know what is happening! I just know that something is, but my stupid brain won't tell me. I'm so done with this! I'm sick of feeling but not knowing!" I carry on pacing the room. "I lost eight months of my life! Do you know what that feels like? Eight months is a fucking long time to have forgotten. It's nearly enough time to grow a human. It's just gone from my head, but I want it all back, so badly!"

"Maybe you should have an early night?" Ben sounds alarmed at my distress. I don't hold it against him. We have never been very good at seeing each other in pain. The only time I saw Ben cry was after my operation, and I had thought at the time that hearing him cry hurt me more than anything I'd been through. Hearing him sound distressed isn't enough to stop me from feeling frustrated at everything.

"I don't want to have an early night. I am sick of not remembering, sick of my stupid brain being so stubborn," I rant. Ben looks like he is going to speak, so I hold my hand up. "The two of you can spare me the doctor talk about how I am lucky it is only eight months, that people have lost decades of their memories, or lost their ability to form new memories. I know it could all be so much worse, but I just want to wallow for a minute."

"Okay. You're not much of a wallower but okay…" Ben glances over to Lily.

"How do I know that I didn't become a person who enjoys a pity party?" I challenge him with a scowl. "Everything in my life appears to have gone up in flames, so why wouldn't I be throwing a pity party?"

"We know you, Beatrice. You were still you," Lily says, gently, and she steps closer towards me and takes my hand. "But if you want a pity party, okay. Tell us what is going on in that mind of yours."

"I just feel like I am missing something important. Someone." I bite my lip.

"Maybe it's Ryan?" Ben offers.

"No. I have hardly thought about him, which is weird considering that when I woke up in the hospital, in my head, the day before we had been together, normal, happy."

"Well, how do you feel about him when you think of him?" Lily asks.

"Honestly? A little disappointed. Apprehensive. I'm glad I don't have to be around him. The idea of being around him makes my skin crawl." I let the emotions pour out.

It feels so weird, as I had loved Ryan. I don't know what happened to change those feelings, but I feel no affection for him. I can't seem to summon enough bravery to contact him and ask him what happened between us. Something holds me back, every time I scroll to his number in my phone. I get the same feeling when I think of people from work.

"Maybe you just miss feeling like yourself." Lily tries again, bless her.

"Which me? I feel like I might have been a whole different person when I was living here."

"What makes you think that?"

"I'm so different to what I remember. I don't know what happened between me and Ryan. I don't know why I quit my job, why I closed my primary social media account or why I have no photographs on my phone when I usually have loads from places I have been, pictures of things that have made me smile. My clothes are different. I know I was doing things, I went out, but I have no idea if I was lonely and sad, or was I happy? Who was I?"

"You should ask Matt," Ben suggests. For a moment, I find myself faltering at the sound of his name. My heart picks up in tempo like I am excited by the idea he could give me a glimpse of who I had been.

"I don't think he likes me very much," I say, and I put my hand to my chest as if to calm the beat of my heart. Despite us spending more time together, there's still something weird when we're together. The atmosphere always feels thick when we are together.

"From what I saw, you have a friendly, teasing banter between you. Maybe you have just mistaken that banter for hostility," Lily suggests.

"He might be able to tell you things. You spent a lot of time together. You probably saw more of him than I did over the last few months. At one point, I even thought…"

"Thought what?"

"Just that he and I hadn't spent a lot of time together. But I have been busy with Lily and work. I was kind of grateful that you were going to and from work with him, keeping him company." Ben shrugs.

"I just wish this hadn't happened. I feel sad right now because something in my body keeps telling me that there is something important that I am missing out on, and I feel…" I start, but then stop because I'm sure they'll think I'm going insane.

"You feel what?" Lily asks, staring at me with an encouraging smile on her kind face.

"I feel a longing for somebody," I admit. Every morning recently, I have woken up feeling like I am missing somebody. It's confusing, to be longing for something but not knowing what, or who. Every morning I feel an ache that I can't explain, other than feeling like I have lost something more than my memory.

"A longing for who?" Ben wonders.

"I don't know!" I exclaim, and the emotions I've been feeling for the last few weeks overwhelm me. My eyes suddenly well up with tears.

"Beatrice…"

"How can I miss something that I don't even remember having, something I don't even know if I really had it anyway?" I choke out, and the tears are flowing fast now. "It's a phantom pain. I feel it in my heart, in my bones."

Ben looks tormented. "Beatrice…" he says again but his voice cracks, seeing me so upset.

"I'm sorry for being such a baby," I cry. I wipe my eyes, but my tears are quicker than I am, and it seems to make no difference.

"You're not being a baby. You're a fully grown adult, as you keep reminding me, you're just going through something, and that's okay." Ben pulls me in for a hug. "We love you. We are here for you."

For a minute, I cry against him, feeling him tense up at every shake my body gives as I cry. Then I remember their fancy night, how dressed up Lily looks, how eagerly they've been talking about this hotel, and I pull away.

"You two get going. Don't make me feel like a sad loser who makes you late. Off you go," I urge. Ben looks conflicted. "Lily, remove him from this house before I sue him for being overbearing." I adopt a teasing stance. Lily, despite knowing me less time than Ben, knows I am serious, and that now I want nothing more than to be alone. She tugs Ben by his shirt sleeve.

"Come on, Benjamin. She's fine."

"If you need us…"

"I am a fully grown adult." I smile, throwing back his words from earlier, trying to make him feel better.

It takes another five minutes of me reassuring Ben that I will be fine before Lily can help convince him to leave. When he goes to the car, she comes back to the living room and puts her arms around me.

"Seriously, if you need us, even as a fully grown adult, let us know. One day, I hope to marry that brother of yours, and I want to look after you like you're already my sister-in-law," she tells me.

"Thanks, Lily. You're so good for Ben. I hope he knows how lucky he is."

"I am the lucky one. I will see you tomorrow. Oh…and do try speaking to Matt. He might be able to help," she says, and with that, she leaves.

I grab a bottle of whisky from the cupboard and a heavy glass from a set of three. I get a jolt, like a tug of a memory. A broken glass on the floor. I stand still, hoping that the stillness might encourage the memory as if moving might disturb it. It appears even recognising this is enough to disturb it, as I remember nothing else.

Frustrated, I sit on the sofa with the bottle of whisky, pouring myself a large measure. I drink this one and then pour myself another, repeating the process again.

"Beatrice?" A voice calls. I jolt awake on the sofa. The whisky glass that I had fallen asleep with tips over me, splashing my top with the whisky I hadn't drunk.

"Sorry," I mutter. I stand but end up swaying, bumping into Matt.

"How much have you had to drink?" he asks, taking the glass from me. He holds me steady with my elbow, and he reaches down to grab the whisky bottle from the floor, holding it in the same hand as the glass, thumb and forefinger around the glass, his other three fingers around the neck of the bottle. It looks like he's used to doing this. I look at him. He's staring at me, waiting for an answer.

"Only three very generous servings, but I am fine. I just got lightheaded as I stood up."

"Come on, maybe some food will help sober you up." He gives me a tentative smile. He guides me towards the kitchen, still holding me by the elbow. He stops when he gets to the breakfast bar, letting me get up onto one of the chairs. He puts down the whisky bottle and glass.

"Are you just getting in from work? I didn't think you were working today." I look at the clock on the kitchen wall. It's nearly two in the morning.

"No, I was supposed to be meeting somebody tonight, but they didn't show up. I swung by the bar afterwards just to see how everybody was getting on," he explains, and he opens the fridge to have a look at what is in there.

"I think I should come back. Staying at home is driving me crazy, you know."

"I've told you, if you want to waltz in there and pretend nothing has happened, it won't work."

"Fine, tell them. Re-train me. I just can't carry on doing nothing."

"Does that explain the drinks tonight?" he asks. He's pulled out of the fridge some leftover gammon, the butter, the mustard. He gets the loaf of bread from the cupboard.

"I was having a pity party."

"Whisky always gets invited to the pity parties," he says, and he refills my glass with a very generous measure. For a moment, I think he is going to tell me to drown my sorrows, but instead, he drinks it himself. He pours another.

"What's your pity party for?" I lean forward on the breakfast bar, propping my head up.

"I think your pity party started first, so what was your theme?" He drinks his new glass and then pours another. This time, he pushes the glass towards me.

"Frustration." I take a sip. "Disheartenment." I finish the glass. "You?" I push the glass back to him. This time, he fills it to the brim, which finishes the rest of the bottle.

"Disappointment." He takes a sip and slides me the glass. We fall into a pattern of sliding the glass to one another, taking sips of the drink and adding a theme.

"Despondent."

"Crestfallen."

"Grief." I take the last sip of whisky. He looks sad.

"Grief?"

"Hey, I never asked you to explain your themes. I shouldn't need to justify." I laugh. I am aware that the whiskies have gone to my head.

"Well, it is a strong emotion."

"So is crestfallen," I point out, but my tongue feels heavy in my mouth. "Okay, I think I might need some food."

"One sandwich coming up." He starts to make sandwiches for the both of us, and for a moment I am quiet whilst I watch him.

"How are things going with the girl?" I ask him as he cuts the gammon. I must startle him by breaking the silence, as instead of answering me, he's suddenly swearing. "Have you cut yourself?" I ask, surprised. He grabs the kitchen roll from the side, pulling off sheets to wrap his thumb.

"Fucks sake," he mutters.

"Wait there." I get off my seat and stumble upstairs to the bathroom where the medicine cabinet is stored. I grab various bits and then go back to Matt in the kitchen. He's looking at his thumb, which is still bleeding, but it doesn't look like it needs a stitch. I stand in front of him and set to sorting out his thumb, trying to focus. I rub the cut with antiseptic; I put on the largest plaster. I pull his hand towards my mouth, and I kiss the plaster. "Poor baby," I soothe.

I suddenly feel very aware that Matt appears to be holding his breath, and I look up at him. There is a moment of absolute silence between us, just staring at each other, and the air suddenly feels thick around us. Before I can stop myself, I lean up towards him, and at the same time, he leans down.

The moment our lips meet, it feels like something else is in control of my body. There is an automatic reaction that I could not have anticipated. As his lips crush against mine, my arms wrap around him, my hands pulling his shirt from the waistband of his trousers, and then my fingers are on the bare skin of his back, searching up towards his broad shoulders. I pull myself closer to his body, wanting to be as close to him as possible.

He kisses me with a ferocious hunger that I have never experienced before, and it feels like my whole body is on fire. I can hear my blood pounding through my body and feel the racing of my heart. Blood rushes and pools in places making everything feel charged and desperate. My breath hitches and quickens, not that I can catch it anyway between these desperate kisses. This is the quintessence of sinful, lustful desire.

My hands travel around his body, down his chest and stomach, connecting to the waistband of his trousers, and I slip my fingers in slightly to pull him by his trousers as I back up towards the kitchen worktop. The thoughts in my head are explicit and commanding. Demanding I unbuckle his belt, screaming at me to unzip his trousers, urging me to take this as far as I can because I am suddenly desperate for him. There is nothing else in the world I could possibly want.

I slip one leg around him, using that leg to pull him into the gap between my legs, and when his body meets mine, I feel that he feels the same desperation that I feel. I hear his throaty growl, and my whole skin feels electrified. He pulls away slightly, and as he moves his face near mine, the slight stubble he has today rubs against my skin, and I feel like I might lose control of my legs.

"I thought you didn't like me much," I pant.

"Trust me, that is not the case," he murmurs. He kisses me again, slower and more tenderly, his tongue against mine, and I have never wanted anything more in my life than how much I want Matt right now. He caresses my face and then he stops, pulling away from me again. This time, it's like a switch has been flicked on him, and he looks conflicted.

"What's the matter?" I ask.

"I'm sorry. I'm so sorry," he says, and he almost sounds bitter.

"What are you sorry for?" I search his face for an answer.

"I have to go," he replies.

Before I can say another word, he turns and walks out of the kitchen. I stand, bewildered, and then I hear the front door, making it clear that Matt has gone, and I am alone.

Beatrice: Then, December

"Have you finished your Christmas shopping?" Kelly asks me. The bar is quiet, so we are taking advantage of the lull and catching up. I'm grateful that it is quiet because the past few weeks have been crazy. Early December, every night, the bar had been packed with people celebrating Christmas. We'd been overrun by people on their office parties, or family catch-ups, or friends catching up when they're home for the holidays. Now, it's winding down, and fewer people are out partying. There are still a few days to Christmas, but it doesn't feel as manic as it was.

"I am all done." I smile.

"You're lucky. I still need to find something for my dad. He's so hard to buy for. I ask him every year, threaten him with socks and generic alcohol, but he never gives me a hint," she complains.

"I don't have many people to buy for, to be fair. Mum and Dad are in Canada, they're looking forward to having Christmas there, so we're going to just do a massive Christmas next year instead of worrying about sending presents. It's the same with my best friend, Jas. She isn't home until next spring, so we've booked a weekend away at a spa instead. So really, I just had to buy for my brother and his girlfriend, nothing too difficult." I don't add that I knew what I would get them, but that Matt was an entirely different story, weeks of deliberation. What do you buy for the man you're secretly dating, the one you're not sure if you'll even see over Christmas and New Year, the one you haven't been brave enough to ask about their plans?

"Are you putting in for Matt's collection? Everybody usually chips together to buy him a bottle of whisky, as a thank you. He's such a good boss." Kelly glances towards the office, where Matt is hidden away, determined to get ahead of tasks before Christmas. The bar closes the day before Christmas Eve, reopening just before New Year. Matt says people deserve time off to see their families.

"He really is a good boss." I smile. "I put into his collection last week, Isaac gave it to me," I add. Isaac had a teasing look on his face when he thrust Matt's collection towards me, like a challenge to see if I would say something.

"Watch out, another team looking worse for wear at the doorway." Kelly sighs, and we glance towards the bunch of new people coming into the bar, feeling the calmness of the night potentially slipping away from us.

The rest of the night is busy, and I'm tired by the time we finally get finished. Matt drives us home, we have the house to ourselves tonight, and I am looking forward to getting into my bed with him, showing him the new underwear that I have on, something I had been teasing him about throughout the car ride home.

We go into the house together, making our way to my bedroom, already entwined together. We are always like this when Ben's not here like we are drawn together like magnets the moment we shut the front door, and nothing is going to force us apart, not even the idea of navigating stairs together. When we get to the top step, Matt sweeps me off my feet, carrying me the rest of the way. He sets me down on the bed, and I pull him with me. He cups my face, caressing my cheeks.

"You are my world," he tells me, kissing my forehead, and then soft kisses on my eyelids, across my nose, making his way to my mouth.

"I wish we could do this all the time," I sigh against him.

"We have a few days at Christmas."

"I thought you were going home for Christmas?" I ask. He shifts from his position, lying back on the bed, pulling me into an embrace.

"I thought we could have gone to my family, but I know you don't want anybody finding out before we tell Ben…so I'm staying here instead. I know Ben's working Christmas Eve and then planning on going to Lily's, so it can just be us two," he suggests.

"Alice must be so disappointed that you're not going for Christmas. You should go." I bite my lip.

"Mum would take one look at my face and know just how I've fallen for you. She knew something when we went last time. She'd be posting messages on her social media pages about how her wayward son has met the most wonderful woman. She'd tag you in her status update. Not exactly the discrete relationship you want." He laughs.

"First, you are not her wayward son," I chide. "Second, this is getting complicated, isn't it?"

"I think we should tell Ben in the New Year. I feel bad that we are lying to him." Matt frowns.

"Me too. I do hate keeping secrets from him. I will tell him," I promise.

"I will just cross my fingers that he doesn't want to kick my ass." Matt sounds like he's joking, but I can sense the tension in him.

"He won't. He doesn't have a mean bone in his body."

"People can always surprise you." Matt sighs. I snuggle into his embrace and look up at him. He moves his head to kiss me on my forehead. Then he freezes, and I can tell he can hear the same thing I can hear, the unmistakable sound of somebody walking around downstairs.

"Ben's home," I whisper, horrified.

"I thought he was staying with Lily tonight?" Matt hisses.

"So did I. Oh my…" I feel sick. "This is not the way he should find out." I scramble out of the bed.

"I'll go downstairs and head him off." Matt gets up and steps to the door. He opens it, listening to see if Ben has made it up the stairs, breathing a sigh of relief. He steps outside and shuts my bedroom door. I hear him walk downstairs, and after a few minutes, I follow him. As I am halfway down the stairs, I pause.

"I don't know what to do." Ben's talking to Matt in the living room, and his voice sounds off like he is in pain. I rush the rest of the way down the stairs to see what is happening. I step into the living room.

"What's the matter?" I ask. Ben looks at me, then his face crumples, and the next thing I know, my stoic, reliable, big brother is crying. I rush towards him, throwing my arms around him. "Talk to me, please."

"Lily says she thinks they should break up." Matt fills in when it is clear Ben can't speak for himself. I feel a pain in my windpipe as Ben sobs softly against me.

"I love her, so much. I thought we were going to be together forever," he cries. I smooth down his hair and swallow the lump that is in my throat. I hate seeing Ben in pain. I can take anything but this.

"I'm sure she will call you in the morning, telling you that she made a mistake, that she loves you too," I soothe.

"I want a drink," Ben mutters, pulling away from me and wiping his eyes, like he wants to pretend he hasn't been crying.

"I'll get the whisky." Matt heads towards the cabinet.

"Ben…" I start, wanting to comfort him. He puts his hand up to stop me talking.

"Just drink with us, and don't mention her name. Not tonight. Please."

"Okay," I reply, and then Matt is back with the whisky, pouring us each a glass.

An hour later, Matt and I drag Ben up the stairs together. Ben is stumbling on all the steps, and when he steps on my foot and falls forward, I curse.

"Jesus, Ben, I thought you could hold your alcohol. I didn't know you were such a goddamn lightweight," I complain. I feel Matt pull Ben's weight towards him, taking the load from me.

"I've got him," he says. I nod, then rush to open Ben's bedroom door. In the time I have been living here, I've never been into Ben's room. He's been into mine for chats, but I haven't been in his. His room is neat as a pin, everything in its place. Above the dresser, he has a large cork board which is filled with photographs. There are some of me and our parents, a few of me and Ben, and the rest of the pictures of him and Lily. I know he loves Lily to pieces. I know she loves him too.

Matt half-carries and half drags Ben into the bedroom. I rush over to the bed, pulling the quilt back, and we work to get Ben in the bed, in the right position. I take off his shoes. Matt takes Ben's phone from his back pocket and puts it on charge. We cover him, and I lean over to give him a kiss on the forehead.

"It'll be okay," I whisper to him.

"Love really fucks you up," Ben mutters back.

"Benjamin Thomas Schofield, don't make me wash your mouth out with soap and water." I try to scold him, but he's already asleep, snoring softly. Matt reaches for my hand and gives it a squeeze. I follow him back out onto the hallway, shutting Ben's door.

"I'm going to tidy up downstairs. You go to bed," he suggests, but I follow him down to the living room. Ben had dropped his glass before we'd dragged him upstairs. Matt guides me out of the way. He gets the dustpan and starts to clean up the glass.

"Poor Ben," I sigh.

"I hope they'll be okay," Matt murmurs.

"He seems so heartbroken," I say, and my voice catches because I'm overwhelmed from seeing Ben like that. Matt puts down the dustpan and gets up to hold me.

"He will be okay. Major hangover tomorrow, but I'm sure he'll be fine. They'll work it out, I'm sure," he soothes.

"You know, I hated Ben when I was growing up. I know we are close now, but honestly, I'd have given anything to be an only child when I was a kid. He used to tease me, like big brothers do I guess, but I was so sensitive about it, and I hated that I could never provoke a reaction from him. We argued all the time. Then, I got sick.

"First, it was something wrong with my heart, something that needed to be fixed 'at some point', and the doctors said it was routine, and okay to wait. Then, a few months later, I got sicker and ended up in A&E; then all the calmness was gone. I was rushed off for emergency surgery. I almost died on the operating table, and for good measure, I had to be resuscitated in the night.

"When I came to, the first thing I heard was somebody crying next to my bed, and I thought, 'my poor parents, what they have gone through', but then I saw that it wasn't my parents, it was Ben, crying like a baby. Before tonight, it's the only time I've ever seen him cry. I wished then that I could take that pain away, and I wish it now, more than I've wished for anything before," I explain.

Matt sighs and holds me closer. One thing I love about Matt, he'll let me talk until I've finished getting everything off my chest, and he'll hold me close whilst I do, giving me the security that I need.

"It'll all be okay, I promise," he vows.

"We can't tell him about us yet, not when he's going through this."

"I know." He leans down to kiss me, safe in the knowledge that Ben's passed out upstairs and won't know. "I love you," he tells me the words he knows I love to hear.

The next few days drag by. Ben hasn't heard anything from Lily, she won't answer his calls, and he looks miserable. Matt takes him out for drinks one evening, and they arrive home late, with Ben wasted and reeking of alcohol, Matt contrite and apologetic that he's in such a state. Around the house, Ben makes conversation with us, but he doesn't sound enthusiastic about anything. He asks Matt when he will be travelling to see his family for Christmas, but Matt remains uncommitted in his response.

The day before Christmas Eve, Lily eventually calls Ben. He disappears to his bedroom, and I pace downstairs, desperate to know if she's breaking my brother's heart further, or if she is just as broken as he appears to be. Matt puts on some crappy romcom film whilst I pace. Eventually, Ben comes down. His face is blotchy and red, but he has a smile on his face.

"She misses me. She says she made a mistake, and she still loves me. She was just overwhelmed."

"I told you so," I point out.

"She's asked me to go over after my shift on Christmas Eve. I just…"

"If you dare say you are worried about leaving me on Christmas on my own, I will smack you around the head," I warn him. "I got invited by somebody at work to spend Christmas with them, now you are going to Lily's again, I can do that."

"Only if you're sure."

"You spend time with Lily and make sure you have everything worked out," I tell him. I glance over at Matt, and the both of us know, our cosy little Christmas is back on.

"Happy Christmas." Matt smiles at me on Christmas morning. We're downstairs in the living room, the room lit only by the fairy lights on the Christmas tree. We'd spent the night in his bedroom, where I had modelled a set of new underwear, a black lace, low-cut bra, matching knickers and suspenders and a pair of black stockings, and I feel like he spent most of the night showing me what he thought about them.

"Happy Christmas," I reply, pulling his hand up so I can kiss it.

"Are you ready for presents?" He smiles and slides over a wrapped box. I reach over to underneath the tree where I had stashed the main present for Matt after Ben had left.

"You go first," I urge him. He opens the gift and opens the box. Inside is a woven bracelet, made with dark tan leather, with a large silver section for the clasp that I have had engraved on the underside. On one section, I have had it engraved with the words 'My heart is perfect because you are inside' and on the other section of the clasp, still underneath, a little bee.

"Bea, I love it. Thank you."

"You don't have to wear it if you don't like it," I say, suddenly self-conscious, but he has already undone the clip, putting it onto his right wrist.

"It's perfect. Go on, you open yours." He runs his fingers over the bracelet whilst he is talking. He watches as I open the wrapping on the present he has given me. Inside is a velvet box, and when I open it, I find the most beautiful white gold necklace. It's a delicate chain, connecting to a white gold circular band. One side of the band is embedded with little white stones, and when I turn it over in my hand, I see that he has had the band engraved with the words, 'you are my sun, my moon, and all my stars'. I throw myself towards him.

"It's so beautiful. Thank you." I kiss him, and he laughs at my excitement.

"I am glad you like it."

"Like it? I love it, I think it is the best present anybody has ever given me." I smile. I take the necklace out of the gift box, handing it to him, so he can put it on me. I swivel around, so I am sat in front of him, my back to his chest, and he reaches around me to put the necklace on. Once the clasp is closed, he pulls me closer to him and kisses me on my neck. I lean against his chest, and he wraps his arms around me.

"I think this is the best Christmas morning I've ever had. I don't think anything can top this." He nuzzles my neck.

"Oh, and there was me, planning on wearing only another set of new underwear whilst I cook you a fantastic dinner," I tease.

"Seriously?" He laughs. He's never sure how to take my comments like this.

"You'll just have to wait and see." I smile to myself.

"Definitely best Christmas ever."

"What's your second best?" I ask. He's quiet for a moment.

"The year Mum got all three of us a bike. They were all brand new, which was a big deal. The house she lives in now, that's a far cry from what I grew up in. At the time, she was a single parent, on benefits and struggling for money whilst she went back to university to re-train as a therapist. My father was no help, so she did everything by herself, and I know now how much she would have struggled to get those bikes sorted. I was ten, Sam was twelve, and Toby was thirteen, and we rode those bikes everywhere, feeling like we were the kings of the town."

"Sounds like a lovely memory." I sit still in his arms. He doesn't often talk about his father. I know Matt was a baby when his father had left, and that they barely see one another. I don't think they have any contact now.

"What about you, what was your best present when you were growing up?"

"Retro quad roller skates," I tell him immediately, and he laughs.

"Roller skates?"

"Yeah, they were white, with a red rose stitched on the side, and red laces. They were awesome. I was so good on them as well, so fast!"

"How old were you?"

"I was fourteen. It was the Christmas before I got sick, the last present I got from my family that could be considered risky or dangerous," I explain.

"I'll buy you some for your birthday," he vows.

"Only if you buy yourself a pair to skate with me." I laugh.

"Deal," he says, kissing my neck as if he is sealing his promise.

That night, we go to bed in my room. Whilst I don't feel a pressing need for them anymore, I have the fairy lights above my headboard on, the lights twinkling above us and the rest of the lights off.

We'd had a lovely dinner, and Matt had taken care of a dessert by showing me the flavours of ice cream that he had stashed in the freezer for us. We'd shared more presents with each other. I'd given him a mug that proclaimed 'this bartender is a fucking legend', and a box set of classic cheesy romcoms, with a promise I'll watch them with him. He gave me two origami swans that he had made, these two are in 3D and when I place them together their necks form the shape of a heart. He gives me a box set of Nightmare on Elm Street movies, a note attached that he'll keep me safe from Freddy, and a beret which he tells me looks adorable when I put it on.

When we went to bed, Matt had grabbed a bottle of champagne from the fridge that we'd not opened at dinner, and he had popped the cork in the bedroom. I'd propped the cork on my dresser, another memento of our time together, and then we'd split our time between drinking champagne in bed and making love, slowly and tenderly. As I drift to sleep, Matt kisses my neck, whispering that this Christmas is the first of many, whispering sweet nothings in my ear until I fall asleep in his arms, never before feeling as content as this.

Matt: Then, December

There is not a chance in the world that there is anybody who feels as happy as I do at Christmas. Waking up with Beatrice on Boxing Day feels like an extra present. When she rolls over in the bed and looks up at me, running her fingers across my chest, a slow smile on her face, there's a burst of emotion in me.

"Good morning," she greets me.

"The very best," I reply.

"What do you want to do today?" she asks.

"Would you think less of me if I told you I think we should stay in bed all day long?" I ask. She kisses my chest.

"I would not. I never want to get out of a bed that you're in. Judge me all you like, I don't care." She smiles.

"So it's agreed; we'll just camp out here forever now. Live in your bed."

"Deal." She kisses me again. We lie in silence for a moment, with me running my fingers down her spine.

"Maybe some breakfast would be good though," I suggest as her stomach rumbles.

"Good idea, I'm really hungry."

"You always are," I tease.

"I can't help it. I don't know how people go without food. Those people who claim they forgot to eat or when they're feeling sad, and they've lost their appetite. How do they do it? I wouldn't last five minutes," she grumbles. She rolls over in the bed, swinging her legs out so she can stand. I roll onto my side and watch her as she pulls on a pair of shorts and a tee, covering up her curves. She throws my trousers towards me. "Stop slacking, Haliwell." She grins, and then walks out of the bedroom, heading towards the bathroom.

As I finish putting on my trousers, my mobile rings. I pick it up from Beatrice's dressing table, checking the caller display.

"Hey, Toby, happy Christmas," I say as I answer the call of my eldest brother. I sit back on Beatrice's bed, preparing myself for a lecture from him for having skipped the family Christmas. This year, my mother, Sam and Andy went to London to stay with Toby and Polly.

"Happy Christmas, bro, missed you yesterday," he tells me. I'd phoned yesterday but barely had a chance to speak to Toby who had been on cooking duties.

"How was the dinner?" I ask. I'd heard him cursing in the background when I'd been talking to Mum.

"Beautiful, I might have missed a career opportunity in catering." He laughs.

"As if you'd ever put down the camera," I point out. Toby's been taking photographs for as long as I can remember. Mum had picked him up a second-hand camera at a car boot sale one morning, and he'd been fascinated by it. It had been no surprise to the family that he had ended up taking photography as part of his school subjects and been adamant that he was going to be a photographer.

"Probably about the same chance you'll walk away from the bar."

"Is everybody up?" I ask, changing the subject. Mum, Sam and Andy stayed over with Toby and Polly last night. I'm preparing myself to speak to my whole family this early in the morning.

"No. People are still asleep. I wanted to talk to you about a couple of things."

"That sounds ominous."

"Well, we'll start with the good news. Polly's desperate to put on social media, but we wanted to tell family first, and as you couldn't drag your ass down here for Christmas, you'll have to live with being told over the phone. You're going to be an uncle."

"Toby, dude, that's awesome!" A huge smile forms on my face.

"We're just past twelve weeks. Had the first scan, one little baby cooking in the oven."

"I bet Mum is unbearable," I comment, and Toby laughs.

"I'm surprised she let Polly lift a finger yesterday once we'd told her. I'm sorry you weren't here to hear the news at the same time."

"I'm so happy for you both. Tell Polly I give her full authority to have you at her beck and call for the next few months."

"I'm always at her beck and call." He laughs. "You'll see what I mean one day."

I hear Beatrice in the hallway. I want to tell him that I'm already at that 'one day', as I would be at Beatrice's beck and call without hesitation. Beatrice hears me on the call, and I hear as she walks downstairs rather than disturb me.

"I'm really chuffed for you."

"I can't wait. The Haliwell boys are producing offspring, the world should watch out," he jokes. There is a little silence, and I know something heavy is coming next. "Speaking of Haliwell boys…"

"If you're not going to be talking about Sam, I'm not interested."

"Max reached out," Toby replies. None of us call Max 'Dad'.

"What now?" I sigh.

Our relationships with Max are complicated and varied. Toby is the eldest. He remembers more, remembers Max's moods, the way Max treated our mother. Sam and I don't really remember anything. Mum and Max's relationship ended when Max hit Toby, and Mum decided she'd had enough. Through the years, and custody agreements, Max fluctuated in and out of our lives. He'd be around and see us, and then be gone for months, sometimes years at a time, living abroad.

When he was around, he was either interested, or distant, but either made us feel awkward and unwanted. As soon as we were able, we stopped interacting with him. When we became adults, he tried reaching out to us all, trying to build a relationship where we didn't really have any foundation. I haven't seen him since I moved away. Last I heard he was living abroad again.

"He reached out through Mum." Toby sounds annoyed. He hates that Max still contacts Mum, after all he did to her. "It's up to you, I don't really want anything to do with him, but I will understand if you and Sam do."

"I'm good, thanks."

"He wrote us each a letter. What do you want us to do with yours?"

"Burn it."

"Matt, take some time to think about it. You might regret not reading it."

"The only thing that man has ever done for me is show me how not to be a man," I reply.

"Just think about it. I'll read the one to me. It won't change my mind about him, but at least I won't be wondering about it forever."

"Alright, if you must, post it to me," I relent.

"Okay. So…are you going to tell me who it is that you're spending Christmas with?" he asks, changing the subject.

"Have a lovely day, Tobe." I laugh. "I will come see you all in the New Year. I'll speak to you on New Year's Day."

"Fine, be a secretive asshole."

"Go give your wife a kiss from me. Speak to you later." I smile to myself. Toby says his goodbyes and then he is gone from the line.

"Is everything okay?" Beatrice asks when I join her in the kitchen a little later after I've got ready and tried to shrug off Toby's comment about Max's letter. Beatrice is making French toast for us both, dipping the brioche into the eggs, cream and spice mixture.

"Toby was just telling me about a bit of family drama, nothing to worry about. Oh, and Polly is pregnant, so Sam and I are going to be uncles soon." I smile, trying to forget Max.

"Oh, that's amazing news," Beatrice says, sounding excited. She puts the soaked brioche slices into the frying pan, then reaches out for my hand. She pulls me towards her. "What's the family drama about?" she asks, her eyes scanning my face like she's searching for clues.

"My father got in touch and apparently wrote us each a letter." I kiss her forehead.

"You know you can talk to me about anything, right?"

"I know," I reply, but she looks at me like she is trying to see if I do really know.

"I mean it. Even if you just want to rant and rave about him for hours on end. Even if you go around in circles with how you feel. Anytime," she assures me. She gives me a small smile, then flips the brioche in the frying pan.

"You are the very best thing in my life. I don't know what I've done to deserve you," I tell her after a long silence between us.

"Funny because I often wonder what I've done to deserve you, so maybe we both just need to accept that we're perfect for one another," she says, looking up from the pan and giving me another smile. She takes the toast from the frying pan and puts it on plates for us. Beatrice scatters some berries over the toast for us both, splashes it with syrup, and then slides me a plate. We sit at the breakfast bar to eat, and afterwards, I pull her towards me for a kiss, tasting the syrup on her lips.

"Back to bed?" I ask.

"Of course. I'm hibernating there with you until Ben's home." She grins.

We go back to her bedroom, and she slips out of the clothes she had worn, waiting for me to do the same and get back into bed with her. I strip off and pull her close towards me when we're under the covers.

"My father hit my mother," I tell her.

She lies perfectly still in my arms, letting me tell her all I can remember, all I have learned over the years. How he'd treat her with disdain. How he isolated her from people. How he controlled their finances. How the last straw had come when he'd hit Toby with the back of his hand.

I tell her how Max had fought Mum for custody, even though it was clear he didn't want us, he just wanted to punish her for leaving. How when his plea for sole custody failed, he disappeared out of our lives for years. How I hated knowing what he'd done but hated that I didn't have a proper father like all my friends. How he'd flit back into our lives, promise us the world, and when any of us seemed on the cusp of forming a real relationship with him, he'd vanish again.

I tell her how my great-uncle Antony had stepped in, emotionally and financially, trying to help shape us as men. How, despite Toby's happiness about Polly being pregnant, he's told me before, he's terrified that he'll be a terrible father. How I despise myself for any time I've lost my temper in the past because it's always plagued with the idea that I could turn into my father.

I've voiced this fear to Beatrice before, at the fair, but not with the context of how awful Max was.

Beatrice listens until I've run out of words, then she rolls over so she can look at me, and she squeezes my hand.

"You're a good man, Matt. The best I know. You'd never hurt anybody, not like him. I know that in my bones. You'd hurt yourself before you hurt me. Whatever you decide to do about your father reaching out, I'll be right by your side, I promise."

I can hear in her voice that she feels this is a promise she won't ever break, and I feel some of the burdens I've been carrying slip away.

Ben arrives home from Lily's late the next afternoon. He looks so much happier than he had done before Christmas. Beatrice throws her arms around him like she hasn't seen him in months.

"How was your Christmas?" I ask as Ben looks taken aback by Beatrice's enthusiasm.

"Did everything go okay with you and Lily, PG version only, thank you very much," Beatrice asks.

"You two are very cheerful today," he comments, extracting himself from Beatrice's hug. I'd love to be able to reply that I'm cheerful because I'm in love with Beatrice, and she's making my world feel brighter than ever, but instead, I give him a little shrug.

"We've both had a few days off work. It always helps recharge the batteries."

"Yeah, Matt has no stamina." Beatrice grins. Before Ben can comment, she swats his arm and jumps a little in front of him. "Come on, you and Lily. All good?"

"All good," Ben confirms and his face breaks into a wide smile.

"When are you next seeing her?" I flick on the kettle, so we can sit to have a coffee together.

"Not until after New Year. We're both just going to put in the extra effort, it's been difficult when we're both on such long shifts and knackered when we get home, but we're focused. We're both looking at other jobs, so we can try to end up in the same place," Ben explains. "Schedules might still be shit, but at least if we're able to live in the same house, that'll be better. Nothing soon, so don't worry, I'm not going to be abandoning the house just yet."

"You have to do what's best for you and Lily. You can't fight what the heart wants."

"Well, if it isn't Romantic Matt making an appearance." Ben laughs.

"Are you working New Year?" I ask before he can carry on with the topic.

"Yeah, bloody night shift. That'll be fun, with all the drinking and what people get up to."

"We'll make sure our customers drink responsibly." Beatrice laughs. She's not worked an evening like New Year before, I don't think she knows what she's letting herself in for.

"Well, if that message could be passed on to every bar in the city, I would appreciate it." Ben smiles.

"When are you back at work?" she asks him.

"Tomorrow night."

"Us too. So, seeing as we're all going to be busy tomorrow night, I was thinking of having a film marathon and a takeaway, what do you think?" Beatrice looks at Ben and then at me.

"Sounds good," I reply.

"Yeah, I'm up for it, so long as it isn't your film choice." Ben laughs.

"What the hell is wrong with my film choices? I have excellent taste in movies!" Beatrice protests. I smile to myself as I listen to them bickering at each other.

Later, we settle on the sofa after we have finished the takeaway from the restaurant that Ben loves. Beatrice sits between us on the sofa, having claimed her seat given she lost out on the restaurant pick to Ben, and the film pick to me. She gives me a small smile when I scroll and select what is dubbed as a romantic action comedy. We sit back to watch the film, about a kidnapped writer being rescued by her cover model, and despite herself, Beatrice is laughing. Halfway through, when Ben's engrossed in the film, Beatrice reaches for my hand, pulling it behind the cushion, and we watch the rest of the film discreetly holding hands, with Beatrice drawing patterns of hearts onto my palm with her thumb. Every so often, I give her hand a little squeeze, and I hope she knows each squeeze is me saying I love you.

"Okay, I know you said it would be busy, but this is crazy!" Beatrice manages to get my attention above the din in the bar on New Year's Eve. We've barely had a chance to talk most of the evening, it has been non-stop since we arrived.

"Do you want a break?" I ask, but she shakes her head.

"No, I'm fine." She has to raise her voice again. She finishes serving the round of cocktails that have been ordered by a large group of people and then moves on to the next order. We're so busy tonight, nearly all staff members are in, and we are still slammed. We're open an extra two hours tonight for drinks service given it is New Year. It's not long until midnight, and people are queuing for drinks to toast the New Year.

I keep serving, customer after customer, keeping one eye on the time, watching the clock ticking closer to midnight, the queue at the bar thinning out as people get their drinks and return to friends in the bar area, getting ready to celebrate. I turn my attention to the woman at the bar in front of me, she's leaning over the bar, smiling at me.

"What can I get for you?" I ask.

"A kiss at midnight," she replies. She pushes her shoulders together, winking at me.

"I've got a girlfriend." I smile back at her. "How about a Long Island Iced Tea?"

"Three gin and tonics," she asks, sounding less friendly than before. I go to the other side of the bar to grab the gin, but Isaac reaches for it first.

"There is an issue in the office. I'll finish this order for you. Three gin and tonics?" he asks.

"Yeah, and she might ask you for a kiss at midnight," I joke. "What's the issue in the office?"

"Just go sort it. Thank me later." He grins. He walks off towards the woman I was serving, and I head towards the office.

I open the door, and Beatrice is sat on the desk, waiting for me. She smiles at me when she sees me.

"I asked Isaac if he wouldn't mind covering you, I hope he's okay with it." She gets up from the desk and walks towards me.

"He told me there was an issue, is everything okay?" I search her face, looking for any sign that there is an issue. She pulls me closer to her by pulling my shirt.

"No issue."

"You know you managed to save me from an unwelcome conversation without even being there?" I laugh.

She frowns. "What did I miss?"

"It was just some woman looking for a kiss at midnight," I reply.

"Did you tell her about your mythical wife?"

"Nope, told her about my girlfriend. I'd have happily told her about how beautiful, wonderful, smart, amazing, and spectacular my girlfriend is, but Isaac took over my order." I grin.

"I called you in here because I wanted to give you a kiss at midnight. I want to see the New Year with you." Beatrice pulls me even closer towards her. I glance at the clock in the office. It is one minute to midnight.

"There is nowhere in the world I would rather be than to be stood holding you." I slip my arms around her. She tilts her head, and her lips meet mine. She gives that little moan that she gives when I kiss her more firmly. I hold her more tightly, she slips her hands up my shirt, and we hear the cheers and singing from the bar as midnight arrives.

"Happy New Year." Beatrice smiles as she pulls away from our kiss.

"The best. Happy New Year." I smile back at her.

"I love you, Matt," she says, softly.

"Forever, Bea, you and me forever. I love you too," I say, and I give her a kiss on her forehead.

"Come on, we should get back before Isaac thinks we're having sex in here." She grins.

"We should get the car out of the way first." I laugh, opening the door to the office.

"Promises, promises." She laughs back, and we walk back into the bar, joining in with the celebrations. For the first time in many years, New Year feels like a promise of happiness.

Beatrice: Now

After Matt leaves me in the kitchen, I'm tempted to run after him, to ask him what the hell is wrong. Instead, I stand still for a moment, letting my body try to return to some level of normal state. My breathing slows. My pulse calms down, and I feel less giddy.

I tidy up the items that Matt had abandoned. I'm not hungry for anything to eat now, so I throw away the buttered bread that won't last. I busy myself with wiping the sides, cleaning away the crumbs and putting the glass into the sink. Normal, mundane activity, keeping my hands busy, whilst my brain is running at one hundred miles an hour, a voice in my head whispering, 'What the fuck was that, Beatrice?' I've clearly stepped over lines and barriers that should not have been touched. Matt probably thinks I am some uncontrollable, wild woman, throwing myself at him.

Yet…he kissed me back.

There may be some woman who is stringing him along, some woman he has a complicated situation with, but I am certain he wanted me. There were two of us doing the metaphorical tongue tango. We were both equally complicit.

My hand jerks up to my mouth, touching my lips, reliving the memory of his lips on mine. My lips feel swollen. It feels like my body sags and sighs in disappointment that I am now alone. I finish cleaning the kitchen, and then I stomp off to bed, feeling frustrated.

He looks up at me from his position between my thighs. My fingers reach for him, curling in his hair.

'Oh God, please don't stop', I plead.

'Don't you want to take our time?' His voice is teasing.

'It's been a long week, I might combust'. I flex my hips. He lowers himself, and his tongue meets me, a slow, luxurious lick against me. I grip his hair again like it's the only thing I can do to keep myself grounded. My breath is coming in

shorter pants, and then he sucks my clitoris, just once, but it has me whimpering with pleasure. He stops again, looking at me.

'Tell me what you want, Beatrice'.

'I want you, in me, right now. I want to come with you, and then do it again and again, all night long'.

'Oh, Bea...' he gives a groan of desire, and I know he has been holding back, that he's as desperate for me as I am for him. He moves on the bed, kneeling above me, glorious and naked. God, he is amazing. He grabs my sides and flips me over. I lean on my forearms, getting into position.

He grips my hips, and the hesitation, the teasing, is gone, both of us demanding. He pushes into me, and I push my body back against him. There's a blissful moment where we both just seem to hold still, enjoying this sensation, this union, then he starts to move, and I grip the bed covers, and he grips my hips harder, and I move with him, matching him stroke for stroke. He slips one hand around me, down my belly and...

I wake, covered in sweat. It takes me a moment to realise I am alone because the dream I was having felt so real. My heart is racing, and my whole body is tingling. It's still dark, still before dawn, and I am still alone. I wish I could fall asleep and get back to the conclusion of this dream, but I'm so hyped up, so alert, that I know it won't be possible. I'm a little overwhelmed at such a graphic dream about Matt, of all people, especially given he walked out on me earlier, clearly surprised by my moment of exuberance in the kitchen.

I wonder what he'd think if he knew I'd had a sex dream about him. Would he be repulsed? Or would he find it a turn-on? My breath hitches again as I imagine this option, imagine him getting hard; imagine him gripping himself in his hand. How he might look at me as he stroked himself. I imagine how he might taste if I knelt before him and took him in my mouth. I imagine how thick he might feel when he pulled me down and finally entered me.

I let my hand slide down my pyjama shorts. I'm slick and wet, and I only need to rub my fingers against my clitoris twice before my body seems to convulse as the orgasm that had seemed so inevitable in my dream becomes a reality.

It takes a few minutes for me to feel like my body is back to normal. I open my eyes again. Still dark. Still alone, and very confused. I've never had a dream like that, not something that has woke me up with such intensity and lingering desire. I can feel the heat rushing to my cheeks when I wonder if the house is as empty as I thought it might be. That'd be the worst; to be overheard masturbating by the housemate I'd thrown myself on, been rejected by.

I get out of bed and walk quietly down the hallway. It's clear that I'm alone in the house, and I breathe a sigh of relief.

What the actual fuck, Beatrice. No more whisky and pouncing on Matt before bedtime for you. I think to myself.

The following morning, I wake with the dream on my mind. I shower and get dressed, ready to face Matt and get over the mortification of speaking to him after the incident in the kitchen, and the memory I'll be holding about my late-night fantasy. The house is still quiet. I'm alone in the house. Matt's car is still parked on the driveway, but his keys are gone, so I assume he hasn't come home since he walked out last night.

I fix myself some breakfast and think about the dream that I'd had last night. It had felt so real, so vivid. My dreams aren't usually that vivid, usually mine are random and unrelated to anything that is going on in life. It feels like it came out of nowhere. Matt and I, whilst we have been friendlier since we went to the cinema to watch The Blair Witch Project and have spent more time with each other doing different activities, he's still guarded with me. I still get the sense that he is holding something back, and our day-to-day interactions are so far removed from the content of my dream.

Feeling frustrated but unsure why, I set myself into cleaning the house. The work is a distraction, as I scrub the bathroom, tidy my room, and set around giving the kitchen a deep clean. Ben arrives home later in the evening, and we have tea together. Matt still hasn't come home. I ask Ben if he knows where Matt is, but he shrugs and says he might be on a date. This sentence feels like it takes my breath away, but fortunately Ben doesn't notice, and he doesn't question why I go to bed early.

That night, I dream again. I dream of being on a big wheel, looking out to the bluest sea on the horizon. The sun was warm on my body, and I became aware that somebody is sitting on the big wheel with me. I turn to see Matt, and my hand reaches for his, squeezing his hand with mine, feeling a moment of complete contentment rush over my body before I jolt awake. I sit up in bed, wide awake. I don't understand this dream any more than the other. It's a different type of yearning from the previous night's dream, but it confuses me just as much, it's strong and intense, and it takes me what feels like ages to settle back to sleep.

The rest of the week carries on in a similar pattern. Each night, my dreams become more vivid and strange. They are either long, drawn-out scenes, or little snippets of conversations that I imagine.

Cool your jets, Goldilocks…
Aw, Beatrice, I man-scaped for this…
I'll keep you safe…
You've been driving me crazy since the day I met you…
God, how can I miss you so much when you're so close to me…
Just because I don't say it often, it doesn't mean I don't feel it, always…
Forever, Bea, you and me forever…

I am starting to think I am going crazy. Each morning, I'm eager to jump out of bed to see if today is when Matt will be home, but he doesn't make an appearance. I feel a longing, a pull, which is impossible to explain. I feel an intense need to see him, but he is making it clear that he doesn't want to see me.

Mid-week, I text him. It's the only text I've sent him. It's short, to the point, asking him what I have done wrong. He doesn't answer. I ask Ben about him, to see if he has heard from him. Ben's responses are brief. I ask if Matt will be coming for the upcoming meal for my birthday, and he promises to ask. I spend the rest of the week feeling like I am on tenterhooks, my head consumed by thoughts of Matt.

On Friday, Jas finishes work early and picks me up. We have planned to go shopping. It's the first time I've seen her by herself since Alessandro arrived. Alessandro seems like a nice guy. It is clear Jas is besotted with him. She apologises for being busy with him as we walk around looking for a dress for me to wear for my birthday dinner the following day. I tell her it is fine because even if we'd been meeting up, I know my mind would only have been half present. Thoughts of Matt are taking over my head.

It is clear both Jas and I feel like we have been terrible friends for the last couple of weeks, so we both throw ourselves into shopping with enthusiasm. Jas insists that I give a catwalk show in the changing rooms for the dresses I've selected to try on. Eventually, I settle on a short halter neck dress, which from the front looks demure, but at the back, there is nothing but the skirt section, leaving my back bare. Jas insists I must have it, telling me that it looks amazing, and I can always use it as a dress to wear in a dating profile picture.

As we're walking out of the shop, we're laughing about how best to avoid accidental flashing, and I feel like somebody is staring at me. I turn and look, and see Anna, Cole's wife, across the shopping centre with their four daughters. I can't remember the last time I saw her, but I'd read on the company website that Cole had left the business in February, to spend more time with his family.

I raise my hand as if to wave, but I stop. Anna is wearing a look of pure hatred, staring at me like she'd happily kill me with her bare hands. Jas notices, follows my gaze to Anna, and sees the look. Jas doesn't know Anna and asks me what her problem is, but I laugh it off, even though I'm unsettled about how I've caused Anna to look at me with such hatred.

That night, I sleep fitfully. I'm dreaming again, but I feel like I am fighting this dream because I keep waking up and falling back asleep. When I'm too tired to fight the dream anymore, I fall into it, seeing Matt. He is staring at me, and I hear myself shouting at him about how Anna gets to do whatever she likes, yet I sleep with a non-disclosure agreement taped to my drawer. This time when I wake, my breathing is ragged. This morning, there is no longing feeling, just jittery anxiety.

It's nearly morning, so I get out of bed and sit in front of my chest of drawers. I feel stupid as I pull open the bottom drawers, tipping it up, so I can see the bottom, and when I see an envelope taped to the bottom with thick tape, I give a frightened whimper. It is with shaking hands that I open the envelope and read through the documents. I see the bank statement, trying not to focus on the figure attached against an unfamiliar account in my name.

I look at the other document, and as soon as I see the words 'pertaining to the alleged incident between Beatrice Schofield and Cole…' I bite my lip to stop myself from screaming out. I pull my knees to my chest, sitting on the floor, feeling overwhelmed as the memory of that night rushes back to me, and it's like I'm in that hotel room all over again, and just like that night, I don't want any of it, but I'm powerless to stop it.

Beatrice: Then, January

January feels like a miracle. Ben has switched to working a couple of weeks on nights, swapping shifts to get some time off at the end of January to spend some time with Lily. It means that for Matt and me, every night, we are free to be together.

Every night when we get home from work, we have the whole house to ourselves, there's no hiding, no secrecy. We spend hours cuddled up on the sofa talking, where we seem to talk about every topic possible. He tells me he's agreed to meet his father once he is back in the UK, on the first day of April. I tell him I'll be there with him. When we're not cuddled up and talking, we spend nights holding hands whenever we move through the house, he kisses me in the kitchen, we take a bath together, we make love every night and wake up together every morning. I didn't think it was possible, but I fall in love with him even more than before.

A week into Ben's night shifts, Matt's awake before I am. When I wake, he's holding me, stroking my shoulders. I sigh in contentment and curl myself against him.

"Good morning." I smile up at him.

"Morning, sweetheart."

"Oh, are we starting with pet names now?"

"Thought I might try it on for size, but I'm sincerely regretting it." He laughs.

"Is that because you remember I'm not very sweet?" I joke.

"Oh, no, you're the sweetest." He leans over to kiss my face. I start laughing.

"You're very enthusiastic this morning."

"I was wondering if you would like to go on a date tonight. Some place other than the cinema."

"A date with a hot, sexy and smart guy? I can't think of a single thing I would prefer to do."

"I did wonder if you might have got a better offer." He kisses my nose. I can't help but giggle. We've barely spent a single evening apart since the first night we fell into bed together.

"Where are we going?"

"Can I keep it as a surprise?"

"I'm fine with that if you give me a clue about what I need to wear."

"Whatever you're most comfortable in."

"Are we getting up for breakfast, we've got about an hour before Ben's home." I check the clock.

"If we have an hour, I can think of something else we could do…" Matt gives me one of his slow smiles, and I grin back at him. I roll out of his arms, and he shuffles down the bed, intent on showing me what he's got on his mind.

Later, I sit at my dressing table to put the finishing touches to my makeup. I feel like I have a swarm of butterflies in my stomach, which makes no sense because this is Matt, the man that I love deeply and completely.

I slick on some lipstick and check my reflection. Unsure of Matt's plans, I'm wearing a knee-length black dress, and underneath I've got on patterned fishnets.

The doorbell rings, and I head downstairs to answer. I don't know where Matt is, and Ben has already left for work. He'd looked shattered, but seemed slightly cheered when I'd handed him the food that I'd packed for him.

I get to the front door, not sure who is here. I've never known anybody visit Matt at the house, Ben's at work and nobody ever calls here for me.

I open the door, and my face breaks out into a wide grin when I see it is Matt on the doorstep. He's holding a bouquet of gerbera flowers, a mix of red, orange, yellow and white flowers. I'd told him once that they're flowers that always make me feel happy.

I lean against the door frame and smile at him.

"Good evening. You look beautiful." He hands me the bouquet of flowers.

"These are beautiful. Thank you." I take them from his hands. He makes no effort to come into the house, and I understand that he's playing a role, the role of a man arriving to pick up a woman for a date. "Would you like to come in?" I ask him, opening the door wider. He nods and steps into the house.

"Lovely house you have here," he comments nonchalantly, following me down the hallway towards the kitchen as I hunt for a vase. I look in the cupboards and give up when all I can find is a tall jug.

"I haven't lived here long, but I like it, it is home."

"Do you have roommates?" he asks, watching as I fill the jug with water to put the flowers in.

"My brother and his best friend."

"Yeah, what are they like?" Matt wonders.

"My brother is quite protective. The other guy, he's nice. I'm pretty sure he's head over heels in love with me though."

"He totally is," Matt replies, and he pulls me by the hand, closer to him. His other hand cups my face, stroking my cheek with his thumb, and then he kisses me, slow and sensual. When he pulls away, I feel breathless.

"I'm totally head over heels for him too," I say, watching him as his face breaks into a full smile.

"Are you ready?" he asks. I nod, and we walk to the front door. I slip into a pair of sparkly high heels, grab my coat and bag, and the two of us head out of the house, hand in hand, towards the taxi he has waiting.

He takes me to a restaurant. It is cosy and quiet, with a small menu of delicious dishes and decadent desserts. The atmosphere seems to shrink so it is just the two of us, cocooned at our table, the light of the thick church candle in the middle of the table bathing us in a soft glow. Afterwards, Matt asks me if I want to get a taxi home or walk, and I opt for a walk. It's cold, but I don't seem to feel it. It's like the bubble of bliss I'm in is keeping me warm.

"That was a wonderful date, thank you." I squeeze his hand as we cut through the park.

"I thought an official dinner date would be nice."

"Yes, funny that we'd not been for dinner, but you've taken me home and introduced me to your mother." I grin.

"You introduced me to your parents first," he points out, and I laugh at the memory. He really had looked pissed off at being there that night.

My phone buzzes in my bag. It's late, so I am not expecting anybody to be contacting me. I pull my phone out of the bag, and I see a notification from a social media site. The notification reads: *Anna has sent you a message.*

The only Anna I know is Cole's wife. We are connected on social media, neither of us had severed the link when everything had exploded. We'd made no contact either since the day she had slapped me in the street. It's been eight months since we have spoken, and the idea of her reaching out makes me feel apprehensive.

"What the hell…" I mutter to myself, and I stop walking, so I can open the message.

"What is it?" Matt stops next to me. I look at what Anna has sent me. It's a picture of her, Cole, and their daughters. It looks like they must have gone to Lapland over the Christmas period. All six of them are wearing thick coats and hats, still red-cheeked in the cold, beaming smiles on their faces, some reindeer in the background. She's written a caption in the message to me. 'You tried to destroy us, but we're stronger than ever. I hope you're ashamed of yourself. Women like you make me sick'.

I almost drop my phone in shock when the phone beeps again. This time, it's an alert that Anna has tagged me. With shaking hands, I click to read it. This one reads 'beware the vipers who try to slither into your home'.

I turn the phone to Matt, so he can see this update. He suddenly looks furious. The lovely dinner that I have eaten seems to swirl in my stomach, and I want to throw up.

"This is ridiculous," he snaps.

"My family are going to see this. My friends…" My voice trails off. There is a small, logical part of my brain that is still functioning, reminding me that my parents don't believe in social media, that Ben's probably too busy saving a life to be checking his socials and that Jas will be in bed given the time zone differences. Then the snide part of my brain takes over, reminding me that eventually, they will see. Eventually, they will ask.

Eventually, I will have to lie about what this means. Even if they don't, this could just be the first shot from Anna. Who knows what else she might want to throw my way?

Matt leads me over to a bench. It's wet from the rain, and he shrugs off his coat for me to sit on. I feel like a metaphorical damsel in distress. He pulls his own phone from his pocket and connects it to make a call. He takes a few steps away from me, pacing. His facial expression is still furious. I hear snippets of his conversation.

"No…fucking indefensible…warning you…sort…immediately… I don't care…whatever…just get it done."

Whilst he is pacing and swearing, my phone buzzes with new messages. Clearly, some of Anna's friends are still up. They add messages to the post.

You okay, hun?
Hope ur okay
You tell the bitches, Anna
DM me, hun, tell me you're okay
Don't let anybody put you down sweetie.

Each one is another pinch of pain. A reminder that in Anna's version of the story, I am the bitch, I am the wolf in sheep's clothing. I wonder how many people she has told her version of the truth to. How many strangers out there hate me and judge me when they don't know what really happened? People who know Cole probably think he is amazing, as that is the way he portrays himself. Family man. Successful businessman. All round nice guy.

I know people see this because it is what I saw. All the years I'd worked for him, I saw him that way. I never expected that he would have pinned me down, wanting to take something that I didn't want to give. I may have made naïve decisions that night, but I am not the bad person here, and it hurts me that people who don't know me believe them.

Matt sits on the bench next to me.

"Are you okay?" he asks.

"I guess it's still true that if you post something cryptic enough, at least two people are going to ask 'You alright, hun'," I scowl.

"Bunch of gossips with nothing better to do with their time."

"Jesus, it makes me so angry! How dare she?" I snap suddenly, standing up. Now I am the one who is pacing around. "I get that she loves him, that she believes him, but to take the time to send me a photograph and messages…"

"What photo?" Matt asks. I switch on my phone to the message and show him the photo and the caption. "I'm sorry, Bea."

"I wish I could reply. I wish I could go on her post right now and tell all the hun warriors exactly what happened, list out everything in graphic detail, so they could see, but I can't. Anna gets to post whatever she fucking well feels like, and I silenced myself. She gets to portray me as some home-wrecker, and I'm the one sleeping with a bloody NDA and hush money taped to my bottom drawer because I'm still too ashamed about what happened to deal with it."

"You have nothing to be ashamed about. They all do! They're the ones in the wrong. Not you, you have done nothing wrong." Matt is on his feet, pulling me close to him. I bury my face into his chest.

"I just wish it didn't happen. I wish I didn't have to think about this. Every time I think I'm okay, something happens to make me deal with it again. I think I have it buried away deep in my head, but then it's back again, and I don't want it. I'd give anything to never have to think about this again," I cry.

"One day, Bea, I promise, it will get better," he soothes.

"This is not how I thought the evening would end. I'm sorry I ruined…"

"Don't even dare finish that sentence. Nothing is ruined, and you didn't do anything wrong." He gives me a squeeze. For a moment, I am quiet in his arms.

"Who were you on the phone to, anyway?" I look up at him. Almost like a sign from the universe, his phone beeps. He pulls away and looks at his phone.

"Taylor says the messages are gone. You won't get any more," he says, and he shows me his phone. There's a message from Taylor, finishing with: *'please tell Beatrice I am very sorry'*.

"Thank you." I didn't know he had Taylor's details.

"I kept his number, for an emergency," Matt explains like he can read my mind.

"Can we go home?" I ask. He goes over to the bench, picking up his coat, and then he puts his arm around my shoulder, and we walk home.

The rest of January seems to fly by. Ben finishes his shifts and then seems to disappear almost immediately to Lily's house. I have deleted my social media profile, not trusting that Anna won't eventually send something else, even if the message had disappeared like Taylor had promised. Matt is busy with work. There is a spate of car thefts from the area near the bar, and he seems anxious that things might escalate, that buildings might be broken into, or that people could be hurt.

Matt and I carry on in our little secret bubble, and I'm still convinced that I might burst from the love I hold for him. When I'm with him, everything else feels so insignificant, and anything that does come up as a problem, I know he will be right behind me. We agree that we'll tell Ben about our relationship in February, as Matt is planning something for Valentine's Day. I'm also keen to introduce him to Jas when she is home.

"Are you ready?" Matt asks as I finish putting away some glasses at the end of our shift.

"All done! Looking forward to getting home. My feet are aching today," I complain.

"I did warn you that working in a bar can be exhausting." He laughs. I stick my tongue out at him.

"I'd like to see you do it in heels," I joke. I follow him out of the building and wait as he locks everything up.

"I think I could cope with your shoes." He smirks and takes my hand. We walk off towards the street where he parked his car.

We are still laughing and joking about switching clothes and shoes when we round the corner, and instead of finding Matt's car parked waiting for us, there is just a smattering of glass on the ground.

"Oh, shit…"

"For fucks sake!" Matt curses at the same time.

"Come on, we can walk home and call the police to report it when we get home," I suggest. He nods, but there is a frown on his face.

"Taxi instead?" he offers.

"Nah, a walk might clear our heads." I pull him in the direction of home.

As we walk towards home, cutting through the park, I can sense that Matt is still frustrated.

"I'm sorry, I should have known to park somewhere else. I knew cars had been stolen from there."

"It's fine. I'm just disappointed we didn't get a chance to have sex in the car," I joke. He starts to laugh.

"I promise, first thing we do in the replacement car."

"I do love your promises." I grin.

"I'll never stop making them for you."

"Soppy git," I tease. We walk further in silence, and I look around the park as we walk. It's dark and eerie, but I love it. "You know, this park always reminds me a little of the Thriller music video," I comment.

"Why am I not surprised that you enjoy a music video that was basically a horror film?" He laughs. I smile to myself because I know I've pulled him out of his annoyance about his stolen car.

"Of course! I know the video is ancient, but I know the whole dance routine."

"You do not…"

"Do you doubt me, Matt?" I stop walking. He looks at me, and for a moment I'm still, and then I start dancing. A smile breaks out on his face, the type of smile I love to see on him. I keep dancing, adding in a bit of singing, and he's laughing hard as he watches me.

"When in the hell did you learn that dance?"

"After I watched *13 Going on 30*." I stop dancing, and he snorts.

"You gave me all that shit back then about romcoms, and you're not only a secret romcom watcher, but somebody who learns the dances in them."

"I'm going to let you into a little secret, my darling Matt, but if you tell anybody, I'll deny it."

"I'm intrigued now."

"I love a dance routine in a movie."

"So that's what I've missed in my quest for a perfect film for us to watch, flash mobs and dancing?"

"If we watch one, be warned, I will make you dance. I know them all," I tease. In truth, I only really know the dance to Thriller from memory as it was a dance I learned when taking dance classes with Jas, but watching Matt's face light up at this topic, knowing I am making him laugh, I can't help myself.

"Yeah, give me an example of another dance you know."

"You should see my Footloose." I laugh.

"You're always a surprise, Beatrice. I love you. Come on, show me Footloose. Maybe I'll surprise you with my version," he challenges me with a laugh.

I take a step away from him, ready to dance something I do remember. I'm laughing at his facial expression, but as I turn and take a few steps forwards, my foot lands on a big patch of ice on the ground. Before I can stop myself and before he can reach me to steady me, I feel myself flip upwards, and as I'm falling back to the ground, the only thought I have in my head is, 'this is going to hurt'.

Beatrice: Now

I stuff the paperwork back into the envelopes. I tape them back to the bottom of the drawer, shoving everything away again. I've been so desperate to get my memory back but this, this memory, I don't want it. I've never wanted it. I cry, silently, and I don't know whether it is minutes or hours that pass before I've cried myself dry. Eventually, I get up, wipe my eyes and head to take a shower. I stand under the cool water, hoping it will help to take the puffiness out of my eyes, as I can't face Ben and Lily for breakfast if it looks like I've been crying for hours.

Whilst I shampoo my hair, I think about the dream I'd had last night, and that the dream had led me to real evidence of something that had happened to me. I'm midway through scrubbing when it clicks in my head. What if all the other dreams about Matt…what if they're not just me having long fantasies about him…what if they're actual memories?

If they're actual memories of time with Matt, why hasn't he said something to me? He's had plenty of time. What if something had happened, but it had blown up in our faces? Maybe he doesn't want to remind me that he broke my heart, or that I maybe hurt his.

I finish showering and go back to my bedroom, sitting on my bed, wrapped in my towel. I think through the snippets of dreams I've had and conversations I'd imagined. Imagined or recalled? I pull out the list of the things I couldn't explain in my room. What if these things could be explained by Matt? Did he buy me my necklace? Did I buy him something expensive at Christmas? If so, what happened between Christmas and the end of January for him not to tell me about us?

The only thing I don't know how to explain by adding Matt to the equation is why I'm following some swimwear model. I grab my phone, it's not an unreasonable hour, so I open the social media app and send a message to Polly.

Short and sweet, a quick: hey, *this might sound weird, but have you heard from Matt?*

I can always claim I sent the message by mistake if she asks me what the hell I am talking about and who the hell I am asking about.

It takes a few minutes for my phone to buzz, and I almost jump out of my skin at the sound of it. On the screen, there is a reply from Polly: '*Hi, Beatrice, long time no speak! Hope you're well. Can you send me your number, can I phone you?*'

I feel my stomach do a somersault. I'm not going crazy, Polly is linked to Matt!

I send a message back with my mobile number, and a minute later, my phone is ringing. It is at this point that I wonder how I'm going to get through a conversation with somebody that I do not remember meeting.

"Hi, Beatrice. How are you doing?"

"I'm good, thanks. How are you and Toby? How's everything going with the pregnancy?" I ask, remembering her husband's name and their pregnancy announcement. I try not to focus on the fact I've run out of information.

"All good, Toby is acting like no other woman has ever been pregnant before, but it's sweet. You know those Haliwell men, they're a bunch of sweethearts."

"They really are," I say, faintly. Toby must be one of Matt's brothers. The eldest. I remember him saying in our game of twenty questions about Sam being the middle brother.

"I don't have long to talk, unfortunately. I'm just waiting for a scan, but I saw your message and popped out to give you a call. I've been a bit worried about Matt, is everything okay? Toby and Sam have barely heard from him though I know they were worried about him a couple of weeks ago when he went home. Alice had asked them to check on him, something about him going through a tough time."

"Yeah, it's not been great." I pull a face, grateful it isn't a video call, as I'm not sure how long I can hold this up.

"I thought you might have gone with him when he went to see Alice. We're all going this summer, are you coming with Matt again?"

"Maybe," I reply. I assume Alice is his mother, which suggests that we went away together. Why hasn't Matt told me anything? Why hasn't Ben mentioned that I apparently met Matt's mother?

"Okay, well, it will be lovely to see you. I don't know what week we're going, but you'll get to meet the baby!"

"I'm looking forward to it."

"Anyway, I'm going to have to get back for my appointment in a second, but I just wanted to say I haven't heard from Matt recently. I know all of them were angry with Max fobbing them all off. That guy is a right dick. I was hoping Matt had rebounded from it, but I know Toby is still stewing. Oh, crap, they're calling me in. Can I call you this evening?"

"I'll call you later in the week. I'm going out for dinner tonight for an early birthday celebration."

"Aw, well, have a lovely time. I'll speak to you later! When you see Matt, tell him Toby's waiting for an answer."

"I will," I promise though I have no idea how I'll casually slip this into conversation with Matt. Polly says her goodbyes, and she's gone. I sit still on the bed, trying to make sense of everything.

"Did Matt say he was coming?" I ask Ben later that afternoon. Jas and Alessandro had arrived an hour earlier, and I've been playing the role of the greatest actress, hosting and keeping them entertained when all I want to do is find Matt. Ben smiles.

"Gosh, you're eager to get out tonight, aren't you?"

"Ben…" I snap. He looks at me.

"I don't know. I reminded him. He didn't answer. Just cut him some slack. He's just been going through something recently," Ben says gently.

I want to laugh at his sentence. Matt's going through something? No shit, Sherlock. All day, more and more things have been filling my brain, more sentences, more snippets, more events, and more emotions. Either I am going insane, or Matt is definitely going through something.

I hear the front door open, and I swear my heart skips a beat at the sound. I whirl around.

"Hi, I'm sorry that I'm late," Matt says as he strides down the hallway. My heart starts to gallop like a thoroughbred racehorse. He looks spectacular, wearing dark trousers and a blue shirt. He is carrying a bouquet of red gerbera flowers.

The moment I see him, it feels like my whole body is screaming his name. It's Matt. It's Matt. My Matt. It's always been Matt. He's always been mine. I want to throw myself at him, to put my arms around him and hold him close. I want to tell him I know, tell him that I remember, that everything is suddenly so clear to me. Instead, I stand still.

"Good to see you, mate." Ben smiles. He walks around me to greet Matt.

"You look good, Beatrice." Matt glances at me. He gestures at the flowers and puts them on the table for me.

I can't bring myself to reply to him because if my face matches my emotions, there is no way I look good. I feel like I've just been knocked off my feet by an avalanche of memories. Things that I had been dreaming and new memories, running through my head. I suddenly feel like I remember everything. I remember the night of the accident.

I'd thought earlier today that something must have gone terribly wrong between us for Matt not to have told me what we'd been doing, but I recall that night so clearly. We'd been fine. I'd been joking and messing around in the park, trying to make him laugh. He'd been laughing, telling me he loved me, and then I'd skidded on the ice and fallen. It was a stupid, stupid accident that led us here. Nothing major, no fight, no heartbreak.

I just don't understand why he hasn't said something to me. He's had all that time to tell me we love each other.

As all my memories are rushing back to me, everything else seems to carry on as normal. Ben and Matt walk to the back garden, over to Lily, like nothing has changed. I feel sick and panicked. This isn't right. How is everybody carrying on like my whole world hasn't just been shaken up?

I stare over at Matt, wondering why he has kept me in the dark for the past few weeks and how it hasn't been a struggle for him. I look at him, as discretely as I can, and I can see the smile he is giving Ben and Lily is fake, something he's put onto his face to hide what he is really feeling. I get the feeling that maybe, these past few weeks have been as bad for him as they have felt for me.

I go into the conservatory, make myself look busy making a drink, watching as Jas and Alessandro cross the garden to Lily, Ben and Matt, joining them in conversation.

I take my phone out of my pocket and send a text to Matt. It's only the second message to him on my phone that I have sent to him, but I remember that I used to delete every message, in case Ben picked up my phone. Whilst there is no evidence on my phone, I know I've exchanged hundreds and hundreds of messages and calls with Matt. Words I had once committed to memory, to smile about when I was alone, words that I forgot, words that I now remember. I remember how I'd smile at every single one, how my heart would soar from the thrill of them.

I watch Matt take his phone out of his pocket, reading the message I sent, asking if we could talk. He makes an apology to the group, stepping away from them for a moment.

My phone buzzes. His reply reads, *'About what'*.

I'm torn on how to answer. I could message him to ask why he has been keeping us a secret from me. I could ask him which colour underwear he preferred on me. I could ask him whether the fair had been in town when he visited his family, whether he had been on the big wheel. I am even tempted to send him a picture of Roger Rabbit given I'd joked it could be our safe sentence. Instead, I reply with a simple *'Please? In the kitchen'* because I don't want to freak him out whilst he is standing in the garden with other people. It's bad enough that I am freaking out.

I head to the kitchen to wait for him. I don't have to wait long. A few seconds later, he steps into the kitchen.

"What's the matter, Beatrice?" he asks, sounding overly polite. I pace for a moment, now he's here with me, and we are alone, I'm not sure the best way to start this conversation. I go for something simple and straightforward.

"I remember," I tell him. There is a long pause between us.

"What do you remember?" Matt sounds guarded.

"Everything! I remember everything!" My previous calm abandons me. I feel my heart racing in my chest, and I take a deep breath to calm myself. He stands in front of me, looking shocked.

"Everything?"

"How could you let me forget you, you tosser," I cry. Matt looks like he doesn't know how to react, how to handle me, whether to keep the distance between us or to cross the room to be closer. He stays where he is standing, staring at me. "Why didn't you tell me? Didn't you want me to remember you?"

"I thought you were better off not remembering everything," he replies after a moment of silence between us, and I know in that instant that he is thinking about Cole, that maybe me forgetting what had happened with Cole and Ryan was the driver behind him keeping secrets. I remember I'd told him I would have done anything to not have that memory in my head. Everything seems to click into place. They were the words I'd spoken, but I had never meant that I'd be willing to forget him as well.

"And you…were you better off?" I challenge him, looking at him, searching his face. He looks devastated. He shakes his head.

"No, Bea, I wasn't better off. It's been killing me. But thinking I was doing it for the right reasons, keeping you safe from things that had hurt you, my pain was worth it."

"You should have told me."

"What would you have done if I had told you?"

"I don't know," I admit. How would I have reacted that first day if Matt had told me what had been happening between us? That day in the hospital, Matt was tired, grumpy, guarded, much like the Matt I'd met at my parents' party. How would I have felt if he'd told me then that we were together, that we were a couple, without me remembering all those times we'd shared together? All those times he was so wonderful, so kind, there for me. Without the context, without the memories, without knowing how we'd grown together, closer and closer, without me knowing the reasons why I trust and love him implicitly, what would I have thought?

"I thought it was for the best, I swear." Matt sighs. He looks exhausted, and I see how difficult these last few weeks have been for him.

"You were in the hospital that night, holding my hand."

"Yes," he admits.

"You were crying."

"Yes, I was."

"But then you left. Why?"

"I heard Ben arrive, heard him talking to a nurse in the corridor. I didn't know how to explain why I was crying next to your bedside, so I went to get a drink, composed myself and came back to sit with Ben. In the morning, you asked what I was doing there. I thought you might just be joking or trying to keep Ben from putting two and two together, but you looked at me like I was intruding, and it was clear you had no idea what we meant to each other.

"Even before they said you had amnesia, I knew it was bad. Everything we'd had, overnight it had vanished. All those memories, those feelings, they belonged to me only, and you remembered me only from the time we'd met at your parent's house. I was left alone with my feelings, feelings I had no right to tell you about, to force that upon you."

"It must have been lonely for you, to be the one holding that knowledge, not able to talk to anybody about it," I say, and subconsciously, my index finger travels to the ring I've been wearing, the ring he gave me, fiddling with the beads. I can see how tormented Matt looks right now. I know now that the way he has been and the way he has looked these past few weeks, that's not how Matt usually is. My Matt is vibrant, the sun in my life, and I feel an ache in my chest when I think about how alone he must have felt. Bound by the promises he made to me, holding a promise not to reveal my secrets, even though I had forgotten them.

"Well, you can't tell somebody that they love you." Matt sighs, and I feel devastated because I've had Ben, Lily and Jas by my side, trying to help me make sense of what I'd lost, but he's had nobody to help him cope with what he'd lost, nobody who even knew he had lost anything. I want to cry for him, and my eyes well with tears.

"I do. I do love you. I remember it all. I felt it. I feel it here," I cry, putting my hand over my heart.

"You do?" Matt falters like he isn't sure whether I do feel anything, given the past few weeks, I've given him nothing.

"Like it's going to burst out of me, like I can't contain it. I'm so sorry," I tell him.

"It wasn't your fault. I wanted to tell you so many times, but thinking that the reason you had lost time was because you didn't want to remember what happened with Cole and with Ryan, I couldn't open you up to that pain."

"Pain... No, look..." I pull my phone from my pocket. I open the folder that was password-protected. I type in MATT. It's all so clear to me now. The folder unlocks, and there is picture after picture of the two of us together and pictures we took of each other.

There is one of me in a bikini, posing in front of the sea on a gloriously sunny day. There is one of him in his florescent shorts, lying on a beach towel, followed by one of the two of us lying together on the sand, shading our eyes from the sun. There are pictures of me dressed as Jessica Rabbit and him as the PI from *Who Framed Roger Rabbit* from the Halloween party at Isaac's. There is a series of us at a concert, dancing, holding cups of lager, and then one where he is standing behind me, me taking the photograph of us, his hands on my waist. The newest pictures are lots of the two of us, a series of photographs where we are curled up together, arms around each other, kissing cheeks, looking happy.

"This isn't pain. This is love. This is happiness. This is everything," I tell him, earnestly, showing him the pictures. "What happened then, it led me to this, to you, and I love this, I love us, I love you." I can't say anything else, as he crosses the room and his mouth is suddenly on mine, desperate, searching, and I respond in kind.

He kisses me like he has been waiting for years, rather than the few weeks I had forgotten. He kisses me like he never wants to stop, in a way that makes me never want him to stop either. I drop my phone onto the kitchen side, and then my hands are up the back of his top, feeling the muscles of his back, the terrain that feels so familiar to me. I pull him closer to me, and he gives a throaty growl.

"God, you have no idea how much I have missed you," he whispers against my ear as he pulls away from our kiss.

"Maybe we should go upstairs, so you can show me how much."

"Don't tell me you have remembered the weeks you lost but have forgotten there are people in the garden, people who are here to celebrate your birthday," he teases and trails a line of kisses down the side of my neck, making me quiver.

"No, I haven't forgotten, I just remember how much I enjoy your room. Or my room. Or any room where it is just you and me." I grin.

"Erm…what exactly is going on?" Ben's voice comes from the doorway of the kitchen. I feel Matt's body stiffen as he realises we have been caught out. There is no hiding this. My arms are still up Matt's top, his arms are still around my body. There is no way to make this look innocent, and I wouldn't want to either. I don't want this to be a secret anymore. I want to shout this to the world. I twist around in Matt's arms, so I can look at Ben. He's stood there, looking confused. I clear my throat.

"Remember me saying that my heart knew something about the time I lost? Well, my head caught up. I'm sorry we didn't tell you before. It was just all new, and we wanted to keep it to ourselves. We have been in a relationship since September."

Ben doesn't say anything. He just turns around and walks away, shutting the kitchen door behind him. For a minute, Matt and I are silent. I turn back towards him.

"Shit." Matt sighs. He bows his head, leaning forward, his forehead on mine. "I knew he wouldn't take this well. I knew he would think I'm too unreliable for you, and he's probably furious that I didn't say anything since your accident."

"Well, he doesn't get to make choices for me," I snap.

"Bea, you're his sister, and he is very protective of you. This was always going to be difficult. We knew that," Matt reminds me.

"It shouldn't be difficult. We are both adults."

"And I am always going to be a gambling addict, somebody who every day has to make the choice not to lose control. Ben's seen me picking myself up from when I was at my lowest. He was always going to be cautious when he found out."

"He knows how hard you work on your recovery." I am frustrated. All the reasons we had discussed keeping our relationship quiet, to have them play out as actual reactions from Ben, is heartbreaking. Matt pulls me closer for a hug, and he kisses the top of my head. We are still stood in the same spot where Ben found us.

Outside the kitchen, we hear the scuffle of footsteps from people, sounding like they're heading for the front door. Then one set of footsteps returns to the kitchen, the door opens and Ben is back. I turn around again, but Matt keeps his arms around me, and I feel secure in his arms though I'm furious with Ben.

"What the hell, Ben, have you just sent everybody away? How dare you? You don't get to make decisions for me! I don't need anybody's blessing! Who I love is my choice, it's nothing…" I shout, but Ben puts his hand up.

"Stop, Beatrice." He smiles, wryly. He looks at Matt. "You love her?" he asks.

"Yes, I do," Matt replies, clearing his throat.

"You're going to treat her right?"

"Like my life depends on it, like it's the only thing I'll ever need to do in life."

"You're going to treat him right?" Ben directs this question at me. I'm startled.

"Of course I am," I say with a frown.

"Okay, well, yes, I've asked Jas and Alessandro to leave. I thought maybe you two needed some time to catch up by yourselves, so they are coming for dinner with me and Lily, and we will leave you here. I ordered you some food to come about seven tonight. I'm going to stay somewhere with Lily, so I will be back tomorrow," Ben explains. I slip out of Matt's arms and cross the kitchen, so I can throw my arms around Ben.

"I remember everything. He's what my heart has been trying to tell me," I whisper. "He's the one, Ben."

"I'm glad you have your memories back. Maybe when I get home tomorrow, you can fill me in on what you were missing. The PG version, obviously, some things you can keep to yourself." Ben laughs softly. "And I know you don't need my blessing, but for what it's worth, you have it. He's a good guy."

"I know," I reply. "I know everything about him."

"I don't know why you didn't just tell me." Ben looks over at Matt.

"I made a promise to Beatrice that I wouldn't be the one to tell you about us," he replies, but I know there is more behind it that we can't say to Ben.

"I don't think promises count when the other person doesn't remember them," I point out.

"Look, I am going to go. You two have fun catching up. Oh, God, gross, sorry. I'll see you tomorrow. I will tell you what time I'm expected home." Ben smirks, and then he turns and walks out of the house. I hear him shut and lock the door behind him, and then it's just me and Matt.

"Google is surprisingly shit about whether you can talk to somebody about a non-disclosure agreement if they have amnesia," Matt says, and I start to laugh. "Or how best to convince an amnesiac who previously said *50 First Dates* was a hostage situation that they do actually secretly love you."

"You are fucking ridiculous," I tut and then I sigh. "Can we sit for a little while?"

"Sure." He sounds apprehensive.

"I just want to hear what you were doing since the accident, please. If you are okay to tell me," I explain, and he nods.

"I'll tell you. Come on," he says, and he leads me into the living room. We take a seat on the sofa together. I slip my hand into his and cuddle up against him. I can't believe I forgot this feeling of warmth and bliss and happiness. Except, I didn't really forget it, my heart kept reminding me that I felt it, but my brain just didn't understand how to interpret it. Now, it all feels simple. There's nothing better than this. He pulls me closer, and he starts talking, telling me everything.

Matt: January to April

When Beatrice falls, there is a sickening crack. I rush towards her, skidding on the ice myself in my haste. Given the noise, I'm expecting that I am going to find her crying and upset, but instead, she's lifeless on the floor. Her eyes are closed, and the features on her face are slack, completely void of expression.

I kneel beside her. Whisper her name. Take her hand. Feel for her pulse. Check she is breathing. Shout for help. There's nobody around, and I start to panic. I can't move her. I know from first aid courses that I shouldn't, but all I want to do, desperately, is pick her up and take her somewhere for help, immediately. I take a steadying breath and call for an ambulance. I plead for help. I take off my coat and put it over her. I feel absolutely helpless, and the most frightened I've ever felt in my life.

The ambulance arrives. I don't even register to start off with that the paramedic is Oscar. I'm just relieved there is somebody there, somebody to help me, somebody who is going to fix her.

"Matt, what's happened?" Oscar asks me. It's only when he says my name that I get a spark of recognition.

"Oscar, help her. Beatrice fell. She hit her head, hard."

"Ben's sister?" he asks. I want to tell him that she is so much more than that. She is the light in my life. She is pure sunshine and happiness. She is the other half of my soul. She is the love of my life. Instead, I nod in agreement.

"She didn't see the ice. She was messing around. Please, Oscar, please help her," I plead. I can tell Oscar understands there is more than her just being Ben's sister. He allows me to travel in the ambulance with them to the hospital. She's strapped to a backboard, I imagine the worst. I hold Beatrice's hand the whole way, silently praying for her to be okay.

The doctors seem to take forever to assess her. Eventually, I'm allowed to sit with her. She is still unconscious. A nurse asks me if I can contact her family. I think of Ben, at Lily's, oblivious that his sister is lying unconscious in a hospital bed, something I know will torment him, make him think of the other time she was lying in the hospital, the time he told me was the worst of his life.

I call Ben. I stay by Beatrice's bed. I hold her hand again. I rest my forehead on the bed, staying like this for what feels like an eternity, thinking of what happened. It was my fault we were walking through the park, my stupid fault for not parking my car in a more secure location given the recent thefts.

It is my fault that she's in hospital, I should have made us get a taxi, I shouldn't have encouraged her to mess about, I should have caught her when she fell. I whisper to her, murmurs of love, and pleading for her to come back to me. I find myself crying. I hear Ben arriving, talking to one of the nurses. I let go of Beatrice's hand and slip out of her room, walking away from them both.

I find Ben later and give him a coffee. He tells me Beatrice is okay, but she's asleep. We both sit with Beatrice for a while. He tells me I should go home, that I look knackered. I tell him I'll stay. I don't tell him that there isn't anywhere else in the world I would be.

Dawn breaks, and Ben and I go to get something to eat. I'm not hungry. I drink more coffee. Ben's phone rings, and I can hear Beatrice, high-pitched and agitated. I curse to myself that we'd left. We rush back to her room, and she looks over at me, asking why I am there. The more she speaks, the more it becomes clear to me that something is seriously wrong.

The day passes, and everything feels like a body blow. Throughout the day, Beatrice glares at me, like I'm intruding. She remembers nothing about us, the only time she remembers meeting me is at her parents' party. Everything else is gone, including the memory of Cole assaulting her. When she says his name, there isn't a flicker of panic over her face, there isn't a hitch in her voice. All I can think is about how she'd cried and say she would give anything to never think about Cole again, and it dawns on me that if I were to somehow make her remember me, I'd be reopening her to that pain as well.

Ben and I take Beatrice home. She sits in Ben's car, scrolling through her phone, frowning. I know there is nothing on the phone about me. She has told me weeks ago that she deletes all our messages and call history because Ben sometimes picks up her phone, and she was being cautious, not wanting him to find out about us accidentally. Beatrice asks more questions on the way home and makes Ben promise not to tell their parents that she has been in an accident. She doesn't want anybody else to know.

We get home, and she goes up to her room, and I'm left alone, wondering what the hell I am supposed to do.

The following morning, Ben and I catch up in the kitchen whilst Beatrice is still asleep in her room. I know Ben has already checked on her. I wish I were able to. I want to hold her and tell her that everything will be okay, but I can't do that. I'd probably scare the life out of her.

It's stupidly early in the morning. Ben is dressed for work, but he looks conflicted about the idea of leaving Beatrice alone for the day. I'm up because I couldn't sleep last night. I'd given up and paced the living room instead.

"I am going to phone my parents later. I think they should know." Ben sounds resolute.

"Don't. She's asked you not to."

"I don't think she is thinking clearly," Ben replies. I wonder if he has ever accepted that Beatrice is always thinking clearly. She knows her own mind.

"She'll be angry with you if you call them. They'd rush home, and Beatrice won't forgive you."

"They should be here. They would want to look after her."

"She has told you she doesn't want that," I remind him.

"I think I am going to call work and see if I can get out of my shift. I should be home, looking after her."

"She told you last night to go in. She said she doesn't need looking after," I remind him again. She'd been firm about this over dinner last night. She might not remember me, but she knows exactly who she is.

"Beatrice doesn't know what she is talking about. She's fragile."

"She isn't as fragile as you think she is," I mutter.

"You don't really know her." Ben sounds frustrated.

I feel like he has hit me. His sentence is a reminder that I am apparently nothing to Beatrice. I want to reply that I know exactly who his sister is. I know how her voice sounds when she is utterly content. I know how steady her heartbeat feels under my hand.

I know she bites her lip when she is engrossed in reading. I know that she cries when she reads her favourite poetry. I know she is braver than anybody gives her credit for. I know why she'll pick a horror movie over a romance, even if she ends up watching it from behind her hands. I know she fusses with every dog she passes.

I know she says the place she feels most at home is when I wrap my arms around her and pull her close. And I know, despite me believing she is better off not knowing some of the things she has forgotten, it's breaking my heart that she's forgotten all about me.

I can't say any of these things to Ben. So, instead, I storm out of the kitchen, ignoring him as he shouts after me.

I sleep for a bit, and when I wake, I can hear Beatrice in her room. I try not to make a sound, getting out of bed, dressing and heading out of the house for a walk. I think fresh air will clear my head, but all I end up doing is walking around for what feels like hours, debating and contemplating. I could go home, right now, and tell her everything that has happened between us, to try to get her to see that we're a couple.

I'm not naïve enough to think that she'll magically remember everything about us, but maybe it's the right thing to do. I don't want to open her up to memories she might be better off not remembering, but it also feels wrong to hold this secret from her, for me to know what we were doing, for her to be oblivious.

I go home, finding her watching *Scream*. I force myself into the living room, to make conversation with her. She makes a comment about me wanting her back, and for a moment, I wonder if she's remembered everything, but then it's clear she is talking about work. I stumble through this first proper conversation with her, coming across as awkward, grumpy, and she calls me a dick. God, I wish she could remember me.

I drop in sentences that I recall, tell her I know she is strong and talk about wrestling bears, each time thinking maybe this would be a key sentence, that she'll get all her memories back, and we'll laugh and joke. Instead, by the time the conversation is over, I'm pretty sure she hates me, and I'm pretty sure she thinks I hate her too.

The days pass. They're painful and tiring. It doesn't matter how long I work, I don't sleep well. Days off work feel worse. I worry that she's still feeling unwell.

She mentions she has been having headaches. I want to scoop her in my arms and hold her close, but instead, I tell Ben that I think she's been unwell, so he can make sure she is checked out. I'm devastated that I don't have the option to look after her myself.

I take comfort in hearing from Ben, via Jas, that Beatrice has no plans to talk to anybody from her old company, or her ex-boyfriend. I had worried she might seek them out and be blindsided. Whilst I had felt sneaky listening to Jas and Ben exchange updates behind Beatrice's back, I can't help but feel more settled knowing she won't. Settled, but still tormented by what is happening.

If I see Beatrice around the house, we make polite conversation. Sometimes she calls me grumpy. Ben seems to have picked up on the change in my mood. One night, he comes downstairs and finds me on my third drink of whisky. I've finished a shift, where everybody was asking when Beatrice was coming back, each question feeling like a personal jibe.

The whisky isn't helping me forget the sting of questions. Ben starts a conversation with me, trying to make sure I am okay. My responses are short, and I hate myself for being rude. Eventually, he gets tired of my short responses, and he takes the whisky bottle from me.

"Are you just stressed because you're short-staffed at work, with Beatrice not there? She isn't doing this on purpose, it isn't her fault." He looks concerned.

"I know!" I snap, with more force than I had intended. Jesus, I know it isn't her fault, but a stupid, freak fucking accident has wiped me from her mind, every memory gone like somebody pressed control, alt, delete. It's taken away the bad memories from her, and I am grateful for that, that the shadow she would get on her face when talking about Cole is gone, but it is killing me because everything else is gone too.

"What's going on, Matt?" Again, there is concern on his face.

"Nothing. I'm just tired. Not because of work. I hired cover for Beatrice, and I've even hired another manager for a few months. I just need a break. I am sorry for snapping."

"I think tensions are just running high. Whisky isn't the way to go."

"You thought it was the answer when your heart was broken," I remind him, and the expression on his face changes. There is a flicker of sympathy.

"I'm sorry I didn't know you had been dating somebody. I've been so focused on Beatrice. Talk to me, tell me what happened. Maybe I can help."

All I want to do is tell him everything, but I'm sure Ben will be furious; for lying to him for months, for daring to believe I was good enough to be with his sister, for being the reason she was in the park. So instead, I tell him I need some sleep.

Each day gets more frustrating until I reach the breaking point, what feels like the edge of everything. I hold the secret of us, and I don't feel like I can tell anybody what has happened. Nobody knows what I am going through, and I'm not sure how to get myself through this. I've lost something that people didn't even know I had.

One night, I walk into a casino. As soon as I get to the reception area, I feel that familiar thrill. I haven't been here before, since I left home I have avoided all places like this, but they're all the same, the same style carpets, the same glitzy exterior, inviting you in, promising you fun, the same beaming smiles of the people at the reception, welcoming you.

I pass over my driver's licence as my identification. This is an act that feels like deception. Quickly, they process my information and then I am inside, with cash burning a hole in my pocket.

There is the usual area of electronic gaming, spin the wheels, cash builder games, all screaming out the jackpot they are due to pay out. These are the types that pay out often enough in the area to convince you to stay in your seat, keep feeding your coins and keep clicking the buttons and convinced that the next spin will be your turn for glory.

To the side of that area is the poker room, there's a tournament due to be played. Poker requires concentration that I don't have right now, so I move away, past the entrance and past the Black Jack tables. I head to the other room, where there are six roulette wheels, each run by a suited casino employee, each surrounded by people placing their bets, spreading their chips onto numbers, staking their money in anniversaries, birthdays, memorable dates, lucky numbers. Others place their bets by monitoring the electronic display that for each table proclaims the numbers from the last twenty spins, the split between red and black, odds and evens, using this like it is a scientific prediction of where they're best placed to land their chips, reap the rewards, instead of accepting that this is a game of pure luck.

Each table increases the stake that has to be placed. Minimum bets on the lowest table start at one pound, the highest table here has a minimum bet of five pounds. I watch this table, watching the guy who places his chips with the swiftness of somebody experienced, playing his usual numbers. Somebody else puts down ten chips on number twenty, betting fifty pounds on one number. I can feel my pulse, pumping fast through my body. It's an instinct like the smell of a newly opened bottle of whisky might cause for an alcoholic, tugging on illicit memories, a darkness saying, 'Welcome back, I knew we would meet again'.

I take a twenty-pound note out of my pocket. Put it on the roulette table with my casino card. They ring me up and pass me a stack of chips. I pick them up. Hold them in my hand. Feel the weight of them. Flick a chip from the bottom, over the stack, moving it to the top. Muscle memory. I remember I explained this to Beatrice once, how I'd missed holding chips in my hand, why I had started learning how to make origami, to distract me.

The thought of this, it's enough. Enough to stop me, enough to make me shake my head, let the clarity back in because I remember her telling me that it was something beautiful I had started, that she was proud of me. I remember her absolute faith that I wouldn't fuck up again. I know that if I throw everything away, I won't ever be able to make myself feel like I was deserving of her.

I walk away from the table. Go to the checkout desk. Exchange my unused chips back into a twenty-pound note. The cashier smiles at me, telling me it looks like a decent win.

I walk out of the casino. I phone Mum. I ask her if I can come home for a bit. She can tell from the sound of my voice that whatever is driving my unprompted visit it is serious. She tells me to drive carefully, and despite the fact she doesn't know just how close I came to throwing away my years of hard work, she reminds me that I'm strong. I drive home, pack a bag, and then drive straight to my mother's, leaving just a note for Beatrice and Ben, telling them I need to go home for a bit.

I stay with Mum for a week. I tell her about going to the casino. I tell her I intended to gamble. She reminds me that I didn't. It doesn't do anything to help the knot of shame I have in my stomach.

I go to gamblers support meetings as many times as I can in that week. I can't fail again.

Mum must tell my brothers, as they're both suddenly blowing up my phone with messages, with invites to stay with them. Toby tells me that he and Polly could introduce me to some of Polly's model friends. I tell him I am not looking for a woman. Sam tells me I might enjoy going clubbing with him and Andy if women are no longer my thing.

On my third night home, Mum and I sit down to the tea that I've cooked. Del-Boy and Rodney sit at my feet, looking at me with their big eyes, hopeful that I'll sneak them some chicken.

"This is lovely, Matt. It's been a while since I came home to tea cooked for me, not since you came that week with Beatrice." Mum smiles at me. I know what she's doing, using an innocent sentence to bring Beatrice into the conversation, looking for my reaction. My reaction must be bad because she sighs loudly. "What happened between the two of you? What is it that has you looking so troubled?" she asks. I push my food around my plate.

"If I tell you, do you promise not to tell anybody else? No telling Toby, Polly, Sam, Andy."

"I promise."

"Beatrice had a fall in January. She hit her head. She's lost some of her memory," I explain.

"How much of her memory did she lose?"

"Since before she came to live with me and Ben," I sigh. Mum is quiet for a moment.

"You love her, don't you?"

"Yes. Yes. I love her," I reply. This is the first time I've said my feelings about Beatrice aloud to anybody but her, and it feels like a crack has been made in my armour, that everything I have been holding inside is about to seep out.

"She doesn't remember anything at all?"

"She doesn't remember anything."

"Have you told her?" Mum asks.

"No, I can't. Something happened to her before she came to live with us. She's forgotten all about that, and she seems peaceful. I don't want to make her remember, as it would make her remember that as well. It makes me feel shitty, as I sometimes think, maybe today is the day she remembers, and then I remind myself what I'd be asking her to remember as well. I can't do that to her. It's so hard, Mum. I miss her, but she's right there, right there in front of me."

"Matt, darling, whatever was going on between you, it has nothing to do with whatever thing happened to her before, whatever it is you don't want her to remember. Maybe you just need to go forward and make new memories with her."

I'm glad that she doesn't bullshit me with sentences about how Beatrice will suddenly remember everything. I've done enough reading to be sure that this is nothing short of a miracle. I mull over her words for the rest of dinner. Maybe she is right. If it is impossible for Beatrice to see what we used to be, maybe I can show her what we could be, instead.

I return home, feeling renewed. Weeks have passed since the accident but nothing about Beatrice has changed, and no memories gained. I throw myself into spending time with Beatrice, to recapture how things had started between us. I don't drop in information I know about her or take her anywhere we have been before. I do my best to keep things new, the only exception is the cinema though I take her to a different one to the one we'd usually go to.

On the first trip, she asks if she could ask me twenty questions. Each one feels more difficult to answer. What can't I live without? Her. Do I want to learn another language? She's already started trying to teach me French, and I've started teaching her Spanish. Do I believe in true love? Of course, I do; she is my true love.

Sometimes, I think she might be on the cusp of remembering something. When she asked me about the leather bracelet I wear during the game of twenty questions, I'm sure she has a reason. She asks a question about it, and I want to tell her that she got it for me for Christmas, to take it off and show her the engraving. I want to point to the necklace she keeps wearing, to recite the engraving that I know is on the side she wears against her chest, to remind her how she'd sat in front of me to put it on her, and she hasn't taken it off since. I'm always a little hopeful, a little fearful, that she might have remembered, but then her face will change, and I know it's just me being hopeful.

I distract myself from everything with Beatrice by going to the meeting I'd arranged with my father, the one I should have gone to with her. He doesn't turn up, doesn't even let me know he isn't going to be there. I wish Beatrice was with me, so I can hold her hand and talk to her about how angry I am with myself for getting my hopes up, and then I feel like I'm being hit again and again when I know I can't speak to her about this because it wouldn't mean anything.

That night, at home, I cut my hand. When she picks up my hand, whispering poor baby as she tends to it, all I can think about is the first time she did this and what happened next. When we kiss, I feel like I am on fire. I want from her much more than I should be allowed to want. I want this kiss to last forever, and it takes everything in me to pull away, not for the first time running away from her.

The idea of showing her what we could be feels suddenly tainted and deceptive. I don't know what way to step or how to proceed. How do I even begin to tell her? Instead, I remove myself from the situation, asking Isaac if I can crash on his sofa.

I debate about how to answer the text from Beatrice. She'd asked what she had done wrong. The simple answer is nothing because she hasn't done anything. The more complicated answer is that something that has happened to her has me feeling like I'm on a cliff top, in the dark, knowing that any step could send me plummeting over the edge.

Is it wrong to keep the secret? Is it wrong to tell her? If she wanted to date me, now, when would I tell her about our past? Straight away? Later? Never? If I summon the strength to walk away from her for good, to let her live in peace without remembering Cole, is that better? Better for me? Better for her?

Ben texts, reminding me of Beatrice's birthday dinner, and I want to tell him I have to work. I've had Beatrice's birthday present stashed away in my bedroom for months, but I still don't know if I should go, and I doubt I can give her my gift. Ben sends a follow-up text message, telling me Beatrice is looking forward to seeing me. I debate all night about what I should do. When the dawn breaks, I still don't have a fucking clue.

Beatrice: Now

I let him finish talking, listening intently as he tells me everything between then and now. At points, I cry. I sit quietly and hold his hand. Sometimes I throw him a look, rolling my eyes as if to call him an idiot. Mostly though, I sit quietly, letting him offload, listening to the pain in his voice at some points, listening to just how much he agonised about what was the right thing to do. When he talks about the casino, I clutch his hand tightly, wiping tears from my eyes, because I know how hard he'd worked to stay out of that environment and how much he would have tormented himself about even stepping through the door.

He talks about his father, the meeting they'd agreed to, and how Max hadn't turned up. I feel like my heart might crack listening to the change in his voice, hearing the mix of anger and hurt in his tone. I know this was the day I'd spoken to Lily and Ben, being adamant that there was something that I should have been doing, and I'm sad that I wasn't there with him, as I'd promised to be right by his side.

When he gets to the present day and stops talking, I climb onto his lap, sitting, so my chest is against his, and I slip my arms around him, pulling him close.

"I'm so sorry, I'm sorry for everything you went through," I whisper into his ear.

"I'm so sorry for what you went through," he replies.

"I'm angry about Max. I wish I'd been there for you." I know I couldn't help breaking the promise to be there when he was supposed to meet Max, but I feel guilty anyway, especially knowing Max let him down, again.

"I knew you'd have been there if you could." His voice sounds even, but even so, I can feel the tears in my eyes.

"I'm sorry you were alone. You should have talked to me, about everything."

"Are you angry with me, for not telling you? Do you hate me?" he asks so quietly I almost miss the last bit. I sit back, so I can look at him properly, so he can see me while I talk.

"No, I don't hate you. I know you did all of this thinking that it was the least suffering for me. That the idea I forgot what Cole did outweighed me forgetting you, even if it meant you suffered. I get it. You were completely wrong, but I understand." I smile. "I still have some issues to work through about what Cole did, but that will be easier in time, I'm sure."

"In the hospital, you said his name, and it was so easy, rolling off your tongue without that change in pitch I hear now. I hate what he did, I hate that he caused you pain."

"Well, I hate what Max does to you. If I could take that pain away from you, I would."

"I know that."

"If the price of him not causing you pain was for you to forget me, would it be worth it?" I ask.

"Never." He sounds firm, and he reaches for my hand, clutching it tightly. "But that is me making the decision for me, it felt completely different trying to decide if I should be selfish enough to force that memory onto you, especially when you'd said you would have given anything not to think about Cole again."

"I get it, but this thing between us, we protect it at all costs. Nothing outweighs how I feel for you, Matt, nothing. Ever," I tell him. "It kills me thinking that you were so alone these last few weeks. I wish you'd told Ben."

"I promised you that I wouldn't tell Ben anything. You were very passionate that you had to be the one to tell him everything. I weighed up whether you'd be more pissed with me for not telling Ben, or telling him and breaking that promise."

"You are such an idiot." I roll my eyes at him.

"Besides, if I did tell him, he might have asked questions I couldn't answer like how we became a couple, or why I haven't told you everything about us to help jog your memory. How would I be able to explain what I was trying to stop you remembering, without breaking promises to you, or violating an NDA?"

"Okay, just, so we are clear, promises you make to me are henceforth null and void if I have amnesia. You can violate any NDA too. Screw the consequences."

"Are you planning on having it again?" He kisses my neck, and I sigh in utter contentment at the feel of his lips.

"No, but I'm going to write down everything from now on, just in case. I'm going to keep a diary, dedicated to you and me. I'm sure it will be filthy, but it would be fun reading if I ever happen to lose my memory again." My hands are now on his shirt buttons. I open one, then another.

"Okay, promises between us become null and void in case you have another memory loss." He smiles.

I pull away from him for a second. "Unless, of course, it's in the future, and you and I are married. I fully expect you to uphold our wedding vows," I tease, and I open a third button of his shirt. I've missed this. This little back and forth between us, the laughter, the moments that are fun, free, the two of us at ease and blissful.

"Bea, I might not have made any marriage vows to you yet, but, just so you know, there hasn't been anybody else. I know Ben told you he thought I was on dates, but no…there is only you." He sounds fierce, and he tucks some loose strands of hair around my ear. "It's always you, it will always be you. I know I will love you for the rest of my life."

I feel my heart soar. "I feel the same as you. So," I say, kissing that little section of his neck that I remember drives him wild. My mouth curves into a knowing smile, as I am delighted I was right, how his breathing gives a little hitch. I still don't know if I have remembered everything, but I feel like I've remembered enough. I remember him. That's everything. I can rediscover the rest with him.

"Yes…?"

"You're telling me that you haven't had sex in some time. Does that mean you're planning on being as fast as that first time?" I tease. He laughs.

"Pre-gaming for a much larger event."

"Promises, promises." I kiss his neck again, and he makes a sound almost like a hungry growl. "I'm still a little fuzzy on some memories so please remind me, did we ever get around to sex in the car?" I ask, opening another button on his shirt.

"No, but there is a new car we can have some fun in," he points out.

"I'm going to hold you to that."

"I know you will. Before we consider the car, are you going to tell me how you got your memories back?" He looks at me, curious. I stop opening the buttons of his shirt because I get the sense he wants to bring the two of us up to the present, to know how things have unfolded before we start making any new memories together. I move to sit next to him on the sofa, sitting sideways, stretching my legs over his lap.

"It was slow at first. I dreamt of you the night we kissed." I smile.

"Yeah?"

"You know me; it was quite a graphic dream. Woke up sweating, and I couldn't work out if I was dreaming something I remembered or something that I desired."

"Walking away that night was genuinely one of the hardest decisions. I knew if I had stayed, where it might have led, and I felt like shit because whilst I have always wanted you, it felt wrong, like I would have been taking advantage of your vulnerability."

"Both of us being full of whisky was probably not a help either." I smile, and it seems to put him at ease. I can feel the weight of what he has gone through since the accident, how every decision has been multifaceted, with no clear best option.

"That reminds me, I owe Ben a bottle of whisky. I've got to pay my debts to my girlfriend's brother."

"Especially now you know he isn't going to kill you for us dating." I laugh.

"I am sure he will have questions for both of us when he gets home tomorrow. Anyway, this graphic dream of yours…?" His voice trails off. He reaches out to me and caresses my cheek, still looking at me like I am something to be cherished.

"The one I woke up from, very disappointed that you weren't here to act out in reality? Dream Matt is very skilled. Almost as good as I now remember real-life Matt to be," I say with a wink. "After that, every night, there were more dreams. I couldn't decide if they were real memories or dreams. I thought maybe they were just dreams, but they were a whole variety of things, snippets of conversation, vivid images.

"One was of us sitting at the top of the big wheel, me looking out to the bluest sea, and then turning to see you. I could almost smell the salt of the sea on the breeze, feel the heat of the sun, and feel your skin as I held your hand. One dream was you clutching at my hips, the way you do when you're pulling me closer towards you on the bed. I wasn't sure if I was making them up."

"Both genuine, one more frequent than the other." He gives me a small smile.

"I am sure one is more enjoyable for you too," I tease.

"You know how much I love the big wheel." He smirks. I swat his arm.

"Every morning, I would wake up with this longing. Each morning, it was getting more obvious that you were what I was longing for, like my heart was desperate to get the attention of my brain, telling me to find you. I know it sounds cheesy, but I missed you and felt the aching in my bones. I wanted to ask you, but I was afraid that it was just me dreaming."

"What made you know?"

"I went shopping, and I saw Anna," I explain, and I see him tense like he is dreading the next part.

"What…" he starts, and I cut in quickly.

"She didn't say anything to me. Don't worry. She looked at me with so much hatred though, and I knew something had to have happened. That night, I dreamt about the time she posted something on social media. Not the actual post, but in the dream I was walking with you, and I said something about how I sleep with a NDA and bank statement taped to my drawer, but she gets to do whatever she wants. I woke up and looked at the drawer, found the paperwork, and that night with Cole came flooding back to me," I admit. He looks devastated.

"Everything I was trying to shield you from, and I made it worse by not being there for you."

"It's okay," I soothe, and then I carry on, moving past Cole and Anna. "I started thinking about the dreams I'd had, and if the one about the NDA was true, then everything else could be true. So I took a massive risk, and I contacted Polly on social media."

"Polly? Oh, God, do I want to know?"

"Hey, I blagged my way through the conversation when she phoned me. I wasn't sure she knew you when I reached out. Then we started talking. It made sense during the conversation why I was apparently fangirling some swimwear model on social media. It was because I had met her…that I knew her in-laws…one of them very intimately. To be fair, her lack of surname, and Toby's arty photography website didn't exactly scream: these are people related to Matt." I grin.

"When was this?"

"This morning. Then this afternoon, you walked in, and I swear it was like a light switch. Every fibre of my being was screaming, 'there he is, that's the man you love! There's the missing piece you have been searching for'. I knew all the things I'd been thinking, they were real. I thought I could last the night before cornering you to talk, and I barely lasted five minutes. I thought I might burst from the joy of remembering you, and I desperately needed to talk to you." My face feels like it is aching from the big smile on my face. He smiles back at me, kissing my cheek.

"Do you want to go upstairs for your birthday present?"

"How was sex going to be your birthday present to me? If I hadn't had a tonne of memories restored in my head, how were you planning on swinging that?" I laugh.

"Well, sex too, but I did get you an actual present. I am a gentleman, after all." He smirks. I get up from the sofa, pulling him up as well. We walk up to his bedroom, holding hands. When we get to the top of the landing, I pause though I don't know why. He scoops me up, and then I remember, all the times he'd carry me the rest of the way to his room.

"I think there are still things for me to remember, as well as new memories to make," I say as he carries me down the hall. I open the bedroom door for him and when we go in, he sits me down on his bed. I close my eyes and breathe in the scent of his room. "Maybe this is the room I should have come to when trying to get my memory back."

I feel a warmth coming over me, something that warms me to my core. I open my eyes. Matt stands at the edge of the bed, looking at me with a smile on his face and a present in his hand. The contrast in him to the man who had arrived earlier is remarkable. Gone is the guarded, grumpy-looking man, the man with a frown on his face. There's a lightness to him now, an aura of happiness. This is my Matt. This is the man I know and love.

"Happy birthday, Bea," he says, handing me the box. It's heavy, just larger than the size of a shoe box. I open the paper, trying not to rip it, it's a paper with little bees drawn on it. Once I get inside the paper, I see the name written on the box, and I take a sharp intake of breath. I open the lid, and inside the box is a pair of quad roller skates. They're white, with a red rose stitched on the side, bright red laces completing them. They're exactly like the ones I'd had as a teenager; the ones I'd told him I had loved.

"You remembered!"

"Yeah, I remembered everything. Some of us don't have memory problems," he teases. I take the skates out of the box.

"You trust me using these?" I ask.

"Totally going to insist on you wearing a helmet, but yeah, who else is going to teach me how to skate?" he asks with a smile, and he points to a box he has in his wardrobe, another pair of skates.

"Oh my God, I love you." I laugh.

"I love you too," he says, and I smile at his words. I want to tell him that the skates in my hand are another way he is telling me he loves me because despite everything, he isn't going to wrap me in cotton wool, he isn't going to spend the rest of our lives questioning if I should do something that I am so determined to do. I want to tell him what these skates represent to me, but instead, I put them on the floor and pull him down onto the bed with me. My hands make swift work of the rest of his shirt buttons. It doesn't take him long until he's just as enthusiastic as I am, pulling my dress off, pulling me closer to his body, and it's like we haven't spent a second apart, falling into our rhythm, everything feeling resplendent, and somehow feeling new and special, as well as familiar and perfectly us.

We don't hear the ring of the doorbell from the food delivery driver. We don't hear the text messages as Ben tells us he's told the delivery driver to leave the food on the porch. We don't hear anything apart from each other. We're too busy making new memories, and I never, ever want to stop.

Beatrice: The Future

"Doesn't she look absolutely stunning?"

"He looks completely besotted."

"I'm so happy for them."

I stand and listen to the voices of the wedding guests around me, smiling to myself. People are milling around, that time after the ceremony, where photographs have been taken, before the sit-down dinner, where people just seem to relax. Waiters pass by with glasses of champagne, family members and friends catch up, young children play together on the grass.

"You look like you are miles away." Jas smiles as she gets my attention. Alessandro stands to her side, looking lovely in his suit. They're a stunning couple together, and I am so happy that my best friend has found somebody who loves her as much as she loves them.

"Sorry, I'm just soaking it all up. It's a beautiful day."

"It's been beautiful, so seamless. Anybody would think that you should go into event planning or something." Jas teases. She's been going on about this for months, as she is sure this is where my talents lie for when I finally make my career move.

"I just wanted things to be perfect for them." I smile, looking over to where Ben and Lily are standing under a gazebo covered in flowers, taking a moment of peace together as husband and wife. They look blissfully happy, and I am so glad everything today has run so smoothly. No last-minute hitches, not for my lovely brother and new sister-in-law, not if I could do anything about it.

Out of the corner of my eye, I catch a glimpse of Matt as he intervenes with two of Lily's young cousins who are about to start squabbling over a game that has been set out for the younger guests to play. He smoothes things over quickly, and I smile to myself. Evidently, Matt is determined as well that Ben and Lily's day will be perfect.

As if he can sense me looking at him, he looks up and meets my gaze. A slow smile forms on his face, giving me one of those smiles I swear he reserves just for me, the type that lights up his whole face. He makes his way over to where I stand with Jas and Alessandro. I don't take my eyes off him as he crosses the garden. He looks divine in his best man suit.

As he walks by a waiter, he picks up two glasses of champagne, arrives in front of me and hands me a glass. He slips his arm around me, turning his head to kiss my forehead. I close my eyes, feeling full of bliss.

"You've lost her attention now." Alessandro jokes to Jas. I open my eyes in time to see Jas roll her eyes.

"It's a good job I love them both," Jas replies. She gives us both an affectionate smile, and I know she's being truthful though I had worried initially that Jas wouldn't warm to Matt.

The day after I had told Matt that I knew everything, I felt like I was on a rollercoaster of emotions, and I told everyone aside from him that I needed to be by myself for a bit. For a few days, my mind kept reverting to what Cole had done to me. I would be doing something mundane and suddenly the memory would be in my head, taking my breath away. Matt kept me going in those days. As soon as I felt like I had control of myself again, Jas and I had been out for dinner, so I could tell her how Matt and I had fallen in love.

The following day, she'd come to the house, and she had grilled him for what felt like hours on end. Jas had asked him question after question, and he had answered them all good-naturedly, but then he had stopped her, saying simply that he would never, ever hurt me. At that, Jas had been satisfied and accepted that the grumpy Matt she'd seen over the previous weeks had just been in emotional pain with everything that was happening. The two of them have a good friendship now.

"Have you thought more about the bar?" Alessandro asks Matt. Alessandro's move to the UK coincided with him getting a university placement as a mature student, but to make some money, he works part-time for Matt at the bar. He plans to stay in the UK with Jas, and I have no doubt that they'll get married in the future.

"I'm signing the paperwork next week for my next instalment, but Antony is on board with the plans for the bar going forward," Matt replies.

During my amnesia, Matt had lost some enthusiasm for the bar. I'd been surprised to know he'd barely been at work during those weeks, having hired another manager to cover his usual shifts on a six-month contract whilst he took unpaid leave and dipped into his savings. Matt's great-uncle had been concerned that he might want to sell his share of the bar.

For the first few weeks after I had got my memories back, I thought Matt might throw in the towel, and it took me a while to realise he was second-guessing all his decisions, sure that everything would come crashing down around him, like it was inevitable that whenever he was happy, something might come along to ruin things. It took a bit of time for him to accept that things could actually go his way. He's purchased more of the bar from Antony, and I'm so proud of everything he is planning. The way he treats his team is exemplary, and they love him. He seems so happy at the bar these days.

I am still at the bar. I didn't return to work straight away after the accident. A few weeks after I recovered my memory, before he went back to the bar as well, Matt and I went away for two weeks. We spent ten days in Portugal, the two of us enjoying the peace and quiet to ourselves in a villa, just being free to do whatever we liked. On the way back to the UK, we stopped with Alice.

Alice had been thrilled to see us together. A heavily pregnant Polly, Toby, Sam and Andy had arrived the day after us for a long weekend stay at Alice's house, and I felt like one of the family, even Toby and Sam teasing Matt the first night it was clear I would be staying in Matt's room rather than the spare room couldn't dampen my happiness.

"Don't forget Tommy will always buy a piece of the bar if you need any assistance," Jas jokes.

"Do not encourage them." I laugh.

Mum and Dad fell in love with Matt when they met him again, as something more than Ben's roommate. They'd come back from the first part of their travelling, spending a few months in the UK before planning on travelling again. When they'd come back to the UK, Matt and I had been together for a year. I'd told them plenty of stories about Matt, and they'd chatted together on video calls, but Matt had still been nervous when they'd come home, and we had all gone for dinner, Ben and Lily, Mum and Dad, me and Matt. That night, Ben and Lily had announced their engagement, and Matt's genuine happiness for them had Mum smiling.

Mum simply adores Matt and Dad thinks Matt is amazing. I tell Matt all the time that he gets brownie points because he looks after both of the Schofield children, and what else would my parents care about? I barely get a look in when he is around though they're off on another travelling stint in a week's time, crisscrossing across Europe this time.

"Don't encourage who?" Mum's voice comes from behind me. She and Dad join us.

"About Dad sinking any money into the bar." I smile at her. I'm glad she's been home for a while, even if she spends her time encouraging me to work out what I want to do with my life. Whilst Matt gets a pass because he owns some of the bar, she worries that I'm not making much money, and I know secretly she'll always worry that I'm overdoing things. At some point, I'm sure I'll change careers, but for now, I'm happy by Matt's side at the bar. Most of my friends are there, and it feels like an extended family.

"Your dad needs to remember how much money he's put forward to this wedding, and our Europe trip." Mum laughs. She looks at Matt. "However, if you need anything, you know you can ask us," she reminds him, and he laughs.

"Fiona, you're a diamond, but everything is fine. Beatrice and I are all good," Matt replies.

"I'll be around tomorrow to help you with that cabinet," Dad tells Matt. He's been so helpful these last few weeks as we rip out a kitchen to put in a new one in our house. Both Mum and Dad are curious how I'd managed to produce an ample deposit for the house that Matt and I are now living in based on my wages. Our house is small, but it's ours, and once I'd reconciled how the money had become mine, I couldn't think of anything better to spend it on than buying somewhere with Matt. I love living with him, just us two, in our own space.

"If we do the cabinet tomorrow, it'll end up lopsided after all the drinks tonight." Matt laughs. Dad grins at him.

"Well, I'm sure you'll be joining me in a tipple of whisky later. It isn't often a father gets to celebrate their child's wedding. Won't be doing this again until it's your twos."

"One wedding at a time, Mr Schofield." Jas laughs, but I remember how excited she had been when I had shown her the engagement ring that Matt had presented to me two months ago. Of all the places, he proposed at the top of the big wheel. He didn't even flinch when the seat had rocked as I'd thrown my arms around him in surprise and excitement.

"I'm just excited about having him as a son-in-law." Dad claps Matt on the shoulder. I'm glad he and Matt have a good relationship. Matt still doesn't talk to Max. Max has reached out a few times, but after leaving him disappointed and waiting for him, Matt isn't ready to reopen himself to that again. I just tell him I'll be by his side for whatever he chooses, and I joke I'll add it to my diary if they do decide to meet, just in case.

"Come on Tommy, time to get ourselves ready to receive guests." Mum slips her hand into Dad's, and they walk off towards the hall. I smile as they walk off. They drive me crazy, but if Matt and I can have a marriage even half as strong as theirs, we'll be lucky.

"Alessandro and I are going to get another glass of champagne before dinner. We'll see you later." Jas gives me a smile, and she and Alessandro also head off, leaving just me and Matt together. We both smile at Lily and Ben as they walk past us, heading towards the hall. They're doing a traditional receiving line for their wedding guests and expect Matt and me as bestman and bridesmaid in the line in a minute to do our duties. I start to step forward, slipping my hand into Matt's, so I can pull him with me, but he pulls me back. I stop in front of him and smile up at him.

"Yes?" I ask.

"You look beautiful," he tells me, and he leans forward to kiss me.

"You're very sexy right now. I can't wait to get you home," I say between kisses. I run my hand down his chest.

"Cool your jets, Goldilocks; we have got a long evening reception ahead of us." He laughs.

"Complete with the cheesy disco they have insisted on. Though, I'm looking forward to doing the Thriller dance with you, maybe a bit of Footloose," I tease.

"Well, we'll be fine, so long as there is no ice," he jokes. I swat his arm.

"It's a good job I love you." I laugh.

"I don't know what I'd do if you didn't."

"You're never going to have to find out," I promise.

"You and me forever, Bea. I love you," he tells me, giving me a full smile. I lean up towards him.

"Forever," I reply, and I seal my promise with a kiss.